KIERAN CORBY

WRITER'S BLOCK

This edition first published in paperback by
Michael Terence Publishing in 2025
www.mtp.agency

ISBN 9781805880202

Cover design (AI)
Michael Terence Publishing

Michael Terence
Publishing

1

As a bright, fluorescent, concentrated beam of light panned across New York's famous formidable rooftops, the security guard's torch flicked across the skyline into an opposing direction, the beam followed by a shuffling unkempt man yawning as he walked. Just as the guard stopped and lowered the torch to light a cigarette, the beam extending from his torch panned across the rooftop garden he stood on. The guard promptly stopped. His lighter held inches away from his face, flickering weakly in the wind. As he remained poised and motionless, his torch brought to his attention a plant pot near the edge of the roof, delicately placed adjacent to a twin pot and a low brick wall. As the guard slowly moved towards the pot, the lighter flicked away and into a trouser pocket, the cigarette wobbling in his mouth as he tip-toed to the edge of the roof. He repositioned the direction of his torch next to the pot, bending down onto his haunches as he noticed crumbs of compost strewn across the otherwise perfectly kept rooftop garden. At this moment, bent over and with his back turned, looking out across the New York skyline, the security guard suddenly noticed a shadow appear on the ground next to his, and the sky seemingly turned darker as the moon's reflection was covered by this ominous presence. Engulfed by shadow, the security guard's lower jaw dropped - and with that his cigarette fell helplessly to the floor, spinning away uncontrollably. Before he could even stand, the guard was swiftly dispatched by a silenced pistol jammed into the back of his head; the hollowing activation of the trigger revealing nothing to the unsuspecting public below.

'The guard on the roof is down.' The killer declared as he pulled up his pistol. He reached down to clean up his bullet casing and slotted the weapon back into the holster situated on his hip. He wore all black, from his woolly hat perfectly pulled over his bald head, his long-sleeved t-shirt and cargo trousers, to his military boots. Within seconds, the killer was quickly surrounded by several similarly dressed subordinates, some armed with assault rifles. 'Alright team, let's get in and out, two minutes, starting…' he paused to pull his watch up to his face. 'Now!' Somehow the killer managed to perfectly execute a whisper and a shout simultaneously.

In the organised chaos that followed, the killer watched as his team of five silently and effectively entered through a glass door into the penthouse after successfully deactivating a series of alarms located on a fuse box outside in the garden. They located a room subtly situated in the corner of the penthouse, with only the room's door allowing people to be known of its presence. After a series of taps and clicks by a soldier armed with a touchscreen tablet, the door made a clicking sound and released itself away from hugging the door frame as smoke was released from the room. As the precautionary smoke permeated through the exterior room, the soldiers placed gas masks across their faces as they waited for their commander to enter the room before them. As the killer pulled the door further ajar, he wandered delicately into the small, closet-like room and remained in awe as he stepped further down the narrow entrance.

The soldiers sauntered through the room in bewilderment, gazing at the walls as if like school children in a sweet shop. The walls were crammed with collectable memorabilia and antiques from game-worn Michael Jordan trainers, to Picasso's, to diamond-encrusted jewellery. Upon reaching the end of the narrow room, all the soldiers' heads turned in unison to gaze in awe at the crown jewel of the collection, placed at the end of the corridor and the only item allowed within the centre of the room. Within a glass case sat a Babe Ruth-worn New York Yankee jersey, perfectly preserved for nearly one hundred years. The jersey itself looked unspectacular, but the historical and cultural significance of such a collectable to baseball fans and the city of New York especially remains unfathomable. However, to the killer and his entourage, this was just another job.

Not a minute later, the last of the soldiers exited through the penthouse glass door and back onto the rooftop garden; the mission was completed as they all began descending a zip-wire erected moments earlier onto an opposing rooftop. As the last zipped across, the killer stood impeccably straight within the garden and removed a flip phone from his pocket. One click and he pressed the phone towards his ear, tapping his foot impatiently waiting for the receiver to answer.

'It's done', the killer said as a wry smile appeared across his face, it was clear this was a rare display of emotion that had swept over him.

'Good.' Replied the receiver. 'I have another opportunity for your team. I think you'll find this time you shall be sufficiently compensated for your efforts. Reach the drop site and await further instructions.' The receiver hung up before waiting for a reply.

As the killer attached his grappling handle to the zip-line, the slightest, quietest of noises forced him to stop completely, his ears pinned backwards like a cat. Then, in one swift, complete motion, the killer spun one hundred and eighty degrees, lifting his pistol as he turned and releasing two rounds into what he soon discovered to be the source of the noise; another security guard holding a pistol of is own, stumbling as he peered down at the bullet holes that had pierced his impeccably pressed uniform. Once again, the killer paid keen interest in cleaning his bullet casings, before glancing towards his handiwork performed on his most recent victim. He stood, tutting as he made one last look at the body. 'Not in the middle,' he mumbled to himself as he shook his head. And just like that, he swung off the rooftop and they were gone. Vehicles buzzed and honked on the street below, drunks slept in doorways, dancers exited clubs, and New York remained as sleepless as always, unaware of what had just occurred: a $4 million heist executed to near perfection.

2

'The forecast is predicting another dry day, with minimal chance of showers.'

'Typical', the man quipped with a snarky undertone as he peered out onto the grim, grey view seen from the window of a stereotypical-looking apartment block; the typical British weather had proved to be unpredictable as ever, with dark clouds swarming the sky and rain ferociously streaming down the window.

If asked, Max would say he was a writer; but to acquaintances, he was a failed one at that. Max was promptly approaching his late twenties and apart from short story success years prior, he was waiting for his 'big break' as he referred to it.

He took a sip of his coffee. Max had brown, medium-length wavy hair that flowed backwards, supported by stubble and green eyes that insinuated inexperience, which he knew all too well. The weather proved a perfect comparison to Max's apartment: drab and empty. The furniture was dated and worn, the cups stained, and the heating broken, yet the cold shower provided a perfect wake-up necessary for him.

As the minutes passed, there was a lack of movement. Max, motionless, stared blankly past his laptop screen and out at the Sheffield landscape. The lack of progress was frustrating Max, which eluded the false impression this was a rare occurrence. Seeking inspiration, he flicked the TV on, only to become immediately annoyed by the news story presented in front of him.

'Shocking news coming out of New York City as two security guards employed at a million-dollar penthouse were murdered last night as possibly one of the greatest items of American sports memorabilia was stolen: a match-worn Babe Ruth New York Yankees jersey, believed to be valued in the region of four million dollars. The NYPD is believed to be investigating the theft, but no new information has been made available at this time,' the newscaster reported.

'I wish I could get my hands on something worth $4 million,' Max mumbled under his breath, his depressing sadness for himself growing, in perfect contrast with his declining writing motivation. It was becoming increasingly likely he'd be wasting another day with relatively insufficient progress, and as the realisation hit him, so too did his head onto the kitchen table.

Max closed his eyes. He hadn't earned a break, but sleeping sounded more interesting than reading the story he had just written. There was a buzzing sound emitting from the table and Max frantically opened his eyes, his head remained glued to the table as he reached for his illuminated phone. The notification was from Max's buddy George, with possibly the sweetest, most heartfelt message Max could ever have considered as he was looking for the perfect excuse to procrastinate. He contemplated the impact of how just three letters formed into a question made the thought of the day completely reverse from boring mediocrity to a world with an abundance of endless opportunities. As he lifted his head and jumped out of his seat, Max swiped his phone off the table and read the message one more time, just for good measure: 'Pub?' Max smiled. *Today might not turn out that bad after all*, he thought.

3

Max shuffled his feet closer to the bar and heckled for the bartender's attention. A casually dressed bartender quickly rose from underneath the bar into a stand. 'Just three more pints please mate,' Max held out an extended arm and dropped his notes onto the bar, looking away to scan the contents of the pub behind him.

This is what locals would refer to as a 'proper pub'. The establishment was dated, with its old stories and anecdotes seemingly bursting out of the walls. Rusty lights clung to the wall, illuminating the dark wooden interior walls with a certain shadiness that made particular crevices within the bar allude to a sense of eeriness. The lights remained the perfect shade of warm to prevent customers from estimating any sense of the time of day. An excellent business model, Max considered as he grabbed three beers from off the bar. He carefully returned to his table, the head on the beer wobbling against the tip of the glass after each stride he took.

'...and that is why Messi will always be better than Ronaldo, just accept it.' As Max bent over and delicately slid the beers onto the table from their previous triangle formation within his grasp, he rolled his eyes before slumping down into the floral-decorated red booth accompanied alongside the table - the booth of which would have hardly looked out of place in a 70s sitcom.

'You guys aren't still on that debate, are you? You started that last week, neither one of you is gonna give up.' Max admitted to his friends as he shrugged his shoulders, taking a sip of beer as he finished. He was sat with George and Will, both old school friends of Max's and they had accompanied each other to a plethora of evenings that often began in a very similar fashion to the one presented in front of them. The duo of George and Will were fairly comparable to each other when judged opposite Max; they had both achieved financial stability through long, grinding work hours and often sympathised with the position Max had shuffled himself into after such a promising start to his career. They did, however, remain nothing but brutally honest toward any upcoming ideas Max happened to be babbling through on any passing day.

'Ha!' Laughed George emphatically as he leaned forward and slapped the table, the almost-full beers threatening to jump out of the glass as his hand came down. George was loud - and for those who sat adjacent to him will inform - he was inevitably louder after a couple. 'I'll forever argue Ronaldo's corner because I know just how much it annoys him!' George appeared to be attempting to speak to the entire pub judging by his level of volume, a mischievous smile creeping across his face as he slapped Will's back as a form of sincerity. 'So come on then, what's the next million-pound idea?' George condescendingly asked Max before reaching for another swallow of beer.

'Okay, erm… what about a story about a guy who witnesses a neighbour commit a crime?' Max's hands had instinctively moved into the 'jazz hands' position in an attempt to add more panache to his presentation. It failed miserably.

'Nope. Hitchcock.' Will didn't even bother to lift his head out from his glass as he sipped his beer, the dead tone of his response indicating his lack of surprise at Max's idea. Will was a down-to-earth and honest friend who kept Max grounded, mostly by highlighting that all of Max's 'ideas' had been made before, in one form of entertainment or another.

'A killer dog?' Max asked inquisitively.

'Movie and book, Stephen King.'

'Bonnie and Clyde rip-off?'

'Thelma and Louise, Natural Born Killers. Oh, and for the real thing, The Highwaymen.'

George's head was frantically moving back and forward between his two friends during this exchange, like he was in the crowd at Wimbledon.

'Something about a lovable alien?' Max shrugged in desperation. Will paused, almost mockingly whilst looking at Max. He took a sip before his smug response followed.

'E.T., Paul, Lilo and Stitch.' Will made sure to count out the numbers on his fingers as he relayed them across the table.

'Shit!' Max exclaimed, his frustration highlighted by thrusting his fist down onto the booth before promptly dispatching the remainder of his pint. 'Three more please!' He shouted across the room this time. As the alcohol began mopping up the last of his constructive thoughts, Max's mind began to wander. Harsh as he was, Will's extraordinary pop culture knowledge benefited Max and he knew that, despite how annoyingly right he was about everything all the time.

'Will, your round', George was waving his hand in indication toward the bar as his face remained in his glass, guzzling the remainder of his beer. After a brief pause, Will reluctantly relented and made his way across the room. As he stood waiting to collect their order, his attention deviated towards the TV hanging in the bar; the same New York heist news story dominating the headlines throughout the day. Will, forever in a pensive mood, allowed his mind to wander about what he'd just heard for the third time today as he made his way back to the table.

'You heard about that robbery in New York? How'd they do it, man?' Will asked with intrigue, Max and George not warranting Will a response to something they assumed to be rhetorical. The three sat in silence for several passing moments, watching as the pub - and seemingly the world - passed them by. 'Maybe that can be your next idea, Max. A heist, like the fellas on the tele?'

It was at this point the alcohol began to impact the conversation to a greater extent than the use of the three brains they all had.

The questions took longer to register, the responses took even longer despite the obvious lack of thought. These three gentlemen had entered the dangerous stage of intoxication: where no idea was a bad idea.

'I'm not sure about a heist,' Max mumbled almost incoherently. 'There's been a loada them before, I wanna do something different, like a search for a lost treasure!' He ended his sentence triumphantly, with genuine optimism regarding his 'innovative' idea.

'That's hardly original, bud. I feel as though they may have thought of that one before..' The sincerity which Will directed towards Max made it clear to him that he was once again spouting drivel.

'But what about a treasure hunt for something Hollywood hasn't made a movie about? Like, a completely new treasure hunt for something people have forgotten about?'

'You know what,' George chimed in as he miraculously managed to finish his beverage at an unsettling speed. 'That actually doesn't sound half bad. A quick Google and you might be well on your way. Not bad, Max.' A smile beamed across his face after approval was granted before his head quickly pivoted towards Will, who always was the tougher audience - Max waiting patiently, like a dog waiting for their owner to throw their ball.

Will took another gulp of his beer. He was a movie fan, he loved to add suspense to his daily life. He knew he need not say anything, but just nodded his head forward towards Max to signal how he felt.

'Alright! Let's get this shit written down before I forget.' Max pulled out a notebook from inside his jacket and began scribbling something that he hoped he'd be able to read tomorrow morning in there. His notebook unfortunately remained relatively new and unworn, he was forever claiming all he needed to be a successful writer was to fill out his notebook with his idea of 'adventures'.

'You never know when your next great idea comes along, that might be it right there,' waving his notebook in the air. Max liked this feeling. The optimism achieved once he had a new idea pleased him, inspired him, and motivated him to keep pursuing his dream.

'Let's worry about that tomorrow. First, I've got to give you boy's a lesson on how to play pub sports. Gentlemen, get your wallets ready. Ha ha!' Max rubbed his hands together ironically to appear mischievous. The other two knew he was vastly superior in most sports, but egotistical men after a few beers inevitably ended in some form of competition.

'Let the games begin…' George retorted as a smugness appeared across his face. No matter how many times Max would beat them both at any form of physical activity or sport, George's bravado and seemingly limitless confidence in victory bordered on that of an ambitious mad man. Whilst annoying, Max did appreciate how much sweeter it was to win when his opponent had confidence.

'I'll get the next round in, 'cus I won't have to buy anymore for the rest of the night after!' Max exited the booth and strutted over towards the bar, spinning his head and dropping a wink he attempted to pass off as cool back to the four people he could now see sitting at the table. This might become a bit messy Max thought as he rested his arms on the bar for support.

4

A golden gleaming beam of sunshine glistened gloriously through the large bedroom window of Max's apartment, who began cursing himself for not only providing himself with the challenging headache that was inevitably about to settle in but for also not closing his blinds. *The one day the sun decides to come out.*

He flipped over and ferociously ripped a pillow from underneath his head and slammed it over his face; rejecting the sun's adequate attempt at brightening up the old, tired decor. Moments passed. Max remained motionless. Before he had a chance to fall back to sleep and push back the hangover, he was rudely awakened a second time, this time by his alarm - the hideous, horrific sound similar to that of a school bell, whilst also providing an awfully analogous sense of existential dread. Max sat up, flicked off the sound and sighed.

Some poorly made coffee and eggs did little to cure the hangover and Max sat looking out his kitchen window feeling sorry for himself - wearing his sunglasses to hide the sun and his bloodshot eyes whilst sipping on his burnt coffee. Despite the previous evening not only turning a profit during the night's pub sports antics, the night was indeed messy, but remained merry and plentiful of shenanigans; Max smiled as he reminisced; he always believed nostalgia was an important stimulant in many people's lives, whilst also acting as a exploitative marketing tool to berate consumers with the 'latest' trends.

The reminiscing continued as his mind wandered aimlessly into the cloudy sunshine of a summer's morning, the beaming gazes of light shining optimism across the city, providing a sense of wonderment that lay ahead. The sun glistened and reflected back off Max's glasses, the aviators doing their best job to make him feel like Maverick from Top Gun. Like his on-screen counterpart, Max had the pressing issue of trying not to throw up, which can be assumed as a feeling not too dissimilar to one's experience during their first F14 run.

As his thoughts trailed off, he began to remember writing something in his notebook yesterday, forcing himself out of the chair and starting to look for wherever intoxicated Max would have been stupid enough to leave it. He eventually found it tucked away in his cutlery drawer, along with an extra fiver. Result.

The leather exterior stretched itself as the book flicked through to its bookmark; revealing some scribbles that Max could easily identify as being made after one too many drinks. As he attempted to make sense of the illegible drivel, it seemed as if a lightbulb flicked on above his head like a cartoon. 'Ah! A lost artefact not already stolen by Nic Cage. That was it!' Max said as the reading trailed off into reactionary excitement. The limbering hungover was promptly replaced with a skip-like run as Max dashed around his apartment collecting his laptop, pen, brain and of course, another cup of coffee and jumped into his seat, releasing a sigh as he flipped his laptop screen open.

Now, let's see what we can find. He cracked his knuckles before the tapping of keys commenced.

5

Two more mugs of caffeinated goodness but the blankness of the laptop screen screamed yet another day with little progress. Max, seeming as defeated as the chewed-up end of his pen, rose out of the slump he positioned himself in and began tapping away at the keyboard. He pondered for a moment, before deciding that a Google would provide himself with the slither of inspiration he so very much needed.

***

After disappearing into a Google rabbit hole, Max stumbled across various potential plots, recognised by sitting up straight and leaning forward in his chair, like a school child waiting for exam results. He came across articles and columns discussing the recent discovery of certain artefacts and treasures - one that particularly piqued his interest was the recent uncovering of a lost Fabergé egg - but he also found literacy containing information regarding lost artefacts that have remained undiscovered. He reasoned a story without its conclusion would allow for greater creative freedom. Max's intensity increased. He began frantically jotting all the potential ideas in his notebook, ferociously flipping each page over as he filled it.

Then he stopped. He came across the story of John Dillinger and his lost fortune. With one hand scrolling in his laptop mouse, the other stroking his bearded chin, he continued reading.

'Dillinger, a 1930s gangster and bank robber, was a celebrity of the era alongside Bonnie and Clyde. His criminal exploits and numerous jailbreaks were dramatised by newspapers, a public enemy number one with bravado and courage comparable at the time to that of Robin Hood.'

Max's eyes widened with anticipation; his chair balancing on its front legs as he leaned excessively forward.

'The theory is that due to Dillinger dying in his early 30s, he must have buried some of his fortune from his escapades. With an estimated fortune of $200,000, the 90-year-old loot is supposedly buried within the vicinity of his safe house lodge in Little Bohemia, Wisconsin. Still yet to be found, who says you won't be the lucky contestant?'

Max leaned back in his chair, sliding backwards slightly and all four legs thankfully rested on the floor once more. Despite almost falling off, Max remained unfazed, the cogs turning inside his head as he considered the possibility of his options. After scooting forward in this chair, running his hands through a bed head that magically still retained its waves and flourishing bounce, Max flicked open an open word document and clicked away his first additions to his newest million-pound idea: Dillinger's Lost Loot.

Standing up, he glared over his laptop, contemplating his construction. He placed his hands on the back of his chair and leaned over it - a man had never been encapsulated by three words for so long - the euphoria of beginning a new project, the endless possibilities, unlimited imagination and the multiple meanders of exhilarating excitement similar to a child at Christmas. 'Let's get started then,' Max said as he sat back down.

He immediately rose out of his seat. *A cup of tea first.*

6

The day went quickly after that. For the first time in a long time, he enjoyed his writing; characters and their backstories being developed, intriguing plot lines with an abundance of possibilities exciting him.

As the ferocious tip-tapping on the laptop proceeded across the day, Max never forgot to add details to his notebook - the pages had never been filled so fast. He always liked to keep key points and notes in his diary, never knowing when he might want to add things or contemplate new ideas.

With the story progressing nicely, Max started to feel like he was being productive for the first time in a long time, the gleam of the sun shining through his window slowly returned to nightfall and darkness as he remained fixated on his computer. It seemed like the whole world was passing him by, like a calamitous earthquake could not deviate his eyes from scanning the screen, nor his fingers from tapping incessantly.

Coffee was promptly replaced by beer once Max finally acknowledged the evening was upon him, before switching later again to spirits, the necessary juices of a writer in desperation, working to get as many of his ideas swirling around in his head down on the page before the inevitable forgetting of thoughts and plots.

He steamed ahead through the evening, only ever stopping for stretches and pauses for spelling mistakes. It seemed at one point the writer in him had taken over. Even as he grew tired, yawning replaced stretching, eyes blinked quicker, and posture becoming more slumped, Max continued with his efforts, determined to keep the thoughts flowing until the keyboard broke.

Then, mid-sentence, Max's head started tilting downwards towards the screen. He tried valiantly to pry his head back up, but it was no use. Blinks were replaced by his eyes completely closing and his head fell lower and lower toward the table…

Maybe just a little kip, he thought to himself.

7

Blank. The following day was different. After making progress unlike any other writing before, Max had managed to seemingly wake up this morning with every writer's worst nightmare: the dreaded writer's block. The most disastrous occurrence of any author, unfortunately, placed with the inevitably of believing it to never end with a timeless loop of worthless ideas congealing like a blocked drain, preventing anything useful from being extracted.

As the afternoon approached, his efforts seemed futile; not enough caffeine in the world, not enough pavements to walk, enough books to read, video games to play, or Google searches to provoke any sense of inspiration in the next step. He had fallen short. He cracked open a beer, defeated. As he swilled back the first refreshing crispness of the wheat and barley, he delicately placed the bottle on the coaster on his coffee table and fell into his sofa. He had not earned the beer, but he thought to himself he had tried everything else.

Max just struggled to connect his dots. He was trying to find a reasonable reason for his protagonists to go in search of the lost fortune. Exasperated, he flicked his laptop back open, the page remaining as empty as he left it, contemplating his steps, and feeling very similar to the heroes in his novel. Wickedly ironic.

He flicked back to his Google tab, thinking he may as well read further on the story and see if inspiration could be found whilst on the comfort of his sofa. Upon finding a YouTube video, his interest seemingly decreased in his own story, almost seeing the video as a final straw before giving up for the evening.

The cheap animation and automated voice recited back the Dillinger story. He was only half listening, his head turned, looking out his window, feeling a little sorry for himself.

He decided to take his mind off everything. A little break; a reward for forty-eight hours of hard work, maybe interacting with something other than a screen will provide some inspiration for him.

As always, his first port of call - and had been for many years - when he needed help, Will was there. Having known each other for so long, it was fortunate to have someone so close, spiritually and geographically. Within the hour, they were both buried on Will's sofa, an ice-cold beer each, Max's refreshment tasting ever so sweeter after all the hard work he thought he had achieved over recent days. *Beer did taste better in good company*, he reasoned.

'How's the ideas going then bud?' Will asked intuitively, the genuine care in his voice was apparent. He had always believed in Max, from the very beginning. He was exactly the friend everyone needed; positive compassion in every instance and a showing of honest optimism for every scrap of paper he was handed with ineligible scribbles over the plethora of years, both good and bad.

'Not too bad, pretty productive I can't lie,' said the somewhat smug-speaking Max as he sipped his bubbling refreshment, leaning back on the sofa as he spoke. 'I'm making decent progress with an idea… I feel pretty good about this one.'

'And what have we got this time? Is it that totally innovative, never-heard-of-before National Treasure rip-off you've been fumbling around with?'

Despite his caring, Will would always prioritise sarcasm over any feeling of affection for Max. He needed to keep him grounded, after all. For all of Max's intuition and inventiveness, Will often found him up in the clouds, like a child's lost birthday balloon, freely floating from one half-baked idea to the next.

But Will understood Max's talent. He could see it. He knew it was there. Max just needed some help to guide him in the right direction, to set him on the right path. Ultimately, Will knew Max had that one great idea inside his short-circuited brain, it was just a matter of time - and a little teasing from Will - until eventually a fully-fledged piece of work was extracted.

'You'll be happy to know, it's still a rip-off,' the tone of Max's voice was not lacking disappointment, Will knew him too well. He took another gulp of beer, before taking a deep breath, readjusting his seating position from a relaxing slump to an upright attentiveness, like a meerkat scouting across the plains.

'But hey, I stumbled across something, I think it could be interesting, I wanted to swing it by you before I wasted more time on it,' Max said with a slight tremor in his voice; he was always worried about just what Will had to say about what he was thinking. Will often became the friend in the group you had to tread on eggshells around, his honesty was often a blessing and a curse.

'So I was reading some stuff…'

'Ooh, steady, that sounds dangerous', Will interrupted, a smile appearing across his face as he was more fond of the joke than Max, who studied Will's face with a familiar frown in response to sarcasm. Will sank a sip of beer, almost in victory.

'Anyway…, I was looking at some ideas, things that were lost, never been found. I wanted something kinda original, some shit no one had thought about, that I could add some originality to.'

'So I found a couple of bits. One that was interesting was the original crown jewels. They got lost somewhere in Norfolk in a bog. Or some water, I can't quite remember.'

'But if they're the first crown jewels, they must be gone for a while, so surely someone would have already tried to grab them?'

'Thank you, my thoughts exactly. I then found a story about John Dillinger…'

'The bank robber?'

'Yeah. So in the '30s, he robbed a shitload of banks, public enemy number one, yada yada, we both know the story,' Max acting as if he knew as much about Dillinger as his biographer after one Wikipedia read, but he knew full well Will knew the ins and outs down to a tee.

'So here's where it gets interesting. He's on the run, got all his loot, and then disappears to his safe house just before he dies in 1934. According to the legend, he buries part of his money near the safe house, just so the police don't get it, and then carries on, pillaging Chicago's banks.'

'As you do.'

'He then gets shot, dies, cus apparently that sometimes happens when you get shot, but then nobody ever knows where his money is, where he's buried it.'

Max could see as he was explaining the story Will was becoming more and more interested. Will was now sat upright in synchronicity with Max, the beer in his hand getting lighter as the sips got considerably more consistent; the beads of condensation streaming slowly down the end of the bottle, edging closer to his hand as the story reached its climax.

Max really knows how to tell a story, Will thought and reminisced, feeling like a child getting a story read by a parent before bedtime.

'So where's the money now?' Will asked attentively. There was a certain hurriedness in his voice, a tremble of contemplation.

'That's just it. Nobody knows. None of his gang knew or even got close to finding it.'

'How much?'

'Supposedly 200,000 dollars.'

'Ah, does that make it interesting though? Just 200,000?'

Max knew what he had done. Managed to carefully construct a story of such intrigue, he superbly sold it and made even Will forget important parts of the story.

'Yeah, you're right, it isn't a lot. Not at all. But this is Dillinger's lost fortune. The money that made him an outlaw, the Robin Hood of Chicago, the people's hero as public enemy number one.' As Max said the last four words, he emphasised each with a slight pause in between, to sell it and what he felt was a home run.

'Not to mention this is 1934 money, notes that won't exist anymore, as well as the sentiment behind what it all stands for.'

Right, Max thought, *time for my own victory sip. Crap!* The bottle was empty, as it came quickly back down from his lips and he shook it, just to be sure.

As Max got up to help himself to another couple of beers for them both in his friend's fridge, he left Will in silent contemplation as he pondered the idea, sipping down the remainder of his beer as he did, clearly signifying deep thought.

Max cracked open the bottles and sat back down on the sofa, this time selecting a more relaxing position nestled neatly and leaning back on the sofa, his feet resting on the coffee table found conveniently in front of the couch. Whilst Max got comfortable, Will finally decided to speak.

'You know what…' the slight pause made Max uncomfortable. 'I like it. I think the idea's great. Original enough story with enough to go off, a relevant character with a really interesting back story, something you can connect a reader with, so long as you make the backstory sweet and the search simple enough.'

This time, as opposed to one of them, they both had satisfied looks on their faces. They both knew, at that moment, that Max had managed to create a legible, imaginative story that could be woven and worked into a creation that had a plethora of potential.

The next sips of new beer bottles seemed like a swallow of new beginnings. The clinking cheers beforehand really sold the idea to them both.

'Well then,' Max said as his beer bottle lowered from his lips. 'Guess we'll get back on it… tomorrow', a cunning smile appeared over his face as he finished his sentence. Will's became very similar upon hearing the news, the idea of celebrating something, regardless of the outcome, whether it was finished or not, sounded amazing. It was difficult to beat the ecstatic euphoria of a couple of jars between buddies.

But this time was slightly different. As Will escaped into the kitchen, his hand reached into the cupboard, exiting back out with a bottle positioned conveniently next to a cheap whiskey. The twenty-year rum, to this pair, was the expensive option.

Both shared another grin, followed by excited anticipation for not only the liquor but the upcoming developments of a project they both felt strongly encouraged by. The drinking was but a metaphor for the grander picture reflected by the fresh, intuitive idea. The incoherency of whatever language the two of them convened with each other for the rest of the evening was inconsequential; they both knew it was work tomorrow. Back to the grindstone. Ideas to develop, characters to flesh out. The brimming optimism, like water boiling out of the pan, the idea was the golden ticket, and Charlie had just opened his Wonka wrapper.

8

The progress of the following day was adequate, surprisingly. Max had decided to crash at Will's apartment, it was closer to the pub they had finished in the night before. Despite the antics of the previous evening, Max awoke positively chipper, with only a strong black coffee required to spark him into existence. He borrowed Will's laptop from the coffee table, flattening his bed head enough for his thinking cap. Waking fairly early and managing to check straight into work mode benefitted the writing developments hugely. Max was in the zone.

Will entered from his bedroom in search of a hangover cure, smartly deciding to remain silent and allow Max to continue working. The anecdote-sharing of the previous evening's antics can wait. There was writing to be done.

He lasted a fair while. The progress made was certainly substantial, elevated of course by Will's pep talk. And then, just as Max was enjoying his writing for the first time in a long time, it happened. Again. The enemy returned. The barrier barricaded itself; seemingly in between Max's brain and his fingers; an inability for creative choices and the lingering lack of literacy left inside his head. As empty as Tottenham Hotspur's trophy cabinet once again.

As soon as it had registered, Max slumped on the stool. A previous upright position of optimism and productivity was replaced by defeated deflation, his head slowly falling and hitting the keyboard, adding a line of indecipherable gibberish to his last sentence.

***

After attempting an afternoon hangover-curing power nap, Max, frustratingly feeling worse, reached across the sofa towards the coffee table for his phone. Wasting his time scrolling through his social media, he began becoming increasingly jealous of anyone he came across - how everyone feels surfing through the brazen self-promotion and almost exploitative strategy users and influencers have alike, despite their own fabricated efforts to distance themselves from this very issue. The endless holidays and travelling, the seemingly better lives people lead made Max feel a little down and out. People were living and exploring; meanwhile, Max remained in an endless loop of failed, big-break opportunities and a notebook made for anecdotes, stories, and adventures, remaining depressingly empty.

Shit. In a fit of pessimistic raged tranquillity, he furiously closed his socials and opened the internet, searching for some holiday destinations. He had no idea where. He did not care. Maybe just somewhere. Anywhere. Something to do, something to see. A chance to fill the notebook, a chance at some experience. Better life, more adventures, better stories. It was for work, was the excuse.

As he had his head glued down towards his phone screen, Max rose off the sofa and aimed his walking towards the kitchen, in search of another caffeine fix, attempting to rid his headache once and for all. As the kettle boiled, he finally raised his head to discover Will seated in his own, plump reclinable armchair with a brew of his own, attempting to spark conversation with his friend. It took Max a few moments and more than an uncomfortable silence to realise his buddy was doing his best to try and talk to him. He quickly snapped out of his trance, placing his phone on the kitchen counter beside him, before a half-smile appeared across his face; showing Will he was now back on planet Earth.

'Sorry mate', he said dryly, 'I completely missed that.' A face of forgiveness tried to crawl across his face.

'Oh, you're talking to me now then?' Will remained as sarcastic as ever. Despite a banging headache, hungry as a horse and bloodshot eyes, the dry wit continued. 'I said how are you feeling man?'

'The nap's never the way to go. I always somehow feel worse after I've slept again with a hangover. I need to power through and sleep it all off at once.' Max was rubbing his temples before brushing his long hair back with his hand. Bedhead or not, the guy still looked like he'd styled it for hours. The natural blonde waviness was something even Dennis Wilson would envy.

'Or you just don't wake up super early after you've been boozing, you psycho.' Despite the pain, both were very much feeling at this point, they couldn't help but smile at each other.

'I thought for sure you were getting us chucked out of that last place,' Max continued. 'Especially after you started hitting on the barman's Mrs!' at this point, Max tried to say this with a disappointing tone, but he couldn't help but smile.

'I can't help it, the good ones are usually taken. I can't help being funnier than everyone else.' They both chuckled. He was right. Will leaned back in his chair triumphantly with his hands interlinked and resting on the back of his head. He was funnier than most. And they both knew he prided himself on his prowess in the game department. It did not harm that along with his razor-sharp wit, Will was a strikingly handsome bloke, in a more traditional sense.

Max shook his head in disbelief. Will always had an ego on him, but the day after a night out on the town was always worse than normal. The smile he had on his face was infectious, however; and he somehow always had the ability to conjure up a great evening of shenanigans. Max couldn't help but smile in unison as he turned his head towards the television.

The kettle was warming up as they both tuned into the news that Will had been watching. It remained the same as it had done over the previous couple of days. The stolen memorabilia from the New York story still dominated the headlines, even across the pond. Still no suspects, still no leads. As NYPD's finest scrambled for any resemblance of clues or answers, nothing showed. Nobody could quite believe someone had managed to get away with such a dastardly and cunning showing of hubris.

'What do you reckon? Gotta be some organised group of tossers thinking they can pillage their way through anything and everything to take whatever they want, surely. And to leave two dead? The audacity is unbelievable.' Will spoke to his friend, attempting to spark up a conversation, which he usually had a good track record of doing, even if the other party didn't want to respond. He just had a way about him, a way with words. But this time, however, his questions fell on deaf ears. As the water brewed, the kettle in the background grew louder. Max, now leaning on the kitchen counter, remained transfixed at the screen. As he was taking it all in, the thoughts raced through his mind, an impossible theory not related to what he was watching at all. As a writer's brain usually was, his mind was elsewhere.

The news report blared through the screen, being drowned out by the rising volume screeching through the top of the kettle, louder and louder as it reached closer to boiling. His eyes remained fixed, despite the noises coming from behind him, his trusted friend trying to speak to him. Max's mind was racing. His eyes began frantically moving from side to side, in desperate thought of options, ideas and plot lines, all of them bad. All of them were not ideas, but Max did not care. Thoughts were free. The kettle grew louder. Ideas were his tranquillity. Still, the water squealed. Plot lines? Well, they were not necessarily a dime a dozen inside Max's big hunk-a-junk brain. Potential? Why not?

Suddenly, the kettle flicked off. The water simmered back down inside its metal cylinder. The room came back into view of Max's gaze, his moment of craziness was over. His eyes flicked over to Will, whose own had remained fixed on Max for several moments, annoyed that once again his conversation remained one-sided. Max could see the annoyance in Will's expression, but the subtle serenity he felt rushing over himself after the intervening moments of thought-provoking enlightenment forced another wry smile to creep across his face regardless.

'I have an idea…' Max said. His eyes had moved down towards his phone, which had conveniently remained on the holiday screen he had been perusing over earlier. Ignoring both Will's flabbergasted reaction and whatever he knew he was going to reply with; sarcastically, of course.

'Oh god, that's dangerous.' Will chose to ignore any more sarcasm and get straight to the good part. He knew his friend was a weirdo, but sometimes in that weirdness, something great can be plucked from it. They both knew it.

9

Will sat in silence. He absorbed it all, every detail of Max's absurd construction. He knew when to be quiet and let him get everything he was thinking off his chest. Often Will was doing the talking for both of them, so this was always a pleasant change of pace. He studied the words, analysed the expressions on Max's face and the feelings he showed upon every word leaving his mouth. Will could read every inch of his face, and Max knew it.

The uncomfortable silence never agreed with Max. He never enjoyed talking for long periods without someone to interrupt his thought process. But Will remained patient. They both knew just how crazy the idea was, there was no doubt about that.

'So, what do you think?' Max managed to finally finish babbling. By this point, both were sat down, Max on the sofa and Will remaining in his armchair. Throughout the whole explanation, Max had made them both a cup of tea; he thought it was the least he could do if he was forcing his friend to listen to him. Before Will entertained the idea of a reply, he took a sip of his drink. The tension was building in the room, Max did not care for it. *Just bloody get on with it.*

'Let me get this straight.' Will put his mug on the coffee table before continuing. 'You want to fly halfway across the world, to a place you've never been before, in the middle of nowhere, to try and find something no one has found for almost a hundred years, in the land of the Yanks, no less too!'

'Well, I mean, when you put it like that…' Max mumbled as he left his sentence trail off. To say Will didn't sound entirely convinced was an understatement. He knew it was a long stretch, and the response was typical for Will, but it remained disheartening to hear, nonetheless.

They both sat in silence for a few moments, but it seemed like an eternity to Max. No, he thought to himself. He'd been idling for too long, his life wandering from one idea to the next. He knew he was thin on the ground. The idea was a long shot, and it might financially need everything he had. His mind flashed back to a pile of overdue bills piling up beside his door back at home, there was a reason why he needed to find himself another big break. He was certainly due a change in fortune and besides winning the lottery he never even entered, a book was the next best thing.

Max, for the first time in his life, was tunnel-visioned. He knew just what he had to do. More importantly, he knew what he wanted to do. Whilst thinking to himself, his head tilted across the room to his notebook, positioned on the kitchen counter. The edge of the book remained intact, the pages pressed together. It looked like it had just come off the shelf.

That provided him with all the motivation he needed. He was determined to fill that book with something. He also acknowledged the opportunity he had stumbled across with this next idea. Every idea he had he believed in, of course. But this one seemed different, it seemed right.

Fuck it, he thought.

'You know what? I don't care.' Will was perplexed, he'd never heard such a brazen response from Max before. He doubled down. 'Yeah, I don't care.' This time, he shrugged his shoulders and pouted his lips, highlighting his carelessness. 'I wanna do it. I've done a load of research for this book, it's going well enough, I think I'm starting to get somewhere.' He was in monologue mode again. Will smugly leaned back in his chair, almost in appreciation for his friend's incessant pestering of his ears.

'The fact that it hasn't been found may become an issue. But is it not worth a try? Even if I fail it gives me an excuse to get out and get some inspiration. Take in the area and the history. Over there, they'll know a damn lot more about it all than I ever will. Imagine being responsible for finding John Dillinger's lost fortune.'

'Well, I guess it's not like he's gonna miss it.' Will's dry wit never skipped a beat.

'I've looked. I think I could really find it. A cranky old farmer had never believed there was anything to find, but the Dillinger gang had used the area as a hideout for a couple of months, that's already well known. The police knew even back then something was missing, it's always been known that two hundred thousand dollars was never recovered. It's already been narrowed down to being somewhere near the lodge. That's the only place we gotta look.' Max was on a roll.

'The area it could be in around the old building is not that big. Either way, I have nothing to lose, and I think getting out and experiencing something would be good. I've spent too long sitting and looking for inspiration on the walls of my lounge. There's only so much you can get from the Vertigo poster.'

'Yeah, a sensational amount of dizziness.' Will was also on a roll. The eye roll from Max didn't deter him. They both knew Max was referring to Hitchcock's masterpiece he'd had the poster of since back in university.

The two of them sat in silence for a while. There wasn't anything more to say, only to wait for everything to sink in. They were like two strangers on the underground, the last ones left, heading for the last stop; the air was thick with contemplation, and anticipation. The line was ending - but with the look they both gave each other in the silence, the wry smile shared - they'll soon be on an entirely different journey.

'Why not?' Will shrugged.

'You coming with?'

'Well I can't bloody well let you do it on your own… you'd die within five minutes,' Will chuckled to himself.

Max rose from leaning on the kitchen counter and swaggered confidently over to the other side of the room. It was rare he had confidence like this, and for now, he was going to enjoy it. Grabbing his laptop, he retired back to the sofa, alongside Will in his armchair. They looked over at each other, a smile slowly appearing across Max's face. 'Let's have a look at flights…' he said.

10

A dark military truck bounced gloomily along a track, its all-terrain suspension causing more bobbing and weaving than a prize boxer in a championship bout. Its sidelights provided a worrisome attempt at illuminating the road that came next, yet fought a losing battle against the inescapable chasm of the dark night.

As it trundled forward towards an obstacle, lights up ahead tried to assist the truck. Two huge spotlights pointed up into the sky, sending beaming tunnels of white to highlight the enormity of the roadblock.

The truck slowed as it approached a metal gate at least fifteen metres up and across, the guards patrolling their watchtowers on either side, even higher into the heavens; thankful for the spotlight scorching a sense of life into their station and keeping their solitaire games alive.

One guard moved a newly discovered ace onto her four foundation piles before peering out from her window down below at the approaching truck. Following specific guidelines, she stood, simultaneously grabbing the assault rifle perched upon the table leg. She whipped it up, observing carefully, scanning what the spotlights allowed her to witness on the ground. Poised with the gun across her body, she waited.

Suddenly, a crackling sound disturbed the silence, and she looked down at her waist to see lights appearing on her walkie-talkie, accompanying the noises. A voice attempted to break through the disturbances.

'Post One… this is… 67… 4… get this gate open, now.'

The guard unhooked the communication device and raised it to speak. 'This is 23, go again. Over.' Her hesitancy was not rewarded or copied. A frustrating tone rose over the machine.

'I said get this thing open. Now!! This is McKenna!' The voice demanded.

The guard became instantly flustered. A wave of sweat crept over her in a flash, and she dropped the walkie in a panic. Hastily bending to collect it, she wasted no time to respond, replying whilst crouched. 'Yes sir. Right away. Sorry sir.'

She pushed one of the few buttons on the wall she was allowed access to, and, without any such noise, the humongous gate began retracting. The two halves separated delicately, yet with speed, whilst remaining impressively quiet for a mechanism of its size.

The vulcanised rubber on the tyres turned once more, and the military Jeep entered through the gates, immersing into the darkness as the spotlights only permitted so much exposure to what lay beyond. With the vehicle not having a roof or covering, McKenna could feel the still, dry air of the desert, despite the wind blowing across his face as the Jeep moved through the complex.

He watched outside the Jeep, paying no attention to the young, clean-shaven driver who he assumed shaved one week prior. He enjoyed viewing what he saw as the car manoeuvred through the tracks in the complex. The part that always impressed him was the stark contrast from outside; the vast emptiness of the Arizona sand, the bleakness that appeared to double once the sun had disappeared. And there, in the middle of seemingly nowhere, a small metropolis blossomed. He could not help looking in satisfaction every time.

It was difficult to see further than the lights protruding from the vehicle, and the blanket of darkness helped to elude any suspicions from an outside party of just what was happening.

McKenna did not require further illumination to see what he needed, his years of experience, added to the frequent trips through the complex made him acutely aware of his surroundings. All along either side of the track, as they snaked around in the bleak night, shadows stood rigid, refusing to permit any more details except their outlines.

Bungalows were positioned and packed tightly along the road, flush onto the track leaving no room spare for pavement or earth. The Jeep bounced through the single-storey buildings, twisting and turning deeper into the maze.

The buildings began to increase in size in every way: depth, height and convolution as they progressed, the tall shadows forming barriers of increasing hostility.

Seemingly driving further and further into the darkness, the Jeep cornered a tight bend and was met with two more spotlights, flashes of light striking their beams towards the grandest building of them all.

11

'Another one!' Will exclaimed as he slammed yet another empty cup onto his makeshift table; everyone else using it to catch up on television series with well-placed tablets at ten o'clock in the morning.

'You can very clearly tell this is your first long-haul flight.' The margarita remnants at the bottom of his cup didn't deter Max from his honesty. His choice of beverage was due to keeping his mind occupied, otherwise his nerves would soon kick in.

Ever since the first booking to his inaugural complementary cocktail aboard the plane; his nerves remained jumpy. Was it all worth it? What was the point? Was there any real reason? And of course, the obligatory, why in the holiest of hell, would casually creep its way into his thoughts midway through his refreshment being replenished.

'I'm gonna make full use of this part while I can. If I need to start dancing like a monkey to get some beers, then that's what I'll do.'

'There's no doubt you'd do anything for a beer.' Max said sarcastically in response to Will's statement. He didn't require a response, but it felt like Max needed to reiterate some reminder of etiquette to his friend.

As they both stumbled further and further into Margaritaville, the drinks continued, the mind pondering. The two gentlemen had time to reflect in between their drinks. Naturally, Max's floated further. What were they going to do once they'd got there? Was it all worth it? And god damn did he need another drink already.

'Bottoms up!' Will was getting progressively louder, despite only being two hours in, they'd drank their fair share of the bar.

The two clinked the plastic glasses together and burrowed some more tequila-filled goodness down their gullets. Ah, that's it. The thoughts drifted further away, out of Max's brain and into the clouds beside him. Losing track of your thoughts after a few beverages can be rather annoying when you feel you've stumbled onto something with potential. But Max didn't chase this one. As his eyes began to blink slowly, his head tilting back into the headrest, he knew he was fairly content to leave his anxiety-driven thoughts drifting 30,000 feet in the sky. And the snoring began.

12

He was trying his very best not to tempt fate, but Max knew they were both thinking it. The first plane journey into Detroit went off without a hitch. Just over eight hours, a subsequent layover for a couple, then back on a short sixty minutes over to Milwaukee. No amount of broken sleep on a plane can successfully recuperate oneself from a day of travelling; they were shattered. They were surprised the guy at the rental car place in the airport gave them anything, as a quick bathroom stop en route to their car confirmed they looked like they were on a comedown from a week of festival festivities.

The two of them disappeared down into the car park underneath the airport, the gloominess of the concrete matching quite ironically with the mood the two shared. Tired, drab and dishevelled, they began wandering around with the car key in Will's hand, frantically pressing the lock and unlock button alternatively in the search for a car lighting up, making noise or any sort of sign of life.

The two turned a corner to see the indicator lights flashing on a Ford Mustang, Bullitt edition. The meanness of the car made itself known even in the darkness of the car park. As the indicator lights dimmed, the blue sidelights took over, illuminating the exit. The car was sitting, waiting patiently, desperate for someone to turn over the five-litre, V8 engine and give the other surrounding cars something to be scared about. As the car sat in all its demonic, ironically coloured British racing green, the two guys shared a look with each other. It was the first time they had smiled since finally touching down in Wisconsin. The look was similar to that of a pair of officers in a buddy cop movie when they stumble across some plot-altering evidence. The look they shared panned to both staring at the car,

The Bullit logo on the back finally allowing the two's jaws to hit the floor. After a few moments, at last, one of them spoke.

'Is this ours?' Was the only thing Max managed to muster.

'Well, I wasn't going to let us half-ass it now was I.'

'Very true, you betta not scratch this one,' Max responded. ''Cus we both know what happened in France…' As he trailed off his sentence, Max peered over to Will with his eyebrows raised, a suspicious look on his face. Annoyingly; despite the day of travelling, his hair remained a perfectly messy but styled waviness, and as always he knew this would further piss off his friend.

'Hey!' Will quipped in defiance. 'I thought we agreed to never talk about France again.' It was Will's turn to raise the eyebrows.

'Just 'cus you don't know how to park, I won't hold that against you.'

'Get in the car, prick.'

In the silence that followed after Will's last remark, Max knew he'd hit a nerve. The story of Will scraping along the side of someone's car in Paris - after a beer no less - never failed to wipe any smile off of his face. Being the only one there, Max was the only one who could hold it against him. He only recalled the anecdote on special occasions, although sometimes it was just funny to see him all flustered, especially in the driver's seat of another rental, feeling even more intimidated once he had hit the start button and heard the engine purring once it had turned over.

Max was disorganised the entire trip, but after hearing Will had already booked the car - being more of the automobile enthusiast of the two - Max had slipped the rental guy a hundred-dollar bill to add the protections on. But it was funny to see a man flustered and not mention this part to him just yet. Hell, it might even mean Max could get to drive the mechanical beast earlier than anticipated. The contrast in emotions on the security cameras as they rolled through the car park exit would have been worth buying, at any price; Max sat in the passenger seat with a wide-eyed grin of smugness, Will looking as anxious as a teenager in the middle of their driving examination. Max remained chuffed as they chugged their way out of the car park.

They navigated through the city in darkness, illuminated by the lamp-posts shining their way through the streets, the noise of the engine roaring confidently and cancelling any street noise within the vicinity. If they ever felt like they were in a movie, this was it. The lights sparkling off the dark green bonnet with an abundance of mystique, the rumbling revs as they pulled to traffic lights, the car begging not to be stopped, pushing to go forward and desperately be opened up on the open road.

They pulled out onto the highway and looked at each other. They knew if there was any time for the horse on the front of the car to start galloping, this was it. Will forced his foot down on the accelerator and the car's back wheel's span, violently screeching in pain as they ran across the concrete, smoke flowing backwards as the car swayed itself into moving up to eight thousand revs. Their heads hit their headrests with a thud and the car growled itself to a very much illegal speed in a frighteningly quick time.

Will had a second to himself as he drove. There was something therapeutic about letting a car open itself up, allowing it to reach its full capabilities. He loosened his grip on the steering wheel and ran his hands around the wheel almost in a caressive way, this car was his baby now. His girl. There was not a chance in hell he was letting this idiot beside him anywhere near the controls.

Not for a while at least.

He smiled and his foot pressed further down onto the accelerator pedal.

13

The truck trundled through sliding doors attached to a hangar, which was so large no less than five commercial aeroplanes could reside comfortably. Despite the space, the hangar was vast, yet empty, containing only two similar Jeeps. On the far wall, opposite the entrance, a set of stairs led to a block of offices. The Jeep killed its headlights upon entering, the overheard fixtures in the hangar bright enough to illuminate the dark sky outside if it sought fit.

Pulling alongside the matching vehicles, the passenger door swung open and McKenna stepped out onto the polished floor before the truck came to a complete stop, seemingly annoyed at the time taken to park correctly. He stormed across the empty space, his boot heels thundering an echo of speedy defiance as he made his way up the metal-clinking stairs and into the office.

The room was open, filled with furniture, technology and fixings, surrounding a large window across one side that overlooked the hanger. Desks were in abundance, yet no table tops were visible, hidden under piles of paperwork that rose like snowy peaks; a large table in the middle of the room appeared as a miniature mountain range.

McKenna stormed across the room and met a colleague, similarly dressed in all-black military regalia, working on a laptop.

'Is everyone here?' McKenna asked with authority.

'Yes, sir. All next door, awaiting your arrival,' came the response from the laptop wielder.

'Good.' He walked to a door that delved further into the structure, opened it slightly, then turned back. 'Get some coffee on.'

'Very good, sir.' The man watched the door close behind McKenna before puffing out his cheeks, wiping his brow with a sigh of relief.

14

They cruised out of Milwaukee with ease. The trip had gone surprisingly smoothly, even if all the travelling was getting to each of them more and more. The only solace Max had as they drove along was the opportunity to gaze out, looking at the vast green forests and fields as they drove through somewhere new. He never enjoyed motorway driving, even if he was a passenger. But now he had an interesting window to keep him company. They had agreed with each other to stop at Green Bay, get some food, swap over, and complete the rest of the journey.

Max did not care. He was impartial to driving the Mustang, his irritation level had peaked. He just wanted to get there. To the lodge. To see if they had any chance of pulling it off. No, more importantly, he wanted to sleep. A nice hotel with a comfortable bed. No, he needed some food, he was starving. He had reached the awkward stage of travel: he could not make his mind up and he was agitated.

The delirium set in as he fidgeted in the passenger seat over and over again. He became annoyed at himself, resting his head on the lip of the door where the window connects and decided instead of losing his mind he would try and get some shut-eye instead. He was hoping Will would realise he was asleep, be pragmatic and drive all the way through to the nearest town to where they needed, Manitowish Waters. He guessed he'd just have to find out how clever his friend was once he woke up. Although he could imagine Will stopping and waking him up purely out of spite. Typical. Max rolled his eyes to himself despite his eyes being closed.

***

Max's eyes blinked open slowly. He rose his head up from the car door and peered out of the windscreen, he felt as terrible as he usually did waking up from sleeping in a car. Horrible. His head hurt, and his neck did not particularly enjoy being in a crooked position for so long. *How long was that, exactly?* He quickly glanced to his left, not expecting to see an empty seat. Once his eyes had adjusted, only then was he finally able to appreciate the breadth of the view outside the window. He blinked once more to ensure his eyes were not deceiving him.

The car had been perched on the edge of a cliff, the nose pointing towards the dangerous drop. A bit further on, Will was sat, puffing cigarette smoke, the ash spiralling into the abyss below and smoke evaporating as it thinned into the atmosphere. Max left the car and sauntered over to his buddy, rubbing his eyes. As his feet crunched on the grassy floor, he sat down to join his friend. They had managed to capture the sunrise at just the right time, just the right spot. They peered over as the sun rose in a promising, golden beam of light, the top half of the fireball illuminating and sparkling a section of a lake below in a perfect, straight line. The pair sat, in silence, no words required. They sat staring as the yellow glow rose higher and higher, the warming light hitting their bodies from the cold air being brushed up from the water. The tweeting of the birds was the only noise they heard, a perfect moment could never have been manufactured. Will knew when he needed to open his mouth. He knew this certainly was not one of those moments.

Even if the trip failed; they could not find anything and Max filled nothing in his notebook but gibberish and empty developments, it might have all been worth it just for this moment alone. The opportunity to have perfect bliss and peace can be found and felt when watching the rise of such a promise all across the globe.

As with most travel companions, the pair of them were well aware that a comfortable silence was often required when spending a significant portion of time with someone. They rarely exchanged words with each other for the remainder of the drive. It was not necessary. Max took over driving the last leg of the trip. The novelty of the car had certainly worn off and his tiredness had resulted in a slow, speed-restricted final journey to their destination.

15

As the car grumbled its way into the car park, the two exited the vehicle promptly. To begin with, the two of them were more concerned with the obligatory shaking of legs and twisting of necks that usually followed the conclusion of a long journey. After twisting and turning more than Chubby Checker, they were finally able to take in their surroundings.

From Sheffield to Wisconsin, it was very obvious from the drive this place was going to be slightly different to home. Travelling in the summer months, the evening drive was relatively cool. But as the mid-morning approached, the fierceness of the sun reared its ugly head on the two northerners, who had obviously forgotten the importance of sun cream.

Will's naturally pale complexion ultimately meant a lobster-coloured sunburn would be achieved without protection in a matter of hours. As Max considered this, a cheeky grin appeared across his face, as the complimentary slap across a friend's sunburnt back was part and parcel of any holiday experience. He can at least try and make it fun whilst they were there.

The hotel they had booked was minutes away from what they all needed. They drifted through the forest-filled landscape and vast, luxurious lakes to their destination; driving past the local airport as they went past.

For how quickly they put this whole trip together, they still managed some research. The Dillinger lodge was situated on the edge of a nearby lake. The airport was too small to fly directly from Manchester, annoyingly. There was a library around the corner for some research. And an Irish pub conveniently just over a mile away from the hotel. This was the first thing they had Googled.

As they began strolling around the car park towards the hotel entrance, Will and Max shared a look. This was the last place they expected to share their next holiday.

'This place is…' Max began… 'interesting.'

'It's a bit hot though, innit?' Will retorted as he pinched the shoulders of his t-shirt, pulling it up and slightly forward, shaking the material in his best attempt to cool himself.

'God, here we go,' Max sighed.

'What?' Will snapped back, fanning away.

'You can never do heat, can you? Even back home, the slightest sight of sun and you're done for. I've never seen a man be so averse to the sun. You're like Dracula, mate.'

'It's not my fault I have sensitive skin.' Will was looking for some sympathy.

'Oh, you're sensitive alright. An hour in the sun and you look like you've played a five-setter with Rafa Nadal! Your back starts to look like a water slide!' Max chuckled away to himself.

'Shut up.' Will took out a cigarette and sparked it up, taking a long, deep drag.

The two strolled through the concreted car park to the entrance. Max decided to be sensible and park out of the way, driving on the wrong side of the road and sitting on the wrong side of the car, he would not take any chances parking next to anyone. The two shared the cigarette as they approached the stairs up to the door.

Gazing up at what lay in front of them, it became quickly apparent that 'hotel' was the wrong terminology. The lodge was fairly large, it must have contained twenty rooms or so, the weathered wood on the exterior provided the structure with an interesting character; the overgrown woodland to the left seemed to attack the edge of the building. Ivy and various other leaves gripped the wall, clearly blocking the view of multiple windows.

Will pointed with his finger, cigarette positioned in between the others. 'Not quite a sea view is it?' He retorted.

Max never responded, he just took it all in.

They walked in unison up four outside steps into the double-doored entrance to their lodgings. The wood had radically changed upon entering the inside of the building. Gone was the aged, unpreserved and weed-ridden wood, as it was replaced by a shiny, dark and glossy interior. After entering the large porch, the building opened up into more high ceilings, expertly crafted, wooden beams propping up an open-planned reception area, complete with a stone fireplace, with low, ruby red sofas and a dark grey, faux fur rug. As they strolled through, they walked to the right slightly to a young female receptionist, with dark, brown hair in a black pantsuit, a toothy smile taking over her face from ear to ear.

'Good morning and welcome to Manitowish Lodge! How can I help?!' The lady seemed to shout towards the two gentlemen, despite only being four feet away. The two of them shared a look, soon realising after interacting with somebody else just how tired and road-worn they both were, the look emulating their energy levels. It would have been rude to just say 'room please, name Max,' but at this moment in time, the Neanderthalic response seemed the most they could muster.

Max replied slowly but kindly and had attained control of room keys at an adequate speed from the bubbly receptionist, soon navigating corridors in search of privacy and reprieve.

Max and Will desperately needed to sleep and shower, as soon as possible. They stank.

16

McKenna addressed the room with a solitary nod, seeming to assume this gesture appropriate for greeting the twelve people gathered around the board room table that took up the windowless space.

A laptop sat on the table's side, its screen already turned on, awaiting instructions, in a similar position to the people. McKenna grabbed the remote that sat next to the laptop, cleared his throat loudly with authority, and began.

'I've gathered you here to tell you all something incredibly important. I have just been in a meeting, and, as of two hours ago, we can now confirm the success of our latest endeavour.'

McKenna was set to continue but was rudely interrupted by an eruption of clapping that engulfed the tight room and his voice, much to his disgust. The people being addressed shook hands with those next to them, smiling ear to ear and gossiping in jubilation, shouting over the clapping.

'And yet..!' McKenna screamed, speaking like a battle-axe teacher to their delinquent students, 'our jobs have not finished. In fact, they have only just begun.' His stare had somehow managed to appear angrier, forcing everyone around the table to remain still, refusing to avoid being reprimanded.

McKenna clicked his remote and the laptop switched slides. Flicking its picture onto the blank, opposing wall, his crowd turned away from him to face the projection.

'In the very same meeting,' he began wandering aimlessly in the gaps of the room, helping to facilitate his public speaking, not that anyone would be able to assume discomfort. He spoke with an authoritative gravel, forcing people to listen and, most importantly, remember. 'We began a discussion on our next assignments.' He clicked his remote again as a scarred bald man reached for the water jug in the centre of the table.

'As I'm sure you are all aware, our itinerary is well planned and constructed, with very little room for manoeuvrability. Or even worse,' he paused his movements and speech for dramatic effect, 'mistakes.'

A small spectacled man gulped with fright as he snatched a look at McKenna's hard stare.

'Yet we felt it necessary to congregate to ensure maximum efficiency with our next endeavour. Before I continue, does anybody have any questions?'

It was rhetorical, and everybody knew it. Still, McKenna witnessed a hand raise and grunted, rolling his eyes impressively far back. It was the spectacled man.

'Yes, Robson.'

The man lowered his shaking hand, hesitant to speak up. 'Erm, it's actually Robinson, sir.'

'Right, Robinson. What's the question?' He sighed.

'Well me and a couple of the guys were just wondering… what the final profit for the previous assignment totalled?'

McKenna shook his head slowly in disbelief. Robinson immediately regretted his decision of free speech. 'Did you get paid this month, Robinson?' McKenna asked with a finger pointed directly into his soul.

'Well, of course, sir,' Robinson moved his glasses up his nose with a finger.

'Good, good. It sounds like that information doesn't concern you in the least then, does it now?' He added a forced smile at the end.

'No sir.'

McKenna began to commence his walking again, but his rhythm was interrupted as soon as he turned away.

'It's just we've heard there were some casualties in our previous assignment,' Robinson spoke again.

McKenna half turned his head, shooting a sparing glance over to the scarred man, who had returned a flickering gaze, his cheeks clenched. McKenna laughed, lacking conviction in its authenticity before saying, 'I wouldn't worry yourself with that. That goes for everyone. That's tabloid journalism and you shouldn't consider anything behind what you see on the news.'

'Yes sir,' squeaked Robinson, lowering cowardly into his chair, wishing the ground could swallow him whole.

'Now, as I was saying before being interrupted,' McKenna shot Robinson a death stare of certain contract termination before reminding himself the confidentiality of their assignments prevented him from performing such an action. 'We have confirmed, from a multitude of various prosperous opportunities, our next decision. Everyone, I present the next fruitful revenue generator.' His finger clicked on the remote and everyone's eyes fixed on the projected screen on the wall, absorbing the new information as it appeared. Light ruffles of discussions began taking place that swept around the table, some nodding heads and eyes widening.

McKenna folded his hands, imitating a man waiting patiently for his audience to settle down before continuing. A brief smile crept in through the corner of his mouth, before quickly realising his emotional blunder and recorrecting his face back to the stern expression of discontent and cruel grumpiness he wore from dusk to dawn.

Once the room settled again, McKenna resumed his presentation. He moved his way towards the projection on the far wall as he spoke.

'Me and the board have spent much deliberation before commencing our next operation. 'Many of you may recognise the face on the screen, although less may be familiar with the intricacies of his story.'

Numerous faces were locked at the screen, the others refusing to move from watching McKenna; like children admiring their presents on Christmas morning. By this time, McKenna had reached the projection and pointed at the photographs on display.

'This, is John Dillinger, the famous American bank robber. If you don't recognise him or what he did or any of his story, that is none of your concern. Our directors are of considerable confidence that there be validation in their sources.'

'You have been given the opportunity to remain an integral cog of our system.'

The scarred man shouted during the pause. 'So what's the job?'

'The job includes the recovery of an asset believed to be located here,' - McKenna clicked to the next slide to reveal several maps - 'a place called Manitowish Waters, Wisconsin. We have expert intel as to its whereabouts, narrowed down to a three-mile radius in a forest thicket.'

'Our communications team have successfully implemented an itinerary for you all to follow when on the ground.'

He flicked the screen off and fully turned to address his audience, naturally crossing his hands neatly behind his back.

'There will be two teams of six deployed to work tirelessly around the area. You will be supplied, as always, with the most cutting-edge equipment and technology we can ascertain. 'We shall station ourselves on the nearby lake to monitor and witness the mission to guarantee success.'

The man moved his stance and somehow managed to appear straighter than before.

'Are there any questions?'

Everyone, including Robinson this time, correctly assumed the rhetorical nature of the question and refrained.

'Head outside to block four to receive your information packs. We leave in twenty-four hours. Dismissed.'

Chair legs scraped as everyone moved at a terrific pace causing the table to wobble; all happy to remove themselves from McKenna's presence. They filed out as quickly as spectators at the end of a sports game, soon rendering McKenna alone and motionless.

Only when the last person had left, and he heard the click of the door shut, did he finally remove a phone from his cargo trousers and begin to dial.

17

As far as rooms go, it was acceptable. The wood decoration did become somewhat repetitive once discovered it was used on all floors, walls and ceilings. Yet the furnishings did attempt to create a sense of homeliness. The dark, chocolate-coloured rug at the foot of the bed complimented the lighter, cream curtains. There was enough space. A couple of chairs, wooden of course, a tall dresser to the left of the entrance with a television placed atop and facing the bed. A wardrobe to the right, opposite the window, on the other side of the bed. Past the dresser to the left, a door with a relatively clean bathroom. A walk-in shower was chosen as opposed to a bath, not expected anymore, the pair did discuss it upon discovery.

To the right of the bed, a door led to another, smaller room which included nothing more than a second bed complete with a second window.

The morning pressed on into the early afternoon. Max and Will had gotten some sleep, recuperated, and most importantly, refreshed with a shower each.

'Ugh, I feel much better after that,' Will retorted as he finished changing into something fresher, exiting the bathroom as he did so.

'Yeah, me too man,' Max was changed, lying on the bed watching some TV; his long hair making not only the pillow wet, but the headboard behind him too. He always air-dried his curls, he did not care much for hair dryers. The heat was damaging, he reasoned.

'Right!' Max got up from his lying position, flicking off the TV with the remote as he stood. The retort was a classic British phrase which meant it was time to do something.

'What?' Will had a confused expression on his face. It was clear he wasn't ready to go anywhere.

'We're doing some research. That library I found isn't too far away, thought we could do some reading.'

'No chance mate. The only reading I'm doing is the subtitles on a TV show.' Will became defensive. 'I'm absolutely knackered, mate. Can we not just chill, have a few beers and relax? Start tomorrow?' Will gestured with his hands to convey a sense of persuasion in his voice.

'Well I wanna get going, may as well start as soon as we can. Come on man,' Max pleaded. 'Just a couple of hours and then I'll buy you a beer.' He began collecting his belongings from the bedside table and shoving them in his pockets.

'Nope. You go and do what you want. I'm staying right here.' Now it was Will's turn to collapse on his own bed, as he started heading towards the door leading to his room. 'You come and get me once you've done all the boring stuff. I'm here to help, but I draw the line at reading.' And just like that, the door connecting the rooms was shut, and you could hear the curtains being drawn in Will's bedroom.

Max stood there briefly, with no movement and no expression. After a moment, he shrugged his shoulders, grabbed his room key and notebook from the dresser, and exited swiftly. As soon as he stepped out of the room, the concentrated air-conditioning of the room disappeared, and he was all of a sudden very grateful for his decision to pack, and wear, a pair of chino shorts.

He wandered along the brief hallway, out of the reception lobby, through the porch and doors, and finally down the stairs. He reached for his phone and Googled the directions to the local library, remaining stationary as he did so. Ten minute walk it said. Max knew very well he was always able to walk quicker than the Google-predicted time. Eight-minute walk. *Okay*, he thought, let's enjoy the sunshine. He stepped out of the building's shadow and into the car park, the sun hitting his whole body as he did so, giving him a warm feeling across his skin. He took a deep breath, filling his lungs, closing his eyes and titling his head back for maximum air. He exhaled with a smile. The wonders of vitamin D. He pulled out his silver-trimmed aviator sunglasses and placed them over his eyes, his hands fell naturally into his pockets as he walked. *And we begin.*

18

As he suspected, the walk was shorter than calculated. It always gave Max a sense of self-accomplishment, he had to admit to himself. He walked through the double doors of the library and it led straight into an open planned room, with little to no flashy furnishings, aside from floor-to-ceiling windows all around, and a couple of doors which he presumed led to bathrooms and offices. There were limited chairs and leisure areas, prioritising masses of books stacked upon shelves that reached as high as the low ceilings would permit.

After snaking through the aisles in a stroll, taking in his surroundings, Max stumbled across a section that caught his eye: 'D'. His eyes zoomed closer as he stepped towards the books and his fingers began to flick through the titles. Like a vinyl connoisseur searching for diamonds in the rough at a record fair, Max's eyes scanned ferociously in search of what he wanted. In next to no time, he had found a hardback containing a biography of Dillinger, pulling the book from its place and he continued scanning for more. After a couple of minutes, he had six or seven books under his left arm, along with his notebook, and began looking for a place to read.

An hour passed. Max had asked the nice woman behind the reception desk for a pen and had got down to work. His research was becoming useful, the pen either scribbling something in his notebook or stuck in his mouth. He was still adamant he wasn't addicted to cigarettes, but he certainly looked like he could do with one now. After reaching a satisfying break in his work, he leaned back in his chair and stretched backwards. He sat and read his notes over again, and began piecing together plot points from history into the fiction he had started in the back of the book. He was starting to get somewhere.

'Hmmm. Dillinger, eh?' A voice came from beside Max, he tilted his head to see his confronter. His eyes met a well-dressed, elderly gentleman, spectacles precariously positioned on the end of his nose and a tweed jacket with his beige chinos. He did not look out of place, and nor would he as a professor, or at a local council meeting discussing the prevention of a village expansion. Max knew he had to tread carefully not to engage the man's Karen-mode wrath he knew these people were capable of.

'Errm… yeah,' was all Max mustered up, his eyes darting back to his progress upon finishing his descriptive statement.

'A legend of such around these local parts, old boy. But I'm sure you knew that already…' the old man's thoughts seemed to trail off, his sentence not finished as he stopped.

'Yeah, so I've heard. Just trying to find a bit more about the local history.' Max chose to keep it vague.

'Well, a rather fascinating story, but I wouldn't have assumed someone as young as yourself to be taking an interest. And from as far away as where that accent is from, too. North England is it, sir?' The man asked intuitively.

Wow. Impressive. 'Errm… yeah. Sheffield.'

'I visited Leeds many years ago. I'll never forget that accent,' the old man replied. Max began warming to the gentleman. He had an aura about him. A selflessness of intelligence, yet not in a snobby way. It was there if people required it, and Max could use the help. He poked the bear.

'So,' attempting to move the conversation in his favour, 'what can you tell me about this guy that I wouldn't find here?' Max gesticulated with his hands towards the papers in front of him. He began moving them closer to him and pointed with his right hand for the elderly gentleman to take the seat next to Max. The man accepted the request, and placed himself on the chair in silence, resting his own books on the table before beginning his lecture.

'Good question. There has been plenty of information written about Mr Dillinger over the years. Personally, my particular favourite is the story involving Little Bohemia up the road, and Dillinger's willingness to hide a reasonably large sum in the dirt to escape authorities.'

Max listened intently. *This guy could prove useful,* he thought. He decided to ask his questions and see what he could find. He would, of course, cross-reference with the books afterwards, just to ensure no bullshit was being fed to him. But somehow he doubted that. The man seemed happy to speak to someone who would listen to his intelligence and poise.

'Yeah, so I've been reading. What was all that about then?'

'Well, Dillinger's Gang had managed to acquire themselves quite the reputation during the 1930s, and a well-known public enemy number one. His number of attempted bank robberies was over twenty, he attempted to rob police stations and escaped imprisonment numerous times. As a result, FBI's J Edgar Hoover was personally heading the investigation with Melvin Purvis in tow.'

'So this guy was in a lot of trouble, basically.' Max interrupted just to let the gentleman know he was still listening.

'Indeed, very much so. Dillinger himself had quite the reputation, too, I might add. Something akin to your Robin Hood fellow; the public believing he was a hero for 'taking from the rich.' But this was manipulated by the media of the day. The gang killed and wounded police and bank employees everywhere they went. Their modern machine guns and brazen approach made it quite the spectacle to exaggerate.

'So, where does the lodge come into all of this?'

'Good question. So, with the police hot on the heels of him and his gang, Dillinger comes out here to one of his hideouts, the lodge, attempting to hide until some interest in him wains. Alas, the FBI found his gang through a local informant, before high-tailing it over to the lodge.

'They staked the building, observing people leaving the lodge and entering a vehicle late in the evening. Assuming it was the gang, and a request for the car to stop falling on deaf ears, the FBI opened fire, killing the driver of the vehicle. Alas, the gang members were not in the vehicle.

'Now. The group of criminals remained upstairs in the lodge at this point, but upon hearing gunshots that were meant for themselves, they decided to scarper out the back doors. They were chased through the forest, and Dillinger importantly got away; not before supposedly burying a healthy sum of depression-era cash in the ground out there somewhere.'

Max took a deep breath in, puffing his cheeks out as he did. 'And no one has any idea where the money's buried?' Max asked as he frowned towards the gentleman.

'Absolutely. No one at all,' the elderly man said with a shrug.

'Not long after this, Dillinger hid around the Chicago area. He remained there until his location was discovered and he was shot dead in the street in 1934, taking the location of his money with him.'

'Jesus. And how much exactly is supposed to be out there?' Max had been waiting for the all-important question. He had read it was in the region of $200,000, but the old boy would know for sure.

'Ah, the important question. Most historians believe there to be more than $100,000 somewhere around the lodge.' The gentleman could see Max's lower jar drop at the information being shared. Sensing he was to be interrupted, he held a finger up in the air before continuing.

'But… judging by the number of robberies made after his last prison escape before getting to the lodge, local residents and enthusiasts suggest this number could be as high as 200.'

'Now that's a lot of money,' Max had been listening intently to everything being said to him. But he had to double-check that part.

'That's what a few of us believe. A lot of money, even by today's standards.'

'Oh for sure.'

'The money has been lost for almost a hundred years, however. Many people, myself included, have tried to go searching for it over the years, but it remains a mystery. Even if it was only 100 dollars, it would be worth more than the original sum for certain.'

'Wow…' Max said, speechless once again. For a moment, the two sat in silence, sharing the information and the story together. Letting both their minds wander, not only regarding the hidden beauty but no doubt about the time period. How different everything was ninety years ago. The utter simplicity of life, how much changing, altering, evolving whilst the money remained breathless under the dirt. As the silence continued, Max started to twitch around the room with his eyes. He really had nothing to say, and no real way of showing his appreciation for the gentleman assisting his research. He doubted the man would actually know how much he had helped. *Shit. Ought to say something, at least.*

'You know, they found a King in a car park back home a few years ago. I think they said he used to be in a church, I can't quite remember. But it was over 300 years ago. Or something like that.' Jesus Christ. Max was disappointed and frankly embarrassed by his lame segue. He could see the old guy's confusion. At least his facial expressions were a little funny to see.

'Oh really?' It was now the gentleman's turn to be speechless. He started to move his head around the room, looking for his chance to exit the conversation he started. 'Fascinating.'

Max could taste the sarcasm coming from the word. Time for a cigarette.

'Well thanks, you know, for all that information. Whilst we're here me and a friend wanted to find out just what happened round here, we already knew some basics. We were planning a wander over to the lodge and the forest around it. Would you recommend?'

'A lovely walk from here,' the man replied. 'If that is your plan, this might help.' The man's hands reached over into Max's book pile in front of him. He picked one from the pile and opened the book exactly onto the page of his desire. 'There you go', he said, his finger pointing at a two-page spread of a local area map, with all the details, including an area that is believed to be home to the fortune.

'Wow… thanks. Much appreciated.'

'But you be careful now…' the man trailed off his sentence in anticipation of Max replying with his name.

'Err Max.' Max extended his hand.

'Jonathan. Nice to talk to you, Max. Take care now.' The man shook the open hand and waved after finishing the handshake, spinning on his heels very elegantly for someone of his age, and strutted off, his book selection tucked under his arm. Max tidied his research section, snapped a picture of the map on his phone and returned the books to their homes. He scouted the building quickly with his eyes as he departed, hoping to exchange a quick nod of appreciation to this afternoon's professor, but the old man was nowhere to be found.

Max swung open one of the double doors, enjoying the hit of warmth from the sun as he did so. He lit a cigarette, taking the inaugural drag with extended gratification, his eyes squinting in the sun and jawline defining as be breathed in the smoke. He exhaled and began his walk back to the room.

19

The bald man with the scar had exited the room swiftly, attempting to hide his hastiness and matching everyone else's speed towards the door. He turned sideways to allow his shoulders to fit, ducking his shaven head slightly under the door frame.

He knew what was coming next. He wanted to avoid the confrontation but knew it to be impossible. With everyone walking out of the first room and into the hanger, the man hung back and accepted two cups of coffee from the man working on his laptop, the smell of the freshly brewed coffee was always an indication of McKenna's authoritative presence.

The man sipped from one cup, the steam still violently exiting the mug as he placed the other on a nearby table. That's when he felt the vibrations in his pocket, looking down and taking a deep breath in preparedness.

There was no contact information on the screen, yet he recognised the number. He grabbed the second mug once more, easily swinging the shut door open despite not having a hand spare.

Stepping through the doorway, he said 'I brought you some coffee, sir.'

McKenna stared at the man as he made the doorway look impressively small. He reached out and took the mug outstretched towards him.

'Take a seat, Decker.'

'Thank you, sir,' Decker replied, taking a seat on a chair, making it appear as though it was built for children. He rubbed his hand over the small hairs on his head and awaited his fate.

20

The plastic key card came into contact with the door, forcing an electronic beeping noise and the handle turned to push the door open. Max wandered through his own space and over to the other side of the room to the connecting door, knocking with his knuckles as he reached it. Nothing. Brilliant. He tried the handle, and the door opened. And there Will was, looking like he had been shot, sprawled across the bed. Max knew what he had to do. Only because Will would do the same to him in this scenario. *It was the middle of the day, the afternoon, for Christ's sake,* Max thought, attempting to justify his intrusive thoughts.

Leaving the door open, he walked across his room and into the bathroom. He grabbed a small glass from the counter and filled it up with cold water from the sink. Slower this time, and with a full glass, he crept back over to Will's space, taking one final look at him resting ever so peacefully. *What a shame,* he thought to himself, erasing any second thoughts of remorse, before throwing the contents of the glass over Will's face.

'Ahhh!'

Will shot up into a sitting position, eyes wide open, along with his mouth, which performed long and loud breaths, puffing out his cheeks.

'You prick!!' Understandably after being woken up, that's all he seemed to be able to conjure.

'Your alarm call, sir.' Max's face scrunched intensely, attempting to hide a smile. No use. There were a few stutters before outright hysteria, maniacal full-body laughing, bending over and holding his stomach before collapsing on the floor to continue.

Will, still skin-soaked, water dripping onto his bed, took one look at Max in pieces, on his bedroom floor. Giggling through his pain, he laughed himself, holding his arms out in front of his chest, palms raised in disbelief.

After ample time to calm down and gather themselves, the giggling schoolgirls had had a relatively uneventful afternoon post-bath time. Max had taken the time to inform Will of all the details he managed to get down at the library, not to mention he was scribbling more in his notebook than he had in years. Perhaps the trip was working.

The pair of them decided to remain in the hotel's dining area for now, the wide-open space off from the reception and main entrance. Despite it all remaining one large room, it felt separate, the dozen or so tables and chairs acting as a territory mark, not to mention the corner kitchen and a bar conveniently positioned in the middle of the space. It ran to the right of the tables, behind the reception, and opportunistically, right next to where Max and Will had parked for the afternoon.

With Will's constant cigarette breaks, it gave Max a great chance to fill his notebook. He was either explaining the history to Will, reaffirming his knowledge; or as soon as it was cigarette o-clock, he'd turn to the back of the book and scribble some new ideas he'd constructed. He was getting close to a semi-solid idea, and he knew all too well that following this stage he'd soon have to start writing.

That was the part that scared him the most. The first sentence. So many hours lost to a pen tapping on an empty page, feeling any choice in the English language inadequate for what needs to be remarked. Like a professional athlete, the weight of expectation heavy on those first impressions.

He never went in blind. He always had the whole story marked out. Of course, he would add parts where necessary, but the core story usually remained the same. So it wasn't like he was going down a creek without a paddle, or on stage without a microphone. Max often just found it difficult to express his thoughts into action and let his true personality be known. He often cited the same justification for struggling when meeting new people, and that new page so often felt like a stranger at a party he wished he could avoid. He much preferred one-to-one interactions and believed this favoured his personality, the recipient of the conversation usually benefitting as a result.

'Looks like you're getting quite a bit down today. That's good mate, keep it up.' Will spoke whilst he walked back to his seat. He did not need to make his presence known; Max could smell the smoke lingering as soon as he stepped through the door. *One later, perhaps,* he thought to himself. He continued scribbling, Will would not mind being ignored. He was used to it by now.

'You wanna beer?' Now that, Max could answer.

'Hmmm, go on then,' he replied, implying there was ever any contemplation of the decision.

Will returned to the table with two bottles, the beads of condensation running down the edge of the glass, like heavy paint running down the side of a fence.

'So, what have you found out then?' Will asked. Max dropped his pen onto the page so he had full use of his hand gestures.

'Okay…' Max began. '… I went to the library round the corner and started reading up a bit more, then some old guy came up, talking to me about it all. Pretty useful.' Max takes a swig of his beer.

Will sat there, waiting for more information than he had already been provided. After a few moments, he knew that was not to happen without probing further. 'What's next then? Go to the lodge, do some writing? Feel the story?' Will moved his hands in front of his shoulders, spread his fingers and swayed them slightly, sarcastically gestured Max would 'write better' in the place he was writing about.

'I suppose. Let's see how we feel tomorrow morning. Cheers,' Max raised his bottle and Will reciprocated.

21

Like most things the pair of them got up to - which included the insane idea of the trip they found themselves upon - they had little planned for what came next.

In your twenties, frivolous imaginations and unrestricted temptation can often result in anarchy of adventure if left unmanaged. The common excuse of 'finding oneself' was a well-trodden path; often with wavering levels of execution and success. Still able to rambunctiously play off any sense of a plan, and like a boat that has lost its sails, can bob aimlessly until either the next brainwave occurs to alter a situation, or someone else saves you. Even as you reach the end of this 'lost decade', as the two friends found themselves approaching, one could assume an acquisition of knowledge and experience could help be implemented to provide wisdom as one approached the years of supposed greater wisdom.

Alas, wisdom can be used for other moments. Max had written for a couple of hours, tentatively teasing with a story that remained relatively uncrafted, but he could see Will getting impatient. After telling himself he was going to get up early to write some more, he closed his notebook and decided to relax with a couple (more) beers with his friend. There still remained no plan, but that suited the both of them, for now.

Will was fairly content and was very much treating it like a holiday. The type of holiday where one has too many drinks and states a true epiphany; threatening to sort everything out when they finish their vacation. 'I'm going to get my shit together. No smoking, no booze. Okay, okay, less booze.' It had become a well-trodden path, a path that often remained pristine and unused. Max could recite the line he had heard so many times before. It was also worth remembering for hungover teasing too, mind.

For Max, the lack of a plan failed to faze him either. Max was becoming increasingly interested in the story. As a hopeless dreamer, there was a small part of him that genuinely thought he was to be the one to find the lost fortune. He was imaginative, and a believer, so why not him? He wanted to go out and start looking. He had taken a photo of the map the old man had shown him in the library and just wanted to get out there and hunt. If there's no joy, they can go to the lodge and have a look at the history. And get some lunch. And potentially another beer. He'd been Googling the reviews of the restaurant and read some good things. There was a notable burger that particularly took his interest. Max just knew Will would probably need a little convincing. But it's not something he hasn't done before. He even knows the exact amount of alcohol consumption to make the job easier for himself.

***

Believe it or not, Will was a little hungover the next morning. As he opened his eyes, they stung, and quickly deduced the day would require sunglasses. He was already grateful enough for last evening's self that he had filled no less than three glasses of water to help hydrate and remove himself from his slumber and placed them on his nightstand.

Max had stopped drinking earlier, claiming that he wanted to be fresh for the day. This was not a problem, only the fact that Will was not going to be bullied and laughed at for being hungover. Fair enough, he thought to himself, he would do the same thing to Max. He gingerly got dressed, drank all of his water and placed some dark-rimmed sunglasses across his face. He opened his door to the main room. Max's bed was empty, already made. He stepped around and out of the room, shuffling across the hotel to the restaurant so he could start attempting to fight his hangover and potentially receive less negligent name-calling. Probably no use, but worth a try.

'Hi there!' A middle-aged waitress of unnecessary volume and buoyancy for Will, came pace walking towards him. 'What can I get for you?' She asked.

'Can I get a full English and two cuppas please, love? Thank you.' Will gave the woman his card, waving his hand as she took the plastic.

'Sure! Coming right up sir!'

Will half pulled a chair and slid past the table onto it, collapsing into a reclined position. He forced himself to sit forward, resting his head and hands on the table. He dozed.

Will's face rose, shot to life courtesy of the two annoyingly loud knocks on his table. And the smell of bacon. Max sat opposite him, grinning gleefully. *Should have guessed.* At least his breakfast was here, although, suspiciously missing a sausage and fried egg; no prizes for guessing where they had gone.

'Thanks for the cuppa, mate!' Max raised one of Will's mugs to cheers him in appreciation.

'Yeah… no problem', Will replied gingerly.

The two sat in silence for a moment, Max enjoyed his brew - never quite the same as being in the comfort of your own home, he always said - and Will tucked into the remainder of his breakfast.

'Ready whenever you are, by the way, buddy.'

'Ready for what?' Will replied in question, in-between mouthfuls of baked bean-soaked hash browns.

'Last night you agreed to come with me around the lodge. So, we can have a gander around, see what we can find.' An optimistic smirk appeared across Max's face that could only drive Will's mood further downhill.

'Yeah? When did I agree to that?'

'Last night, before I went to bed. I double-checked with you when you were at the bar, getting a drink and trying to flirt with the 60-year-old bartender. That didn't go well for you, by the way, mate,' Max chuckled to himself. Will deliberated, his food for thought being mushrooms, chewing away.

'For Christ's sake,' he said eventually. 'Let me eat this, then we go.'

'Take all the time you need.' Max reclined in his chair and sipped his tea in victory.

22

McKenna would have usually stood for this conversation. He liked to force others to sit, to make himself appear dominant and in a stronger position, looking down like a big cat watching its prey. This time, however, he made the decision to sit, indicating his level of respect for Decker, who now sat across from him.

Decker watched McKenna sit and appreciated the respect, having been made aware of the man's eccentricities. He saw the battle-hardened face stare at him through the steam of the coffee, each mug attempting to blur Decker from getting a full view of his superior.

'I would like to congratulate you, Decker.' McKenna began, the compliment taking Decker by surprise.

'Thank you, sir,' he managed in reply.

'Our last endeavour was successful, and you'll be pleased to hear we have now attained a considerable profit margin as a result.'

Decker was struggling to hide his confusion, so settled for grabbing his mug. 'Glad to contribute to the success, sir,' he said after a sip.

He has had conversations with McKenna before. He has heard other people's interactions with him. They are never usually like this. Traditionally, it is a dressing down for the slightest infringement - Robinson got the hairdryer treatment in a specific example for too many buttons undone on his shirt, exposing too much chest hair - and you are supposed to sit and take the talking to, leaving hurriedly with your tail between your legs. This conversation was unsettling Decker, the compliments were not normal and he shifted uncomfortably in his chair.

'I have read your report,' McKenna continued. 'You felt the casualties were justified?'

Here we go, Decker sat upright. 'We believed so, sir. Having constructed the mission plan myself, I believe everyone was aware of the risks. We always try to avoid that conclusion, yet sometimes there isn't an alternative.'

McKenna attempted his best impression of trying to put someone at ease. 'Do not worry, Decker. I have been in your position, it is not always easy to make these decisions in the heat of an endeavour. We are talking about milliseconds of time to assess and judge the situation. The report you turned in confirmed everyone we thought would happen.'

Decker cleared his throat. 'Well, I'm glad you agree, sir.'

'How long have you been with us now?' McKenna asked. He grabbed his mug for the first time, taking big swigs.

'Five years, sir.'

'And you were in the CIA before we recruited you?'

'Special Ops, sir,' Decker corrected.

'Ah yes, I remember the file now. Very impressive record, not to mention your invaluable work with us.'

'Thank you.'

'You are on a good path, Decker. I am expecting some interesting news to develop in regard to your future when the forthcoming endeavour will undoubtedly be as successful as the previous ones.'

McKenna stood, indicating he was finished with the interaction. Decker obliged and stood promptly.

'I look forward to it, sir.'

'You're dismissed, Decker.'

'Thank you, sir,' Decker stood and began walking towards the door.

'Oh, Decker?' McKenna called to him across the room, forcing his subordinate to turn to face him. 'The next job. You know we have attempted a peaceful resolution for the relevant parties in regard to compensation, I'm sure.'

'Yes sir. It's been made aware to me a claim to the land the asset is on is owned by a local. A local who has not been forthcoming in accepting our offer.' Decker had thoroughly read his briefing prior to the morning's meeting.

'And as always,' McKenna pressed, 'you are to be made aware that this requires utmost caution. We shall be operating in the shadows of the forest.'

'Agreed, sir.'

'And, if necessary, you will be given the all-clear to terminate anything that may prohibit the acquisition. This includes the supposed landowner. It may be required to silence any negative publicity.'

'I understand, sir.'

'Good. Now, on your way, Decker.'

Decker replied with a nod and slinked out of the room as subtly as his large body would allow.

McKenna sat back down and attacked the remainder of his coffee in the mug. He shouted through the wall to the man working in the other room, who appeared in the doorway with a coffee pot to replenish McKenna's refreshment. He said no more to the man and he left in a hurry.

He sat back and enjoyed a moment of peace and quiet, savouring the first sips of a new brew in the mug, the quietness of having a room to himself and being about to remove any thoughts. The first parts of a hot drink he thought were always the best, the start of something new, a refresh, a turning over onto a new sheet of paper.

No sooner had he relaxed, the moment had passed and that was all he allowed himself to switch off. He grabbed the telephone from the table and began making another phone call. He gulped the hot liquid as the phone dialled; the only parts to enjoy were the first, the rest became merely sustenance.

The line picked up on the other end.

23

The pair of them walked to the lodge. It was not necessarily far, but Max knew he had chosen the more favourable option to help combat Will's hangover. It took just over an hour, which annoyed Max as he had seen the walk was estimated to be as long on Google. In his mind, he blamed Will's current state for slowing him down.

The walk was mostly pavements running adjacent to the road, but the views were impressive and tranquil; specifically when there were no loud, American, boat-sized cars going past. The greenery was lush with an intriguing quality, and the depth of the forest cut through so sharply and suddenly by the human necessity of a bland, grey, concrete road.

Just out of sight, the airport remained in earshot, planes cruising vertically into the clouds above their heads; there were even a few helicopters, which surprised Max. He knew from his research that the Manitowish Airport was relatively small and he certainly was not able to get a direct flight from home. Nevertheless, the number of helicopters was more akin to the arrival of numerous celebrities to a red-carpet affair, or the constant surveying choppers found on Australian coasts (Max had visited Australia in his early twenties and discovered the surveillance was a particular type of shark watching). He tried to find a logical explanation behind the phenomenon. They were walking for sixty minutes and the pair had seen three planes and five helicopters. Why? He knew he could never find a direct answer, but the mystery intrigued him nevertheless. It became a convenient solution to pass the time whilst they walked, as naturally, Will had not been in much of a talkative mood.

It was just past midday when the two switched the concrete pavement for a turning off the main road into a sandy-coloured dirt car park, a car park where cars churned up smoke on the dirt and gravel, a very unfavourable position for walkers as the smoke clouds grew thicker and larger the more vehicles drove through it. Being lunchtime, the cars were of a constant frequency, perfectly timed for the duo as they were coughing and spluttering as they reached the main entrance to the building.

'How are we feeling now?' Max asked.

'Yeah… that walk really helped actually. Think the full English too. Just… give me a second.' Will was bent over, his hands on his knees in a crouch-like pose.

'Well,' Max crossed his legs over and leaned back onto the railing to the side of the entrance, smiling. 'Just let me know when you're ready.'

'Yeah, cheers mate.' A few moments passed. The gasping escaping from Will started to sound more like natural breathing and his figure slowly became more upright. 'You didn't tell me we were walking the whole way. And I definitely didn't realise it was gonna be this far. A little warning would have been nice! I'd have got some water to take.'

'Oh stop being a little baby. Just be grateful I didn't make you run it.'

'You've done it before, fucker. Can you not remember the endless 5k that turned into 25? No warning. Worst day of my life.'

'I did you a favour that day.' Max pointed as he replied.

'Yeah? How so?' Will moved closer to Max and slapped away his finger in jest.

'Yeah. The amount of times I've heard you use the fact you done a half marathon to flirt with women.' Max rolled his eyes. 'Thing is, I've never seen it work!' Max laughed; the smile visibly seen in his eyes through the aviator sunglasses he had on.

'Ha ha,' Will said sarcastically. 'Stop mucking about and let's get this over with so we can get back and do nothing else for the rest of the day. I'm shattered already.'

As the two of them stood by the entrance, Max took a moment to stop jibing Will to take in their surroundings. The lodge seemed superior to the one they were staying in, yet this one was clearly smaller. The dark wood trim accented the light wood encasing the building perfectly; the chocolate colour of the darker wood weathering slightly, leaking down into the light wood panels.

As the doors opened, the wood began to blend into one colour, settling for something in-between. This was covering everything; the walls, tables, chairs and bar in the far-left corner. There was a main hall-type room which held the customers, with two doors on the right which included one for a kitchen. The ceiling was low enough that one could assume there to be a second floor, but there appeared to be no sign of stairs.

Max recognised this and thought aloud. 'I read that when the gang was here, they were on the second floor, playing cards when they heard someone outside before they escaped. But…'

As he trailed off, Will helped. 'Where are the stairs?'

The pair of them looked like children in a sweet shop, their jaws both open. Max just loved being in places of history. He enjoyed attempting to imagine what a specific period would have been like. In that sense, if provoked, he would admit his favourite place to visit was the Cavern Club in Liverpool. It was not difficult to imagine the swinging sixties and early Beatlemania when you were in an underground sweat bunker and sixty years of partying and clubbing stuck to the bare brick walls.

The lodge, now converted into a restaurant, seemed relatively pedestrian compared to its well-publicised history. It is unclear how long the Dillinger Gang used the lodge, being from Chicago. It may not have been longer than a few days before the authorities found them, but those select few days had such an impact on the building that has stood for more than one hundred years. This was clear from the newspaper cut-outs all across the walls, the Dillinger merchandise available by the cash registers and topped exquisitely by the 'Dillinger Gang' burger that had made its way onto the menu.

Max moved across the open main room to the bar in the corner and introduced himself to the barman. He was not middle-aged, but slightly older if he could guess. His hair was silver and thinning on the top, but remained perfectly slicked back with a comb. His shirt fit him perfectly. One could assume he dressed well and took care of his appearance, just by judging by his top half, as the rest of him remained hidden by the bar. Will hung back slightly, he figured he had already spoken to enough people today, the sunglasses still covering his eyes.

'Good afternoon, how can I help?' The barman started the conversation. His pronunciation was proper and polite.

'Hi, mate. Wondering if you can. My friend and I,' Max's thumb pointed behind him to Will, 'were just looking for some extra information on Dillinger. We've come here on holiday and we just really love the story, and we thought there might be some more information here. But it seems you don't have much more than we already know.'

'Ah, some more budding enthusiasts.' The man seemed unimpressed, but there was a hint of uneasiness, almost a tremor, in his voice. It was slight but noticeable.

'Yeah, sorry man, I bet you get this all the time.' Max laughed, trying to help the bartender feel more at ease.

'Of course. We usually get lots of people asking to see upstairs, but in light of recent circumstances, we've been forced to stop this service for now,' the disappointment was clear in his voice.

'So, there is an upstairs? I knew it! Wait. What do you mean by stopping it?

'We had an incident.'

'Oh…' Max thought quickly. 'What sort of incident?' Will was only half listening, but after hearing the word 'incident', he sprung to life and moved closer to the bar so he could hear clearly.

The barman sighed. 'Some gentlemen came in when we were closing yesterday. Wanted to see upstairs. We said we were closed, but they were more than welcome to come back tomorrow. They threatened us if we didn't let them upstairs. So, we did. They went up, came back down 10 minutes later and shot right out the front door. They didn't take anything, but it has made us nervous if you can understand.'

Suddenly the barman's change in behaviour after being asked the question made sense. 'Jesus, that's crazy,' Max's idea of compassion wasn't particularly inventive. 'All you guys all alright afterwards?'

'I think so. One of the girls took the day off. She seemed to take the brunt of the abuse from one of them. It's strange. They looked like professionals, all dressed in black, military boots, and what have you. Seemed awfully strange, there isn't anything valuable up there, so it wouldn't be worth stealing anything if they did. Thank you, though. I appreciate your concern.'

'Yeah, of course, not something you expect I imagine.' The old man shook his head in response. There was a brief silence while Max tried to collect his thoughts. 'So, there isn't any way we could get up there and have a look any time soon? Just we've come an awful long way, it'd be disappointing to go back having not seen it.' Max went into his pocket and produced a twenty-dollar bill. He placed it on the bar and smiled.

The barman's eyes flicked from the note to Max's teeth and back to the note again. He took a few seconds to consider the situation but eventually relented. 'This,' he took the note, folded it delicately, and filed it away into his trousers. 'Plus, you have some lunch, and I get a good tip for serving you as well, and I'll take you up after.'

Will pushed past Max and spoke up. 'Look man, I've just eaten, is there any way…'

Max cut him up before he could finish. 'No problem, we'd love to have some lunch.' The trademark smile reappeared. Will's face showed the opposite of a smile.

'I have grandchildren's college funds to help with.' The barman walked to the other side of the bar and met the pair of them. His trousers were freshly ironed, perfectly seamed down the centre, and his dress shoes were recently polished so impeccably they looked new. He showed them to a table.

24

After a quick lunch, served with a generous tip to their waiter, the pair of them were shown upstairs by the older gentleman. He had stated to them that there were, in fact, two staircases, and they would be using the smaller ones located in the back of the building to try and avoid running into the lodge's manager as they went.

Up the stairs, the main room they came into was smaller than the largest room downstairs. The room's furniture consisted of a red sofa in the middle along one of its longer walls, and four wooden chairs surrounding a square table. Aside from this, there were several wooden cabinets built waist-high with glass tops, all of which contained artefacts from the 1930s, including a Thompson machine gun. There were more newspaper cuttings decorating the walls, which apart from this and the windows, were completely bare. Upon the table, there was a card game being played, next to a fabricated newspaper with the front page containing the date of issue as April 22nd 1934: the date at which the FBI attempted to arrest the gang before they absconded.

It was clear that the lodge had attempted to keep the room in the state that it was in at the time Dillinger's Gang had found refuge there. Max wandered the room, making his way to the corner where the table sat. Upon closer inspection, looking out of the corner window, he noticed the lodge continued on the ground level, beyond the length of the first floor. He peered through the glass, looking down and seeing the roof of the lower floor connecting to the wooden outside wall he now stood on the other side of. The barman had followed his path across the room, and before Max could ask any questions, the older gentleman interrupted his thoughts.

'The theory is,' he began, talking over Max's shoulder as they both looked out the window, 'they jumped out the window once they heard gunshots, onto the first-floor roof, then the grass and escaped into the woods out there.' The barman's finger pointed towards an area of dark forest to the left of the building. 'They couldn't have gotten far; I wouldn't have thought.'

Max took his chance to show off his recently found knowledge. 'So, the FBI supposedly came in after a tip, but they didn't call for backup or had many of their own numbers. So, the chances are, the gang had someone who was able to sneak back around the front to get a car, and go round the forest sweeping everyone up. But not before Dillinger got nervous and buried his money.'

'Not bad kid,' the old man replied, Max's face remained pointing at the window, so no one could see the smug grin across his face. 'You're right. That is more than likely what happened. Dillinger was supposed to return and dig it up, of course, but didn't make it to even the end of the year.'

The two shared a moment in silence, both looking out the window. In the near distance, straight ahead and beyond the tree lines, you could see the lake the lodge backed onto, yet there remained a considerable number of trees between the two objects, despite the distance being less than thirty metres. Max could see numerous small fishing boats bobbing their way along the water, some attempting to move, some happy to remain as still as the water would allow. During this shared appreciation of their surroundings, Will had taken to perching himself on the sofa, which faced the room in the opposite direction, and looked around, confusion visible across his face.

'I still don't understand what those guys could have possibly wanted yesterday,' Will spoke up. It was a statement but aimed as a question towards the barman. After coming back to earth from his daydream, he responded.

'We have no idea either. We have security cameras, of course.' His right hand opened and pointed in the direction of a camera in the opposite corner in which he and Max stood, the camera fixed on the set of table and chairs. 'But all we saw when we looked it back over was, they came upstairs, had a look around the room and came over to where we stand now. After talking for a minute or so, gesticulating with their fingers outside the window, they ran back down the stairs and left. A very peculiar end to a day, I must say.'

Max turned around to face the barman, placing a hand on his shoulder as he spoke. 'At least no one was harmed, that's the main thing. Hopefully, you can all just forget about it soon enough, and let people back up here. This place is really quite something.' He looked over at Will, the two of them sharing a glance, and Will rose. 'We'd like to thank you so much for letting us come up here and look at this stuff mate,' Max continued. 'We'll get out of your way so you can get back to it downstairs before you get in trouble.' And with that, the three of them took the stairs, and the two of them left the lodge.

Outside, Max immediately took a right, walking parallel to the side of the building, following round the corner and coming to a stop directly underneath the window he had just stood at. He inspected what he had just seen from upstairs, a small area of trimmed, freshly mowed grass and then the plethora of dark trees and shrubbery that trailed off in the distance. The forest was tall, as from the ground Max could not see the lake in the distance. He remained there, staring and in thought, before he was interrupted.

'Hey man, wait up.' Will trailed but eventually caught up. Within a few moments, standing next to Max, Will's brain caught up as well. 'Ohhh. You wanna go in there now?' Will looked at the same view as Max and smiled in anticipation. 'Let's do it.'

'Well, look who's finally decided to wake up,' Max retorted.

'Hey, I had that coffee at lunch for a reason. I just didn't know what for. But if you wanna, let's go.'

'Alright.' The two of them shared a look, smiled at each other and took the twenty-yard walk across the grass, the cut grass smell hitting their noses as they trod in the new ground, feeling like sports stars entering the field from the tunnel to begin the game. After this, the grass seemed to dissipate instantly, replaced with a mixture of dirt, mud and tree trunks, some popping out of the earth. Within a few strides, they were completely in the forest, and neither from the window or the place they had most recently stood, would you have been able to see them anymore.

25

McKenna had waited patiently enough for the respondent to pick up on the other end, so wasted no time and proceeded to jump into conversation, sparing no additional words, using only what he required to get the point across.

'This is McKenna. I have spoken to all relevant parties relating to the beginning of our next endeavour.'

'Very good.' A gloomy, incoherent voice crackled back through the poor signal of the line. 'Have we had any further developments in our predicament?'

'Yes sir, I believe we have.' McKenna spoke crisply and professionally.

'And what may the decision be?' Enquired the voice.

'We are to commence with Operation Turntable right away sir. We are to perform this alongside our upcoming task,' McKenna replied definitively.

'You believe Turntable can be achieved successfully without compromising everything else?'

McKenna cleared his throat. 'I believe so. I shall consult the others on the board and deploy our best to ensure significant results.'

'I have faith in everyone under my tutelage. I look forward to hearing news of a positive outcome.'

And with that, the call was cut from the other end, leaving McKenna to sit and poise, reflecting on the implications of the interaction he had just had, the wheels he had just put into motion.

He reflected, as if an old cowboy smoking a cigar on their porch. He had made a difficult decision, yet he knew he had made far worse with more severe circumstances, but still felt the pain sear through him, piercing his thick skin. He wondered if it may be his advancing years making him softer. Not yet fifty, McKenna understood he was in a young man's game, his experience allowing it to take him to the position he held now.

Pushing the negativity away, he stood and wandered through to the first room, stopping in front of the large window that engulfed one side and overlooked the empty hangar below. The resentment he held towards his subordinates annoyed him. They were far worse off than he was, yet the emotion clung to him, like a sloth on a tree, lazily clinging to the dignified structure.

The feeling was buried and replaced by a fire striking inside of him as he turned his thoughts back to the conversation he had on the telephone, ruminating as he looked out into the empty hanger. He knew he was making the right decision, ensuring his future and guaranteeing an early retirement. It was a shame, he admitted, having to remove someone who had become of such paramount importance to the organisation's development. Yet he would sleep soundly knowing his selfishness enabled him a prosperous future, which, will begin sooner than anticipated.

He liked Decker, but he knew too much and therefore had to go. He would make sure no one would replace him until the time was right. It would be quick, and clean. It was the least he could do for Decker, who had not put a step wrong during his time under McKenna. Apart from getting too close, and threatening everything he had worked so hard for. He was not going to allow that.

26

They trod lightly and carefully through the forest. Even in the middle of the day, the canopy of trees restricted the majority of the sunlight from penetrating, leaving the air cool on a hot day and creating an independent climate that, if one stayed in long enough, would create an eerie chill to run down one's spine. The ground was damp, despite it not raining in the two days since the pair had got to Wisconsin, meaning careful footing was required. The old, historic trees and their branches whistled in the wind, their roots growing out of the ground like snakes across trodden down paths creating an obstacle course of resistance to newcomers in their home. Upon every couple of steps, there was a leaf crunching or a twig snapping, resulting in foliage being shaken, and frightened animals scarpering from a pair of big-footed humans intruding. The forest was not overly large - its growth restricted by the nearby lake - but Max got the sense that they could very easily get lost if even the slightest lack of concentration crept into his mind.

'Do you have any idea where you're going?' Will began whispering from behind as they continued walking.

'Sort of. I have a map on my phone. Wait, why are you whispering?' Max responded, semi-confident, but it soon changed to confusion.

'I dunno. Just kinda seemed like the best volume to remain respectful of the surroundings.'

'It's not a cemetery, mate,' Max turned his head and smiled back.

'Yeah, duh. But you kinda get it though, right?' Will's volume never rose above anything heard in a library.

Max stopped and stood up straight. He angled his head and looked at the highest branches at the top of the trees, listening. The silence, as tranquil as it was, put him at ease, the air inside this place cleaner, refreshing his nose as he took deep breaths and filled his lungs. He closed his eyes, 'yeah, I kinda do,' responding to his friend behind him. He held this position for a few moments longer, before snapping back into action and reaching for his phone from his jeans pocket. Will pulled closer to have a look as soon as he realised Max was pulling up a picture of the map he had been shown by the old man in the library.

'That's what you're using? That doesn't look helpful at all,' Will said, scratching his head.

Max chose to ignore him and kept his attention on the screen. He was, in a way, right, and Max knew that. All the map entailed was an outline of the area, including the lodge, the lake, and the tree area they currently found themselves in, and just beyond the trees on the other side of the lodge were two houses, a considerable distance away from each other. According to the map, the forest was around twenty times the size of the lodge. Within the darkened colour which indicated the trees, there was a circle covering about fifty per cent of it; this, of course, being the area where the money was estimated to be located.

The more Will stared at it, the angrier and more concerned he became. 'So that's all you've got to go off? Jesus Christ.' His hand remained on the back of his head and he turned, wandered a couple of meters, and paced slowly in a chaotic circle. 'By the looks of it, the forest looks like it'd take an hour to walk through it. And that area is half of it. If we don't have anything else to help us look, we're screwed, mate. I'm sorry, I know that's not what you want to hear. But that's a lot of area to cover, and I'm happy to do it. I'm happy to help you, I just kinda thought you'd have more to go off that would at least give us a fighting chance.' Will paused. 'If this is all anyone knows about this thing, there's no wonder it hasn't been found yet.'

Max remained silent. As much as he wanted to find the money, as much as he wanted to believe they could do it, he knew Will was right. They did have themselves up against the wall, a whim, tasked with the impossible that had stayed as such for almost a hundred years. He hung his head slightly lower than the height he held his phone, his eyes flicking briefly to his notebook in his other hand, before staring blankly at the floor. He tried his best to clear his mind, to not think and just block everything out. *They were going to at least have a look*, he thought to himself - but he just wanted to rid himself of the negativity before they carried on.

As his eyes scanned the floor just beyond his feet, his blank expression soon turned to confusion, creasing his face and frowning with his eyebrows. He noticed, just a couple of feet further ahead, the leaves on the dirt path a slightly different shade of green to others surrounding it. Will began talking behind him, but the words were at the back of his head. 'Look, I'm sorry, man. You know I don't mean it when I say these things. I just try to be as honest as I can with you. You see-'

'Shhh,' Max finally realised Will was interrupting his thinking. He pointed at what he could see, and said, 'what the hell is that?'

They dropped lower to the ground and leaned towards the strange disturbance on the floor. Max moved to the side of the path, stepping on tree roots to get himself directly next to the side of it. Now he was on top of it, he could now make out what he was looking at. It appeared to be artificial leaves, stuck together to form an area the size of a plastic shopping bag. The colour match to nearby leaves was not quite right, despite being credibly similar. If he had not looked at the ground, there was no way they would have seen it.

Max glanced over to Will, who had stayed on the path, far enough back, and Max stretched out an arm, lifting him the leaves, lifting up together to reveal what it was hiding.

Dug into the ground, a circular brown metal, the top of which protruded ever so slightly above the ground, the rest of the earth beside it untouched. In the centre of the metal object, an even smaller circle the circumference of a ring, delicately higher than the rest of the object, menacingly red in colour and looking poised and dangerous at the same time.

'Is that what I think it is?' Max spoke first.

'Is that a bloody land mine?' Will, his voice raised way above a whisper, frozen and flabbergasted.

The two of them remained frozen, attempting to absorb the information and the object that lay in front of them, Max's feet just inches away from the deadly incendiary. Max, sweat beads forming on his forehead showing the level of panic as his mind raced through the possibilities he could have just found himself in, a few more steps away from being thrown across the path, in God knows how many pieces. The sweat now began to drop from above his eyes, hitting the ground below him.

'Max?'

'Yeah?'

'We need to move. Slowly, but also very quickly.'

Max heard these words and struck into action. He placed the artificial leaves that were still in his hand onto the floor beside him, leaving the object uncovered. Being aware of the tree behind, he moved further away from the mine and Will, sneaking to the other side of the tree, covering his view of the object. Will crept in his crouched position to meet his friend on the other side of the tree.

They both raised themselves slowly, walking away into the collection of trees and away from the path. They remained in silence as they walked for a minute or so, the only noise created being the crunching of leaves to accompany the unwavering sounds emitting from the ecosystem. When the two of them felt they were an adequate distance away, both breathed in a large breath and let out a sigh of relief, still in shock.

'Why the hell was that there?' Will was not expecting a response of any kind to justify what they saw, not a constructive one and certainly not a joke to lighten the mood, as much as both needed some imaginative foolhardiness Will knew both were capable of at a moment's notice. Together, the two friends stood silent and Will, most certainly no longer hungover, looked around the trees attempting to gauge a sense of where they were. His eyes met something else he wished he had never seen. For the second time in a matter of minutes, he wanted his eyes to deceive him.

As Will observed the branches and the canopy of leaves high above, he noticed not all was as it seemed.

He scanned the surroundings above him with a little more detail. He was not entirely positive, or whether it was his subconscious second guessing everything in front of him, but it seemed like some of the leaves above him were a lot closer than the high, extravagant trees he could see around them. Max still had his phone in his hand, grasping it so tightly his knuckles were white. His heart raced his body in a cocktail mix of fear, adrenaline and shock.

'Erm, just a quick one,' Will began, 'do those leaves look a bit weird to you?' His finger pointing upwards, his eyes following. Max snapped himself out of his gaze and focused his attention on what Will was waffling about, raising his head to the blanket of branches of the heavens. He remained in contemplation for several moments, but he could begin to see what Will was talking about.

There was a section of branches – accompanied by leaves – that appeared to hang slightly lower than the rest. The trees in the forest appeared to be at least seven metres high, with all of the branches extended to create the covering that operated on the peak of the trees alone. Having seen no difference to this status quo throughout, it was rather peculiar to have such a low-hanging collection of green, no more than two metres from the earth. As his eyes studied the subject, they began observing the tree they clung to. The bark of the tree seemed affected, different to all the other trees, specifically in the area connected to the low-hanging leaves.

And it was then, whilst looking at the side of the tree, Max saw it. Not everyone would have seen it, even after studying the situation in as much detail as they had. But there was one particular blemish in the bark, from which extended a metal hook that held a clear wire that ran diagonally to the floor. Again, despite the panic, sweating, brain racing and racking, thinking of every worst possible outcome, Max remained calm on the exterior. With his eyes remaining fixed on what he could now deduce as a fake canopy, he grabbed hold of Will's arm and pulled them both backwards a few steps.

'Is there a reason you're taking us back in the direction of the exploding device in the ground?' Will asked confusingly.

'Just trust me,' Max responded but chose not to add context to a very reasonable question.

They had walked back around ten paces. Max reached down and produced a rock the size of a tennis ball from around the shrubbery. After shaking it up and down in his hand, he tossed it further on from where they had once stood, directly under the low canopy of leaves. Will's expression was replaced with amazement. And fear.

The rock, once it had finished its trajectory, impacted with the ground, followed by a snapping noise of either string or wire. In the blink of an eye, the canopy had fallen from its perch and collapsed onto the ground, smothering the rock and its vicinity of at least two metres. The fake canopy was easily identifiable once it had come into contact with the ground, but high up in the trees, it had blended almost perfectly with its surroundings; no doubt helped by the darkness that covered it.

Will spoke first. 'I'm glad we saw that, otherwise we'd have been completely buggered.'

Max pointed with his thumb behind him, followed by his index finger pointing at what lay in front of them. 'Yeah, either that or this, I think we've been a bit fortunate today,' letting out a brief sigh of relief.

'You can say that again.' Will laughed as he spoke, a nervous but appreciative chuckle, as he turned to survey the surroundings.

Max suddenly heard a smacking sound, followed by an almighty thud, spinning to see his friend collapsing to his left, face down in the dirt.

'Will!' He cried, but just as he began to bend down and tend to his friend, he felt a poke hit the back of his head. The sensation was cold, a small circular object remained glued to his skull, keeping him indefinitely frozen in his upright position.

What followed next was the most painful gut-retching noise Max had ever heard. It was strange to him how a noise could inflict pain, despite the clear inability to incite any physical altercations at a low decimal level. He remained a statue upon hearing the noise, despite his favourite person in the world lying buried in the dirt, fighting off every natural reaction that was telling him to go and check on his friend.

The noise Max heard was the click of a hammer being pulled, the gun pushed against his head, milliseconds away from his brain looking like a Jackson Pollock painting.

'What the actual fuck is happening?' were the only words Max could muster, as he stood and waited impatiently for the fate that had been drawn up for him.

27

McKenna had moved himself across the complex, enjoying a brisk stroll outside surrounded by the Arizona desert as dawn peered through the clouds. His walk ended with him sitting in a different meeting room, this one of a much grander size indicating the importance of the six people inside it. The room was the size of a tennis court, with a simple table well-proportioned in its centre, and arrays of various technologies placed around it.

All six, three men and three women, were turned slightly to face a wall which showed a projection. They watched the figure move around, constantly walking backwards and forwards across the screen, a headset attached to its face to ensure everybody heard and everybody listened.

The figure on the projection spoke first. 'Thank you for joining me so early this morning. It is a little later here in New York and my day is very busy.'

Everyone in the room nodded a head of gratitude, knowing more followed.

'Having heard of the success of our latest endeavour, I would very much like to find the final number we have achieved, minus expenses. Jones, if you can get us started, please?' The figure continued pacing the screen.

A woman sat in black military regalia and her hair tied up cleared her throat, before leaning over the table to consult the notes she had placed in preparation.

'Thank you, sir, and good morning. We can now confirm that, minus expenses, our total profit achieved is estimated to be in the region of $24 million.' Jones optimistically smiled upon finishing her statement, looking up from her notes to see similar expressions shared across the room. Her eyes made their way to McKenna, who remained emotionless.

'This takes our total profit for the year to $50 million, an improvement of $7.3 million at the same point last year,' she continued.

The figure on the projection took over proceedings. 'Thank you, Jones. That gives for very impressive reading indeed.' The voice came through the transmission as direct and with sufficient poise. 'The upward trajectory of our figures is very positive, yet I am still more excited when we extrapolate and see just how much we can achieve next year, and the year after, and so on. I am very pleased with the progress. So, what is next for us? McKenna, you are the most informed about this. Please.'

McKenna rose from his seat, thus allowing him to sneak in a deep breath to settle some nerves that dug away every time he addressed a group.

'Thank you, sir. We are all aware, to varying degrees, of our next endeavour. Everybody that needs to be informed has been this morning, and they have received their information packages. We shall be leaving in less than twenty-four hours to head toward the destination.' McKenna seemed to be speaking with an increased directness, the bouncing on his heels helping to replace strolling the room, not wanting to appear unprofessional.

'Our current estimations believe we should have the asset within forty-eight hours of arrival.'

A woman spoke in a query. 'What is the asset to be this time?'

McKenna looked rapidly towards the screen, the figure listened intently and replied with a subtle nod in reply to the look he saw.

'The asset,' McKenna continued, 'is the lost fortune hidden by John Dillinger.' The bouncing no longer sufficed, and, feeling more at ease, McKenna began strolling in the emptiness of the room. 'Sources indicate he buried $200,000 of stolen cash in a forest somewhere in Minnesota.'

McKenna knew the secrecy of the organisation and its tasks. It was a strict, need-to-know basis, of which McKenna recognised not everybody in the room needed to know every significant detail.

'The cash, buried in a wooden chest, has been lost for almost one hundred years. Recovering it would be of great value, both financially and promotionally for the organisation.'

The figure nodded its head on the projection in agreement.

'The idea has been constructed that the organisation, if successful, publicise the endeavour, helping to continue building a reputation we have carefully managed for public consumption. Some of our activities are, in our best interest, kept in strict secrecy, as you are all aware. However, it has been decided that this endeavour will be promoted upon successful completion.'

The nods of agreement were now being shared amongst the room.

'We have been made aware that despite the land the asset sits on being public property, to our knowledge, our assessment team surveyed the area two days ago and found a local homeowner laying claim to the land.' McKenna paused for breath and was set to continue, but was rudely interrupted by the projection.

'Having sent the team there,' the figure continued, 'I allowed them the option of confronting the owner to gather information and the potential for settling the business through peaceful negotiation. Cooper, you were the leader of that inquiry, correct?'

The conversation pointed toward a man of no discerning features. He rose to address the room. McKenna remained standing.

'Indeed I was. We led a team to evaluate Little Bohemia Lodge and the surrounding areas. We successfully located the territory and confirmed the allowance for focused and, most importantly, discreet, excavation. Having spoken to the female landowner myself, we were not able to sufficiently guarantee her cooperation.' Cooper knew the negative nature of his statements and pushed forward with pace.

'This problem, however, has become a minor infraction. We contacted the local government within the town, and the land records have been changed accordingly.' Cooper's chuffed expression of accomplishment absorbed his face.

'And I am correct in believing they shall trouble us no further?' The projected figure queried.

'No, sir,' Cooper replied defiantly. 'It was brought to my attention that the man in charge there was a fan of fishing. He should be enjoying his new boat as we speak.'

'Thank you, Cooper,' the retort came from the shadowy projection. Cooper nodded and took his seat once more.

'As you should all know your relevant tasks for the upcoming operation, I believe there is nothing further to add.' McKenna chirped, eager to retain his control of the conversation.

'That should be all, everyone. Thank you for your cooperation.' The figure on the screen, for the first time, came to a halt. The face was still impossible to see, hidden expertly with positioned lighting. 'And McKenna, I appreciated your call this morning, no matter how early it may have been. I am glad to have your unwavering support.'

'Thank you, sir. I am glad we agree,' McKenna nodded.

The bodies strolled out of the room and the projection was shut off, McKenna waited for everybody else to vacate, sharing glances and gestures of greeting. The information regarding Decker's future will have to be kept top secret, with no one, even the board, the highest employed in the organisation, allowed to understand the severity of Operation Turntable.

McKenna's mind thought forward. He just hoped the job could go as smoothly as planned. He had performed similar tasks many times over the years, but he had worked his time in the field. It was now someone else's job to do the dirty work. Killing a member of the team on the ground was not easy, and he had previously lost many nights of sleep wondering if he had made the right decision. Now, he slept like a baby. His age cleared his conscience and he was too far away from the field to bother second-guessing his choices. A choice he knew this time was the correct one, as his gut was telling him.

28

'Turn around. Slowly!'

The characteristics of the voice sounded strange to Max, yet threatening all the same. That, paired with the obvious gun barrel pointed at his head, made him want to comply and follow every instruction this person gave, no matter how ridiculous. Max would happily run a mile backwards dressed as Daffy Duck if it so appeased. This person was in charge now, that much was clear.

He suddenly felt a hankering for chocolate. Maybe the sugary boost would help his leg stop jiggling like Elvis.

Doing as he was told, moving his hands above his head as a gesture of goodwill, Max stole one last glance at Will helplessly flat on the floor. He closed his eyes, wishing one last time he was caught in a dream he could wake up from. Turning, he soon discovered that if he were in a dream, the very last thing he wanted to do was wake up.

The first thing he saw was not the double-barrelled, brushed metal, polished wooden death machine. Max was transfixed. He was frozen. And not by the lethal weapon, but rather by the transcendental beauty he found difficult for his eyes to comprehend.

Just a few steps ahead of him stood a woman. She had dirty blonde locks tied in a messy ponytail, strands of hair escaping and flowing delicately across her face and shoulders. Not one hair seemed out of place; even as the wind picked up, rustling the trees, her hair blew but never restricted her vision, politely returning to its original position.

Within his eyeline, Max could see she was wearing a red flannel shirt, long sleeves curled up before her elbow, the top few buttons of the neck open to reveal a simple yet graceful gold necklace where a circular pendant hung. Max attempted to absorb all of these details from his periphery, as his gaze remained locked at the centre of her face.

He saw an eye colour quite indecipherable; a colour that allowed the viewer to imagine and see their own favourite colour. A tapestry of shades and flavours which would seem able to change to mood and emotion. Her face was perfectly symmetrical with the big, round, ambiguous eyes surrounded with delicately light freckles and dainty cheeks, above firm lips pressed together to signify her current feeling of animosity; the rage remaining in her eyes as Max's soul danced happily amongst the crashing waves of her idyllic irises.

'Who the fuck are you then?' The words spoken woke Max out of his waking dream, his first acknowledgement being the opposing beauty and harshness of the vocabulary chosen.

Secondly, and more importantly finally, he registered the shotgun barrel that was still pointing at his head.

'Okay, easy. We're not here to hurt anyone.' His words were soft but it was obvious from his tone it was a plea.

'Even so,' she shrugged, 'you're still on my land and I'm well within my right to shoot both of you.'

Despite the severity of his predicament, Max could not help but smile. A small grin crept across his stubbly face, spreading into a toothy smile. He liked to believe his smile to be an attractive part of his charm but he usually left it up to everyone else to decide. Playing the odds, he knew he usually got favourable feedback.

'Ha, America,' Max muttered with an exasperation under his breath.

'What did you say?!' She angrily shouted, accompanied by a glare that indicated she did not appreciate Max's sarcasm or new found confidence.

'I'm sorry,' Max attempted to start again. 'Me and my friend are English, we're not used to seeing your trans-Atlantic firework sticks. We're just on holiday enjoying a walk.' Max's smile began to appear back on his face. There was no need to explain the situation further, it probably helped if he did not.

His head moved down towards the lifeless Will. 'Although I'm not sure how much walking he's gonna be doing the rest of the holiday.'

After taking a second to stand in silence, absorbing the stranger's information, and quite possibly translating their English, she replied defiantly.

'And why should I listen to you? Why should I trust you?' Her voice wasn't necessarily loud, Max had observed, but rather stern and resolute. It made him believe in the possibility of getting shot. *Great holiday*, Max thought. *Perhaps Benidorm next time.*

'I don't know what you want me to say, love, to get you to put that thing down, but I would appreciate it if you considered it.'

'I've just about had enough of you people coming here, disturbing what's not yours and bothering me. Just leave me in damn peace!' This statement came from a place with more emotion. For the first time, there appeared to be a slight tremor. Max's confusion spread from across his face to his response, his frown created a perfect wrinkle in between his eyebrows.

'Us lot? I can assure you I have no idea what you mean. We're here alone!' Max was starting to feel the situation slipping away from his clutches. His coolness dried up, replaced by sweat reappearing on his forehead. 'You have to believe me! We have English passports in our hotel. Do you need proof?'

The barrel lowered slightly, the stern expression she wore switching slightly to apprehension. 'You seriously have no idea what I'm talking about?'

'No!'

'I must admit, you do look pretty different to the other guys I've been seeing. And you sound totally different, too.'

'We're just the two of us, we're just trying to enjoy the area,' Max paused a moment before continuing slyly, 'not including the hospitality of the locals,' finishing with a sarcastic tut in her direction.

'Well don't think I'm gonna turn my back on you just yet. Knowing those people, this all might be an elaborate set-up.' The gun remained hovering in Max's direction. He noted to himself she used the words 'those people' as opposed to 'you people', giving him some relief. She may be starting to believe him. *Not out of the woods just yet. Wow, that was a terrible pun*, he smiled at his own imaginary dad joke.

'Can I at least just check on my friend, please?'

'Yes,' the response came after a small delay in comprehension. He could sense a slight remorse in the tone.

'Thank you.' His hands came down from above his head, jumping to the floor to Will. His face was still in the mud as Max checked the pulse on his neck. He looked up from his crouch, past the gun barrel to its owner. He wanted to see her reaction to what he had to say next.

'He's still breathing.' To add to his growing reassurance, he noticed a minuscule tension release from her face and shoulders upon hearing the news. Everything remained the same and she had hardly moved, but the twitch was enough. *Not a killer*, he thought. *At least she would have needed a lot of convincing to shoot me*. In his mind, his eyes rolled. *What a day*.

'Can't say I've ever had to deal with a concussion before, my drinking habits have never been that bad,' Max said, trying to lighten the situation, more for his own benefit than anyone else, as he rolled Will over onto his back.

Away from Max's view, her body language changed. The gun lowered further, adopting a more relaxed position. She took one hand off the weapon and brushed her brow with her forearm. She couldn't help feeling slightly guilty. She had had to deal with people coming round here for long enough, but recently it had gotten a lot worse. But these guys didn't look anything like the recent pests. She had gotten a little too defensive and hurt somebody as a result. She sighed. Not just at the situation, but at herself. She decided to extend an olive branch. Of a sort.

'He'll be alright', she began. Max sensed the friendlier tone again. 'I didn't hit him very hard. He just needs somewhere comfortable as soon as possible and some water when he wakes up.'

Remaining crouched, Max could now see the gun barrel dangling, directed towards the floor a few feet from him. He knew he could try and grab it, but the distance he had to reach was too far, and she would pull it away before he could. The distance hardly seemed accidental. Close, but far enough. The gesture of lowering the gun was there, but she was testing if he'd bother going for it. A smile appeared across his face again. *Smart*, he thought. He was not going to take the bait.

Quickly getting out of the way of his own hubris, he reminded himself to take care of his friend first. 'Our hotel is over an hour's walk away.'

'He began the next part already knowing the response. 'I guess I could call an ambulance and tell them exactly what happened. I'm sure they won't ask too many questions about a concussion –.'

'No. Wait,' she interrupted. As strong as she was attempting to portray, Max sensed trepidation and uncertainty despite her previous comments indicating regular visitors.

She clearly had not had to deal with something like this before. Max decided to try his luck.

'You know of anywhere close I can take him, just to wait until he gets up?'

'Well…' she began.

'Not too far, though. This guy will be bloody heavy. He had a full English for breakfast.'

'I know somewhere', the kindness returned momentarily. 'But you won't be able to stay there for long', she snapped back, aware of her previous comment. 'Just till he gets up.'

'How long would I have to carry him for?'

'Only five minutes. It's this way.' She turned, facing the opposite direction Max had come from, which included the obstacle course, Max noted.

Letting out a sigh, he straightened up, before bending back down and pulled Will's arms across his back. Using his knees, he stood, throwing the remainder of Will's top half over his shoulder. When standing upright, he threw the limp body up slightly to allow it to move into a more comfortable and secure position and held the back of the knees. In this firefighter's lift, he turned to face her, waiting to begin the journey, holding his free palm out, indicating to her to show the way.

'No way.' She shook her head. 'You first. I can watch you from behind. Just follow the path.

'As you please.'

Off the three of them travelled, deeper into the forest, deeper into the unknown. Max didn't have much of a choice: either walk this way or the gun behind him. He was happy to take his chances this way.

29

If Max had any feedback, it was more like ten minutes. But it felt like hours. Will was a lot heavier than expected. The two of them walked until finally approaching a clearing. The path continued beyond the tree line, the branches stretching towards the ground to leave the opening hidden; if it was not for the path, no one would have recognised the walkway continued. Max waited diligently, awaiting further instructions. Without conversing, she caught up and pulled back a branch with her spare arm, revealing an opening of tidied grass, appearing respectable and presentable in contrast to the beyond forest they found themselves in.

Sweat was beading down Max's back, he clutched the legs of his friend, who remained hopelessly drooped over his shoulder, his arms swaying, flailing upon each step; Max was the vessel transporting and protecting him across the terrain. It felt like a moment to ponder for Max, before entering what lay before them. If only a brief pause for recollection, as he quickly remembered how heavy his luggage was. His shoulders burned and his legs resisted every further step forward in defiance to the added weight. Max let out a deep breath, puffing out his cheeks and ducking under the branches and her arm to see what lay next on their travels.

They had survived death three times. Will was immobile and Max was quickly becoming the same. Their forest experience left a little to be desired and, so far, the holiday had been anything but relaxing. Stumbling across the tree line to the continuing dirt path, Max managed enough strength to pull his head from concentrating on his steps to look at what stood before them.

Thirty yards away, an eighteenth-century farmhouse remained standing strong, in spite of its age and natural surroundings. It had dark wood panelling across its sides, which were perfectly square to form its cube-like shape. There was a balcony - also wooden, this painted white - that extended all across the four sides and windows sparsely dotted on both levels of the building. The roof was tiled, with one third-floor window visible. One side of the exterior wood seemed darker than the others, so Max presumed at one point would have had an accompanying barn or outhouse attached to it. The ground level copied the first floor with its porch around the edge of the building, the white paint flaking and discolouring across the structure.

Of the thirty yards of well-maintained, lush grass standing effortlessly between the group and the structure, the seclusion was completed with one single dirt track that exited the clearing back into the green metropolis of forest in the far corner, showing only a flicker of availability – but, more importantly, privacy – from the rest of the world.

It was clear that in its day it would have been quite the residence for the occupants of the surrounding land. An impressive and recluse escape from any danger that hung outside its borders. And that strength had carried through the centuries, where even then, the building remained impeccably worn and yet not tired. It was a mansion of its day, a stoic representation of stability and endurance across centuries of adaptation.

'Come on!' A cry came out from behind Max, and promptly she overtook him again as they neared the house. 'Just up here.'

The ground floor had five steps from the earth to the porch that ran underneath the second-floor balcony, five steps Max did not want to take. She hopped up the steps, placing her gun near the door. She stood and watched as Max got closer to the insurmountable wooden steps that he assumed would prove to be his downfall.

She noted the dejection of defeat on his face and came back down to help carry Will on the final leg of the journey, each holding a top and bottom half of the body. Walking backwards, she kicked open the door. 'Just drop him down here,' as they manoeuvred as one to get to a felt sofa that would have once been red and had clearly seen better days. Lowering him delicately, Max spun around to leave Will's head resting on the arm of the chair, noticing no cushions. Upon laying him down, he stood up and finally had a chance to look around.

'Wow', he began. 'This would be a perfect place for a zombie apocalypse.'

'You reckon?' She twisted and walked away as she spoke.

'I'm telling you. I bet a tenner that's the first thing he says when he wakes up.' Max could not help but smile. 'Can I get some water for him, please?'

'Yeah, one second,' he heard the reply but was not looking as his eyes flicked back to Will and then his surroundings.

The windows helped create an abundance of light, aided by the lack of interior walls in favour of support beams to thrust the light across the living space. The bright, lightly tanned, hardwood floor also helped, although this was hidden in numerous places with large, traditional, carpet rugs. It was now clear they had entered through the back door, into a kitchen with a separate, adjoining island to the left. To the right, a spacious living room, hosting two sofas, an armchair and a television backed up onto a wood-panelled wall, which one could only assume was the rear of the staircase. A faded royal blue rug divided the two areas, a hallway leading deeper into the house, presumably towards the stairs. The inside, whilst decorated modestly, held both old and new furnishings seemingly complemented each other; a range oven next to a smoothie maker; a thick oak coffee table with an e-reader sitting atop; a fireplace to the right next to a flat-screen television; it remained painfully clear some renovating was in order.

Max, scanning quickly, saw the bare-brick fireplace having parts of brick falling off, floorboards hidden in between rugs showing signs of warping and irregular colour, and the window frame rotting above the sink overlooking the garden, the aged curtains desperately clinging beside it. To Max, it looked like whoever was maintaining the house was trying, but appeared as though the current number of hands was not sufficient, the house dismantling quicker than the repairs. Max, being nosy, needed to find out more. Once she returned with the glass of water, he began.

'Thank you', he said. He sank the water in seconds, holding the glass out for a refill. 'Please?' She tutted disapprovingly, taking the glass and returning to the kitchen area, like a toddler being sent to the naughty step.

'So, this place yours?'

'Yeah,' she replied. 'Sit down if you want.' The gesture was polite, but it seemed rather forced. Max made his way over to the second couch and flopped, rather exhausted and grateful for the weight to be off his feet, no matter how weathered and worn the seat was.

He watched with intrigue as she made her way from the kitchen to the vacant armchair to the right of the space, and closest to the fireplace. The chair was a grey colour, with a dark green throw over the headrest. She glided effortlessly across the space, weaving in between the furniture – she ran her fingers delicately across the kitchen counter and the sofa Will rested upon – before the dirty blonde back of her head rested on the green throw. She afforded herself a moment with her eyes closed, hoping to keep herself together, and opened them to retain a wary stare towards her unexpected house guests. She leaned to place Max's refilled glass on the coffee table.

Max couldn't help but watch the entire movement, transfixed by the beauty even in her walk, flowing like a summer dress in a breeze, so clearly free now the gun had no physical hindrance or mental energy taking away from her elegance.

'Thank you,' he reached for the glass before continuing. 'I never got your name,' Max said with relaxed pronunciation. He moved to cross his legs.

'Penny,' she replied with a smile.

'Well, it's a pleasure.' Returning the gesture. He pointed to his sleeping friend. 'That's Will and I'm Max. The smile grew into his trademark grin.

'Charmed,' she replied somewhat sarcastically, but she took note of the charming smile. 'Your friend should wake up anytime now, then you can go.'

'Thank you, I appreciate it.'

'Don't mention it.'

The bluntness was beginning to bother him. They had nothing better to do, so why not be friendly? He was determined to get something out of her. *Her number would be an excellent start.*

'So, how long have you been here?' As he said this, she brushed her hair away from her face, allowing him to see all of her features. The hair played in synergy with everything underneath, the freckles seemingly more prominent than before and providing the perfect addition to her indescribable eye colour. He hung onto her every word.

'Erm, about seven years.' She looked away as she spoke, then turned to face him once she had finished. This was the first time they were both still and she had a chance to look at his features. The chairs placed them only yards apart, so she assessed diligently. The light brown hair bounced happily around his forehead, the natural golden skin allowing his light blue eyes to glow towards their recipient. And the smile. As she looked, she saw the confidence, but also the unknown, the disarming nature of it. The cheekiness in it would help other people smile, almost making her smile herself.

She felt herself release and let go. What it was, or how, she could not be sure, but she felt more at ease. She blinked slowly and continued. 'Seven years in this house, but I've lived around the area my whole life.' She pushed some loose hairs behind her ear.

'You like it here?'

After a brief moment, she replied. 'No, not really.'

'No?' Max could sense a conversation developing. 'How come?'

'I don't know. I guess I just kinda got stuck, like most people.'

'Yeah', Max agreed. 'I feel the same sometimes. You feel like whatever you're doing can't just be it, as if there should be something more, whatever that may be.'

'Yeah, exactly,' she replied slowly, with a sense of surprise. She smiled diligently towards him, holding her gaze a moment longer than she intended. 'It's not like I didn't like the thought of being here at one point or another – many times, in fact,' she corrected herself. 'I don't know,' she continued, 'it's starting to feel like a different place. A place I don't see myself in anymore.'

'And where can you imagine yourself being now?'

'That's the problem. I have absolutely no idea.' She let out a laugh of almost sarcasm and Max obliged with a laugh of agreement and sympathy.

He observed as they sat in relative silence for a moment. The only noise was the heavy ticking of a wall clock, the loud careful clicks alluding to its age and wisdom. It sounded almost as old as the house, a constant presence amongst generations passing and memories fading, everything changing throughout the passing of time, the one constant being the never changing time piece.

He noticed a slight distortion on her face, she looked at the floor almost in a silent embarrassment. He was keen to change the topic as if the current subject was becoming too emotional for her. He was enjoying the conversing and did not want it to end. Or Will to wake up. *Just a couple more minutes. Maybe ten. Best wingman ever*, he thought. Max smiled towards his friend as he began another conversation.

'You said earlier that we didn't look like people you had seen before. Might I ask who you were talking about? It seemed like you weren't on about more lost tourists,' he added at the end, remembering to continue his façade.

'Well,' she began after a moment of pondering. 'That all seemed to have happened in the last couple of weeks. But before I talk about that, I'm gonna need a cup of coffee. Do you want anything?' She smiled at him as she rose from the chair. His eyes lingered and watched with fascination once more as she danced her way to the kitchen; the smile enough to render him speechless momentarily.

After gathering himself, he smiled, his plan had clearly worked. 'I'd love a cuppa, thanks.'

'Milk and sugar?'

'Just milk would be great, thank you.'

'Sure.' They both shared a smile before she turned towards the kettle and Max leaned over to check on Will.

30

The following morning, with the darkness of the desert sky to cover their tracks, the operation had moved into action. One of the company's jets was chartered and the team of twelve fled, under McKenna's tutelage, to the nearest commercial airport to the target.

Landing at the Manitowish Waters airport, it's small size and the flight's early arrival time ensured the group could land without prying eyes, boarding the waiting Jeeps on the runway.

Within twenty minutes, they arrived at a nearby lake, littered with boats that had been left by the inquisition team a month earlier. Inflatable boats bounced on the water, adjacent to a small pier exiting the forest. Having travelled onto the lake to reach larger boats, McKenna had told the group to get some rest, informing them they would commence the search at dawn.

Being only hours from the sun arriving, McKenna saw no sense in sleep. As he walked around his private cabin, he had to admire Cooper's handiwork.

Cooper had managed to move four boats over to the lakes they now stood on. Consulting a map that stretched across the entirety of one wall, McKenna noted they now floated on Little Star Lake, which connected to Manitowish Lake and two additionally named lakes further north. He recognised Little Star Lake to be extremely close to the airport, so could not give Cooper too much credit; as he assumed he had only flown the boats in.

During a briefing, McKenna was informed to keep as many of the boats moving as possible. He did not press any further in the matter, accepting the request. As he stared at the map, he planned an itinerary in his head for the coming days.

The boat they all now resided on was of considerable size, especially when compared to others on the lake. With its specific design, it could comfortably accommodate eighteen people. There were three shared cabins of six beds each, followed by three private cabins. Instructed to leave the largest suite untouched, McKenna had naturally selected the second biggest.

He sat in its living space, complete with a desk, sofas and a large television placed opposite the wall of maps. Further along, a door separated a king-size bed and en-suite lavatory.

The couch was an annoying shade of cream, McKenna had scanned the room with success, standing to collect a bottle of scotch and a glass before reclining once more. He took generous sips and sat contently in silence, swilling his glass bringing him enough entertainment. With that, he patiently waited for the morning to begin for everyone else.

31

Brews made, thanks given, the two resumed their positions, the hot liquid in their hands rising upwards in a steam that gently blended into one as it rose higher towards the wooden-beamed ceiling.

'Okay, so it all started, like I said, a couple of days ago. Or maybe a week, I'm not quite sure. Some guys were poking around in the areas not far from where I found the pair of you, real annoying electronics beeping away. I approached them and mentioned that the land was mine, all friendly. We sometimes get tourists, or dog walkers, strolling through. Doesn't usually bother me, and we get used to it, especially being so close to the lake. But these guys looked different. Dressed in military stuff, fancy tech, they weren't here to fish, if you get me.'

Max sipped his tea, diligently waiting for the story to continue.

'They started being nosy, 'is this your land?', and 'how long have you had it?', and then the real kicker, 'would you be interested in selling?''

'And what did you say?' Max replied.

She took a small and precise drink before going on. 'I told them I wasn't interested in selling, of course. We've had our fair share of offers before, believe me. These looked just the type that would want it to be a giant hotel, a shopping mall, or whatever else of an eye-sore you can make ten stories out of.'

'That would destroy half the forest if not all of it.'

'Exactly. Hence why we always said no. That and the community around here would probably murder me if I took the money and sped off in a yacht.'

They shared a laugh whilst both imagining the situation. Max could picture torches and pitchforks, which amused him further.

'Did you see these fellas again?' Max pried.

'No, not them specifically. I saw some others, on a couple of occasions. Same scenario, and I knew the affiliation as they stood out like a clown at a funeral. I watched these from a distance, but they mostly just stood around, pointing and looking at their screens.'

Max nodded, ensuring she knew he was following. 'Then one day, a knock at the door,' she continued. 'Five of them, on my porch, the leader of them asking me if I was the homeowner. He then had the audacity to invite himself and his entire gang inside.'

He shook his head. 'Then what happened?'

She pursued onwards with added intensity. 'The leader of them was working up a fuss about the 'fruitfulness of the property and the surrounding areas',' she gestured with quotation marks throughout the last words and Max smiled at the implication. 'He was saying how much I could get for such a piece of land, and how it couldn't possibly be maintained by someone independently such as myself.'

'So let me get this straight,' Max interjected for a moment. 'The guy invites himself in, with all his interns, and insults you about your house?' He laughed in disbelief.

'Yep.'

'Well, he sounds like a nice bloke.'

They both smiled at each other in agreement of the audacity, spending a few moments in silence and drinking their beverages. It was easy for both of them, each accepting an understanding despite being from entirely separate worlds, the right from the wrong remained clear, the obvious disposition and intrepidness of this group of people being a pest to this woman. Max was eager to discover the conclusion.

'So, what happened next? As friendly a welcome as we received with booby traps and concussions?' He smiled slyly and sipped on his tea, watching her reaction through the corner of his eyes. His tea was now empty. *Let's hope I can get another*, he thought.

'Well, naturally I told them nothing around here was for sale. I've had more than a few people come over and offer me ridiculous amounts for this place, and its reasoning is obvious, but these guys just seemed…' she could not find the word suitable enough for what she was looking for, so opted to gestate uneasiness with her hands and facial expression.

Max picked it up immediately. 'How were they not like people you had seen before?'

'They seemed more intense. Like they'd never heard the word 'no' before. And even when I said it, it wasn't like they took any notice.'

'I suppose that's why you kept seeing them afterwards.'

'Exactly,' she continued. 'After I'd seen them a couple of times, I decided to increase security. I can't say our family traditions are the most usual of ways.' She smiled through the last part, almost aware of the insanity. Almost.

'Yeah, most people just get cameras,' Max mocked.

'I've tried to get rid of all the particularly dangerous ones. They were put there a long time ago, but there didn't seem much sense in them being there now. I mean, the forest is beautiful, and so is the lake. It's perfect for dog walkers and forest animals. I wouldn't want to cause any harm. I decided on a more modern approach that would require less cleaning.'

'How do the dog walkers know where their presence is no longer welcome?' Max needed to find justification for all this, it was crazy.

'There's a well-trodden path all throughout the place, it's fairly easy to follow, for most people. The area where those idiots were looking wasn't near there, and once I'd seen them a couple of times in the same area, it became very obvious the reason for their interest. Not to mention they started moving boats the size of houses onto the lakes around here.'

She could sense the apprehension in Max's face, realising he required further reassurance. 'Don't worry, the people who live round here have been here their whole lives. And generations of the same families have always lived here. They know how crazy we can all be around here, and for that reason, they stick to the path.' She smiled like a nurse to a sick child towards Max, attempting a warm comforting gesture, becoming aware of how insane it all sounded.

He smiled back. *How nice to keep tradition*, he thought as his eyes dropped, staring at the bottom of his cup. He was attempting to process everything at that moment. A woman had just attacked his friend and now she was making him tea in her home that was guarded by traps the Ewoks would be proud of. *But man was she hot.*

'What's with all the boats then?' Max pried again.

'No idea. There must be four new boats on the lakes, it's pretty easy to tell which ones are theirs. There used to be regulations about how big and how many there could be, but I assume that's all been changed so the council can get more money.'

She stood up in front of him, his eyes darting upwards to meet hers. 'Another?' She asked, pointing at his cup.

'Yes, please. Thank you.' He handed his cup over with a grin and she pirouetted off towards the kitchen.

After a moment, he got up and followed, leaning against the counter with his arms crossed. 'You said the reasons why you get people here are obvious. How come?' He asked innocently.

She stopped making the drinks and turned to face him. 'What do you mean, you don't know?'

He shrugged nonchalantly, before adding a smile.

She rolled her eyes before adding her own. She liked it when he did that. Smiled. She continued. 'So you're not familiar with Dillinger?' The drinks making resumed whilst the discussion grew deeper.

'You mean John Dillinger, the famous playwright?' Max joked.

She picked up the sarcasm immediately. 'Around here we grow up with the stories. So much so that we could win Jeopardy if all the questions were about it.'

Max frowned, confused, having no idea the rules of Jeopardy. He tried to rationalise. 'You mean it could be your subject on Mastermind?'

This time, she was confused, neither having any idea what the other was talking about. They both shared a laugh before Max carried on, knowing domestic game-show comparisons could go on forever. 'Yeah, I've been fortunate enough to speak to a local already about it, fascinating stuff.'

'Where did you say you were from?' It was her turn to pry.

Max liked it. 'I didn't', he said with a smile.

'Well, where?'

'Sheffield,' he replied.

'England?'

'Yeah, sunny England.'

'And you came here for a holiday?' She questioned. She knew he knew; she was not stupid. She wanted to call his bluff.

'Yep,' he defined the 'P' of his word, he knew where this was going, but he enjoyed the cat and mouse.

'You're telling me you came all the way out here for a holiday, and never once came across under the 'stuff to do' there was any mention of the name John Dillinger, and the fact that we have very little reason for international tourism, other than there was a gangster that shot a few bullets here a thousand years ago?' She added a sarcastic, wry smile as she finished, stirring the tea.

He grinned, noticing she also opted for tea as her beverage of choice. 'Wow, you really wrapped that up nicely. You should get a job down at the tourism office, people would love to hear that descriptive attention to detail.'

'Shut up', she replied with a grin, handing him his mug back, the steam once more exiting the top.

He spoke as they walked in unison back to their seats. 'If you're referring to John Dillinger, famous bank robber and former short-term resident of the Little Bohemia Lodge, who raged a rampant vendetta against all bank security he came across, not to mention leaving presents of bullet holes everywhere, then I think I've heard of him.'

They sat. 'That's him. Seemed like such a nice guy. The locals around here love the story. I couldn't care less if it were me.'

'Not interested?' Max wondered.

'It's just we get told that stuff when we're growing up, the legend and everything. I'm just bored of it; it hardly seems fair celebrating the life of someone like that.'

Max nodded, what she said made a lot of sense. 'But he was considered a Robin Hood-type of his day, no?'

'He was, you're right,' she said, pausing for a moment. 'It's common knowledge the media spun every story they came across of him into a celebrity, it was the only way they were gonna sell papers. At that time, too, after the crash and everything.'

'That's very true,' Max replied. Even for someone with no interest, she knew a lot about the subject. Very similar to him and his knowledge of cricket, no thanks to an unhealthy family obsession with a particularly boring choice of sport, in his opinion.

He knew he had to ask her about the lost money. The old man in the library was extremely helpful in providing information he may not have come across by reading articles online. The last couple of hours had been a whirlwind, he had almost forgotten his reason for being here until the conversation had been brought back around to Dillinger.

He had gotten distracted by Penny. And the near-death experiences. And Will. He could not forget about Will, his eyes flicking to his friend, still resting on the couch. He knew he had to tread carefully, as Penny did not seem particularly forthcoming or entertained by the idea of discussing the Dillinger story any further. He was also dying to look at the map he had taken a picture of back in the library. They had started into the forest going the right direction, but after the events went south, he had no idea if he was even on the map anymore.

'So, what do you know about the lost money?' Max interrupted his thoughts, sensing the time to ask was now.

She took a moment to ponder before responding, almost caught off guard by the question, but practising a well-spoken response in her head before beginning out loud. 'I know as much as I heard from bedtime stories and books I was forced to read at school,' she began with a calmness. 'I know the story, and people think there is a fortune buried around the local area somewhere, but nobody really knows exactly.'

'So, nobody knows the location definitively?'

She was becoming agitated by the line of questioning. 'No, not specifically. He could have buried it anywhere between the lodge and Manitowish Lake, which is about a mile, and anywhere along the edge of Little Star Lake. People have been looking for ninety years, but no one's found anything yet. I'm doubtful that anything is out there at all, to be honest.'

'How come you don't believe the legend? If you don't mind me asking.' Max could see the resistance she was holding regarding the conversation and chose good manners as a tactic to keep her answering his questions.

'I don't know. I guess just because I've seen hundreds, if not thousands, of people look for it even in my lifetime, not to mention the years before. It just seems to me like a story the media created at the time to help in growing the story into legend, and people have run away with the fairy-tale of it all.'

'I guess if you've been around the story all your life, it could have gotten quite annoying.' Max understood and sympathized with her. It made sense where she was coming from and the sheer number of people that would have poked around her land just to see if they could find something no one had ever been able to discover, it must have gotten old very quickly.

'Do you mind if I use your bathroom?'

'Down the hall to the right, under the stairs,' she pointed deeper into the house as she spoke.

He nodded in a gesture of thanks and made his way down the hallway. He had acknowledged he had probably gotten all the information he could out of Penny regarding the Dillinger story. He was surprised he managed to get as much as he did, eventually. She had not been particularly forthcoming, which seemed rather strange to Max, but once she explained and he had time to find the reasoning, it did make sense. Living under the shadow of such a story could soon prove a burden, as he remembered when he was briefly staying in Whitechapel,

London. He could not walk home from the pub at night without passing at least two or three tour guides for Jack the Ripper.

Upon locking the bathroom door, he had a moment to splash his face with cold water, grabbing the hand towel and staring in the mirror as the towel dried his face. It was then he first had a moment alone since the debacle in the forest, and it was now the feeling of dread, uncertainty, bemusement and overall anxiety that rushed over him. Letting out a deep sigh, his mind wondered back to leaving home and beginning this strange experience.

He wanted this. He told himself he needed to go out and find a story. To live one. To be a part of something, to get him attached to anything of particular interest. He would not admit he signed up for land mines and concussed friends, but Will agreed to tag along, so it was his own fault.

Gathering his mind, he was probably in there for too long. *God knows what she must think of me*, he thought. He rushed around in the small space, placing the towel back, hurriedly attempting to fold it back the way he found it. It was no use. Whatever origami she had performed, it was too technical for Max. He pulled it through the loop, opened the door, then stretched across the room, remembering to flush the toilet, just as the door was pushed open past the limit considered rude. Jesus did he need a cigarette.

32

Max walked back through the hallway, noticing the family pictures on the wall below the staircase. There were particularly old photographs in rustic, yet timeless frames, many of them containing wedding pictures. As he continued proceeding, the photographs became more recent, until the wall ended, leaving the last photograph undoubtedly the newest. His eyes flicked towards it, then away, before returning for a longer and more intense review.

She was younger, but it was unmistakable. It was Penny. And she looked incredible. All dressed in white, her elegance extending in a dress that covered her feet, running across the grass and out of frame. Max looked and looked, before realising he had only been staring at half of the photograph. He swallowed and took a step backwards, seeing a dashingly handsome gentleman at her side, complete with a top hat under his free arm. Max knew it was a wedding photograph, but he did not acknowledge this with any certainty until seeing the man beside her. His heart sank. She was married. *Damn. Hardly surprising*, he thought. She had managed to look like a movie star in her ponytail and dirty chequered shirt, no wonder she was taken.

Max's mood did not change, walking back into the kitchen, and meeting Penny at the sink. She turned and smiled at him and he shared one in return. He now looked at her necklace again, the necklace he had noticed when Penny held him at gunpoint. The jewellery dangled adjacent to the open buttons of her shirt, just above a white undershirt. He caught the detail in the better light, the black 'R' inscribed delicately in calligraphy on the gold.

Fuck you, R, he thought. *Wait. Good job I didn't say that out loud, I sounded like a pirate.*

Always being good at deflecting and never revealing, he was in the thought process of striking up a new conversation with his lovely host when a noise came from somewhere. A jostling, rummaging sound broke their gaze as their eyes followed the noise. *What was that?* They looked over toward the living room, when something, or rather someone, rose from the sofa, the back of which faced the kitchen.

'Will!' Max shouted and leapt over to help his friend. There was grumbling and grunting of nothing decipherable nor understandable, but he was hell-bent on moving, that much was certain. 'No, you mustn't try and move, mate. You need to get some rest.' Max forced him back down, pushing his chest so he fell back to lying on the furniture. He grabbed the glass of water that was on the nearby coffee table, assisting Will and holding the back of his head as he drank. 'I assume you've got a headache, so this will help', he added.

Penny came rushing over, holding out a tea towel. 'Here,' she said, 'put this on his forehead. The towel was warm but not hot, and Max gratefully took it and followed the instructions. Will smiled, his eyes closed. When the towel made contact with his skin, like Dracula from his coffin, he forced himself upright, waving his hands to avoid further restraint.

'I need a wazz!' he said, pushing Max away and standing up with the shakiness of a toddler learning the new skill. His head scanned his surroundings hastily, quickly realising he was in the unknown. 'Woah,' he said, much calmer, 'this place looks great for a zombie attack.' Max, still crouched by the sofa, widened his eyes and thrust a stare of disbelief towards Penny, with an outstretched arm pointing at Will. And with that, Will hobbled off down the corridor and found the bathroom with ease, as if he had lived in the house all his life.

'What did I tell ya?' Max stood up and smiled. 'Ten quid, please.'

Penny pushed his hand down and replied. ‘Technically, that was the second thing he said.’

Max tutted. ‘Dammit.’ She was right.

33

The toilet flushed and Will emerged, still fiddling with the fly on his jeans, he walked back to the other two positioned on the sofa and armchair. He looked more than a little confused, but for someone who had just dealt with two life-and-death scenarios, and a concussion, he epitomised perkiness. He wandered to the spare sofa and dropped himself into a relaxing slouch.

'What the fuck happened?' He began abrasively, but it seemed rather justifiable.

'In essence,' Max started, pointing at Penny, 'she tried to kill you and I saved your life. More than once.' It was said with smugness, matching his expression. A life-saver. He liked that.

'Not quite', Penny defended herself.

'Yes quite,' Max interrupted. He could see a look of confusion appearing on Will's face, so decided to help him. 'She's cool, though. She's letting us stay here to till you get your head screwed back on.'

'Hi, I'm Penny.' She leaned out of her chair and over the coffee table with an extended hand. Will, doubting the gesture's validity, remained motionless momentarily. It took another glance at his friend, who gave a reassuring nod, for him to get up and accept the friendliness.

'Will,' he smiled back.

'I know,' she said. 'How are you feeling?'

Will took a second to ponder the question. 'Erm, okay, I guess. I have a headache, but it only hurts right at the back of my head.' His hand followed his words and he let out a wince when he made contact with the source of his pain.

'That doesn't sound like a hangover headache. You're not still hanging, are you?' Max smiled a best friend's smile to Will. Only true friends can find pain and suffering amusing.

'Well, it feels like someone's thrown a brick at the back of my head, which isn't usually how a hangover feels.' Will replied back with sarcasm. He would have much preferred to insult Max, but his brain was still not up and running.

Penny cleared her throat. 'So will you guys be okay to… you know… head off in about an hour.' She was having difficulty with the sentence, seemingly arguing with herself throughout. 'I'm just a bit worried, it's gonna start getting dark soon.'

'Yeah…' Max was brought back to reality. They needed to leave. God knows when her partner was supposed to return and how would he react if two random strangers were relaxing on his sofas and flirting with his wife. 'What do you reckon, Will? Think you can make a run at it?'

Will began to stand. 'I'm not so sure about running, how far away is the hotel?'

'Erm, I have no idea,' Max replied honestly. 'Penny?'

She snapped into action. 'Where are you staying?'

'The Lakeside,' Max responded.

'Oh, not far at all. Maybe a thirty-minute walk.' She considered her words, before extending an olive branch. 'I can drive if you like. My trucks parked out front.'

Max smiled at her, at the gesture. Despite being threatened with death, she was a nice lady. It was a shame the situation was not going to extend beyond today's interaction, but he was grateful to have spent time with her regardless. 'Thanks for the gesture, but it's okay. I'm gonna call us a taxi and we'll wait on the main road.' He smiled, moving towards Will to help guide his steps in the direction of the door they had arrived in.

'It'll be easier for you to go out the front,' Penny replied, gesturing with her hands to the hallway.

'Okay, great,' Max said. 'Can I just trouble you for a bottle of water, just for Will? Please?'

She laughed as she walked to the refrigerator. Handing him the bottle, she said, 'bo'oh'o'wa'er,' in a mocking tone.

Max chuckled back sarcastically in response. 'Fuck you,' he said jokingly with a smile.

Her smile remained as her head shook. They made their way through the hallway as she continued. 'I did hear that the English use swear words as terms of endearment to their closest friends.' Her eyes flashed up to meet Max's, who was still holding Will as he was swaying gently from side to side, as if on a boat.

'I have no idea where you've got that from,' Max smiled back, looking into her eyes. Having reached the front door at the end of the corridor, he waited for Penny to turn the handle. She pulled it open, allowing Max to usher Will through. He turned to face her and she stared back as the sun set in the distance and shone a ray of orange glow through the opening.

She stood just near enough to the door to get an orange beam bounce across her golden skin, lighting her up as Max examined every last detail on her face, for fear he was never going to be able to see it again.

She held his gaze, the sun casting darkness over his face, but the light shone atop his hair, the blonde starting to dance in the breeze.

'It was a pleasure to meet you, Penny. Thank you for your hospitality.'

'My pleasure. And do apologise to him for me again, when he realises what country he's in.' She smiled and they both broke into laughter, staring at Will before Max led him down the porch stairs and onto the dirt path. He stopped, for he had to steal one last gaze. He spun to see her, standing with her shoulder resting on the door frame, her arms folded. They shared a look of amusement at the utterly bizarre circumstances that led them to each other and how unintentional all of it was.

He turned and walked away, his arm wrapping over Will's shoulder as they followed the path into the trees. She watched with intrigue until they disappeared under the blanket of green, before finally closing her door.

Max reached into his pocket, took out his phone, and loaded up his maps. Before he called a taxi, he needed to do something more important. The app had his location on, the blue dot beaming whilst surrounded by a sea of green. He zoomed out slightly and took a screenshot, knowing that tomorrow he would need to remember where they were, and he could resume looking for what he came for from this spot. *Sticking to the path, of course*, he thought to himself. He didn't fancy getting blown up tomorrow.

His hand reached into Will's jacket pocket. *Result.* He pulled out the cigarette packet and lighter. He sparked up and took a long drag. That was needed after a long day. Now he just needed to get them back.

34

The following morning, Max awoke early but slowly. He had not slept much, replaying his afternoon exploits with Penny. Aside from his friends, he seldom laughed like that with anyone, at least not in a very long time. The thought of her made him restless, the thought of never seeing her again providing an inconsolable anxiousness, making sleeping difficult. He lay in silent contemplation for a long while, yet, even when he got up, the hotel restaurant had not yet opened, so he found himself at a diner across the street for mediocre coffee. Judging by the cups of joe, he certainly was not going to test the quality of their tea.

He sat in a booth overlooking the empty car park from his window, scribbling whatever he could conjure every five minutes in his notebook when the daydreaming stopped, sweeping him back to reality.

Despite the tentative process, he had consumed enough coffee to wake a dinosaur fossil and had sat for more than a few hours to transform the morning into productive, all whilst watching the sunrise. After returning to the room to shower, he felt relatively optimistic about his day. He dressed and waited for Will in the restaurant. It was not long before he joined him.

‘Morning mate. How are you feeling?’ Max begins.

‘Like I need a cig,’ Will replied, ‘but not bad, otherwise. Back to normal.’ He sipped the coffee Max had bought for him while he was waiting.

‘That’s good, at least you’re alright.’

‘Yeah, clears your guilty conscience doesn’t it,’ Will added with a chuckle.

‘What do you mean?’ Max asked, offended.

'You're the one who wanted to come here. You're the one who dragged me along with ya. Anything happens to me, that's on you brother.'

Max smiled. 'No one forced you to come.'

'Well suppose I didn't. You'd be dead already.'

'How so?' Max contemplated.

'The bird,' Will took another sip, 'she would have killed you, but 'cus I was there, she took a liking to me and couldn't go through with it.'

'Oh yeah?' Max replied. 'She hit you. With a gun.'

'Yeah, that was before she saw my face,' Will replied slyly.

'You're an idiot,' Max said.

Will laughed it off. 'So how long was I dead for? Long enough to not get in the way of your flirting, I hope?'

'An hour or so, so you did alright. I would have preferred a little longer.'

'Oh I do apologise,' Will retorted sarcastically. 'I'm sorry me waking up from a concussion got in the way of your grade-B flirting.'

'Hey. We both know it's not grade-B,' Max snapped back from joking to seriousness.

'Err…' Will weighed up his options. 'You're right. So what happened? You get her number?'

'Nah,' Max replied disappointingly and dropped his head slightly. 'She's married.'

'Shame. Next time I get a concussion, I'll play dead long enough for the girl to get a divorce too then, hey?'

Max laughed. 'Good. If I agree to send flowers to your funeral, can you shut up long enough to order breakfast?'

Will placed a cigarette in his mouth and stood up. 'Of course. Only if you order me a full English.'

He offered his packet of smokes to Max, who shook his head in reply, and then headed for the door.

That's a lot of cholesterol, thought Max. He sat in contemplation for a few moments before he had his answer. *Eggs. That's what I need.*

***

'So what's the plan for today?' Will had returned, and breakfast had arrived and been eaten.

'What do you want to do today?' Max asked.

'Me?' Will was slightly taken back. He leaned backwards in his chair. 'I say relax. Hire a boat, take some beers, get out on one of those lakes. Maybe hire some fishing gear, too, make it look like we're there for a reason.'

Max smiled. 'Yeah, we're not doing that.'

'Why not?'

'We've got to go back to where we were yesterday.' Max held his phone up, showing the screenshot he had taken of their location.

'Why would you ask me then?'

'I kinda thought that's what you were gonna say. You'd say it with enthusiasm and you'd be excited. It'd have been a good way to start, but you've ruined it now.'

Will thought of his response. 'You're so stupid', he laughed. 'Also, why would I want to go back to a place I nearly died?'

'Oh, stop whining. It was only a mild concussion,' Max said, the sympathy never lost between the two of them. 'Plus, we have new information now.' He noticed Will still looked slightly disinterested. Max rolled his eyes. 'Come on. I'll buy you the first round later.'

'First round?' Will scoffed. 'You're buying all the rounds till we go home.'

They both stood up. 'Fine,' Max said reluctantly, before adding a smile. He punched Will's arm in jest as they made their way to the door. 'Today is gonna be a good day,' Max added, putting on his sunglasses and they set off on their walk.

35

The group were travel-worn and tired beyond belief, almost appearing unrecognisable to each other upon exchanging morning pleasantries. McKenna, however, managed to never cease expectations, remaining impeccably well kept, his shirt perfectly tucked, boots freshly polished and a fresh shave. He did not need sleep, he was too concerned with ensuring completion. Much like a postman, he took pride in always delivering.

Having delivered a stern, morning briefing, the twelve had been split into two distinct groups, the theory behind McKenna's decision was the fewer investigating, the more incognito they would become. All would be drafted to help set the operation up, but when commenced, one group would be on land at a time, the other working on the boat.

Rising with the sun had a strategic advantage, allowing the early morning dusk to evade local witnesses investigating just what they were getting up to. Moving swiftly and using the jetty that was masked by the thickness of the forest, they transferred equipment from boats to land slowly enough to not arouse suspicion with any early morning waves. By mid-morning, everything had been implemented, with a base set just inside the forest where they were permitted a strict, time-regimented breakfast, supervised by Decker.

The group shared hardiness and optimism, in spite of the drowsiness sweeping across the camp. Having all had responsibilities in a number of previous opportunities for the organisation, it was clear to see a sense of camaraderie amongst them all. They were all grateful to be away from McKenna's menacing and unscrupulous gaze, hanging over their every move like a bird watching its prey high in the sky.

McKenna had ensured the movement across the water was completed without a hitch but had elected to delegate the overseeing of the first ground movements to Decker. Everyone, including Decker, graciously accepted the news, everyone aware he still demanded respect and his orders should be followed, but he had remnants of a personality, unlike McKenna.

They sat around the supplies and food they had prepared in a circle, exchanging anecdotes and nostalgic tales of many adventures they all shared together. The feeling was pleasant, and they savoured every moment of relaxation before the hard work commenced, inevitably like a train travelling on its tracks, with no time to stop, ploughing ahead.

36

Upon leaving the hotel once more, the pair trundled further along the main road, advancing east, parallel to the lake situated in the south. After a while and in a brief pause in conversation, they were both in agreement of having walked far enough, not to mention they could see the eastern lake appearing in the distance. They found another trail and made their way through. The discussion naturally dispersed, settling for the returning naturalistic sounds for white noise whilst they concentrated on their footing and surroundings.

This area of the forest was much denser and more verdant, for reasons unknown. The blanket canopy of leaves and branches hindered the sunlight to pierce through, creating a darker, seemingly more treacherous path. The heat of the day was reaching its peak and what sunlight that had been granted permission through the thicket proved inescapable, bouncing off the highest line of branches back towards the ground. This created a particularly humid environment, which – when paired with the consistent concentration and stress the pair shared – created a sweaty atmosphere that culminated in moisture across their brows and backs.

This all added to their discomfort as they carefully constructed a path through a series of overgrown greenery that had taken possession of the track leading to the southern lake. It did not, however, slow any progress. The pursuit continued, and the pair soon found themselves at the edge of the treeline, staring at the open waters of the lake. Its vastness could not be overstated, the size resulting in the inability to see the shoreline on the other side.

They reclined on the water's edge for recuperation under the shade of the trees, watching the sun glisten and play on the subtle waves the wind blew across the water.

Resting for only a few minutes, they soon decided to use the rest of the sunlight to pursue onwards, back into the thicket of wildlife to venture further into its depths. It was on this return journey into the forest that something in particular caught Max's eye. They had been frequently stopping to investigate potential areas of significance throughout the day, much in vain. This time, it seemed like no other. A routine, yet careful, inquisition into what appeared a trodden path over shrubbery and plants.

After multiple tentative steps took him no more than ten paces from the path Will remained on, Max scanned the area around him swiftly, imagining the vicinity to be as regular and boring as all the other times they had performed this manoeuvre. But, just as he began to turn his head back towards Will, he noticed a tree, a little further in the distance. It was the same as all the others, a green and brown moss-coloured bark with various branches and twigs extending. Yet, the trunk seemed to display an odd formation, certainly not naturally occurring on the wood. He decided, with a nod to his friend, to walk the additional steps over to the tree to inspect.

Upon reaching the tree, Max pushed his face to within a few inches of the bark and studied it in impeccable detail; incessantly scanning, ensuring nothing to be missed. He scoured every centimetre he could see, before returning his eyes to what had initially caught his glance.

Just below his eye-line, at his chest height, was a carving in the bark. It was spherical, with a diameter of no more than ten centimetres. Within the circle, there was a pattern, a symbol or insignia of some description, but it was not possible for Max to decipher what it could possibly be.

He twisted his head and looked back over to Will and gave him a wave, gesturing for him to join him. Making sure to follow every step perfectly, Will moved like a cat in the snow, stepping exactly where Max had, across to his friend. Upon reaching him, the beads of sweat across his forehead started to drip onto the dry leaves at their feet, thudding onto them as they stared at the tree marking.

They stood for longer than necessary in total silence, both gazing at what lay before them. Will was the first to speak. 'What do you think it could be?'

'I have absolutely no idea', Max replied honestly.

'Hmm,' Will pushed his hand under his chin and posed thoughtfully.

'Do you not find it weird that it's all the way out here? It seems nowhere significant,' Max added.

'Yeah. Really weird,' Will replied.

'We should have a look around, see if we can see anything else.'

'Okay, good idea. But slowly,' Will added.

Precariously, they searched the ground and every tree, searching intensely for something similar. Or anything. This seemed like a lucky break, a pivotal, paramount moment of which Max was hoping to exploit full advantage of. Yet, it seemed in vain. The pair carefully looked in every nook they could find, eventually circling back to the original tree.

'Crap!' Max let out a frustrating scream. Exasperated, he fell on the tree and slid down, sitting with his back resting on the trunk.

Will remained productive. He snapped a photograph of the carving. 'Come on,' he finally said after a few minutes. 'Let's carry on looking over here. We haven't been this way yet.'

'Okay,' Max replied, reluctantly getting to his feet. And the two set out searching for something again. As they began walking, Max remembered to take his phone out and once more take a screenshot of where they found themselves. He wanted to be absolutely sure they could recollect where the carving was, just in case its importance was greater than the conclusion they came to. *One can hope.*

37

The group's spirit had slowly drained, as opposed to a sudden dramatic decline. The first group had been searching since dusk, with no return in sight. McKenna, believing the task to be unchallenging, had unsurprisingly become cantankerous and rageful after being updated with constant defeat throughout the day.

Under strict orders to remain as quiet as possible whilst in the forest, the exchanges between everyone developed into strictly professional, consulting technological findings and detector readings as they searched every blade of grass and pile of mud they could see, on the surface and six metres deep.

Working in two alternating groups of six, they attempted to use radars and maps to methodically investigate the entirety of the three-mile forest, searching closely in as many places as their feet would allow, the more difficult-to-reach areas were investigated through detectors and sensors they had spread thoroughly across the ground's surface; a decision which also aided in making sure neither group scrutinised the same place twice.

The day passed with relatively insufficient progress and they were all beginning to feel the pressure by McKenna and everybody else back in Arizona. The organisation prided itself on punctuality and it was unheard of for an endeavour to ever run behind schedule, and, understandably, the group of twelve were worried they would soon be in search of new employment. That being the best-case scenario. Mutterings and rumours had always been in abundance during everyone's time there, the water-cooler talk usually denoting fear of reprimand if a job was unsatisfactorily performed, the punishment presumed to unimaginable lengths.

McKenna was becoming increasingly frustrated. The lethargic and passion-less exercise had gone on long enough, so long he was certain it was starting to make him look bad. He had placed faith in Decker, who, for the first time, had disappointed him. Eager to get back on track, he opted to inform one group that he intended to oversee the next morning's attempts to locate the asset. Understandably, the group worried about being overly scrutinised when their time came to venture into the forest, the evening chatter on the boat soon became quiet, replaced with a hanging sense of dread.

To add to McKenna's despair, the first group, tasked with beginning the search, had failed to return to the boat at their scheduled arrival.

McKenna attributed it to a lack of enthusiasm and drive to achieve the organisation's goals. He stood on the edge of the deck, looking out over the water towards the forest's entrance. Having followed instructions - seemingly the only person there capable - he had continuously navigated the boat to various destinations over the four connecting lakes throughout the day. Due to this, McKenna was an awfully long distance away, not being able to see the pier particularly clearly. He paced for a few minutes in avid frustration before retreating to his room.

He grabbed a glass and poured a generous scotch, knocking back the amber liquid. Consulting his gut, he made the decision not to ponder too much on this particular predicament. He would go over himself the following day and ensure that both groups would work together to find this thing sooner rather than later.

Having poured himself another, he reclined in the chair, the whisky making his mind dance more than he usually cared for. The lack of sleep did not concern him, he knew he would not be sleeping tonight regardless. It was Decker. He was supervising the group that had not returned. Had Decker heard what McKenna had planned? Had he found out about Operation

Turntable? He finished the fresh glass and leaned forward for a refresh.

It was impossible. There were only two people privy to that information. He waved off his accusation with a shake of the head. He took another sip. All the more reason to go over tomorrow, to see exactly what these imbeciles have been up to.

His phone buzzed. He leaned towards the coffee table, examining the screen lighting up, vibrating on the glass table. It was Decker. He picked the phone up. He wanted a very good explanation for their tardiness.

38

Sometimes, things can change very rapidly. Max and Will were enjoying their cigarette together, talking about whatever came to their mind at that moment, before their enjoyment came to an abrupt halt. As quick as it took Will to take another burn of his cigarette and bend down to tie his shoelace, they were expertly surrounded by a group of men who looked very unhappy to see them at this late hour. Not to mention they seemed to all be carrying guns.

Will bolted upright, as if getting a telling off from the headmaster, his back straight, the cigarette dangling in the corner of his mouth. They both stood frozen, their eyes frantically searching in an attempt to comprehend what had just happened. As their eyes continued scanning around, they instinctively raised their arms above their heads, just waiting for whatever inevitably came next. Soon, they were approached from behind, two men kicking the back of their legs and forcing them to drop to their knees in unison. A gun remained pointing at both of their heads as they waited for the shouting to stop. It seemed as though all of them were screaming at something, heightening the tension as much as a silence would.

Suddenly, in the height of the frantic shouting, one voice rose louder than the rest. It was obvious he had not been shouting before the interjection, and the rest of the group silenced themselves within an instant of his mouth opening. The silence was only momentarily, as in the distance, sounds of the forest returned and the birds chirped once more.

The man with the loud voice walked slowly up to the pair on their knees. He was holding a telephone, speaking only in response to the person on the other end. There were nods of agreement, grunts of acceptance as if he himself was receiving orders. He stopped directly in front of Will and Max. As he listened on the phone, he bent down and snatched the cigarette from Max's mouth with hands covered with black leather gloves, putting the cigarette to his own mouth and taking a drag of satisfaction.

It was only at that moment that Max's head tilted upwards and he was able to see the man. He wore a black military uniform like the rest of them, but his seemed to fit slightly better, accenting the muscles that were trying to escape around his arms and shoulders. His face was scarred. He had both acne scars and a long, thin scar that ran from the side of his forehead to below his left ear. His black stubble made him appear darker, blending into the shadows of the scenery around him.

'Yeah, that's fine. I've found some people lurking in the forest, what do you want me to do with them?' He finally spoke. He had an American accent, but it was one of deepness and too many cigarettes. He awaited a response before an ugly smile took over his face. Everyone was motionless waiting for the verdict. 'Okay, yeah. Yeah, I'll bring them with us.' He hung up. He pointed at Max and Will and indicated to the men who stood behind the pair. Nothing was spoken but understood clearly. They were forced to their feet, guns pointed into the bottom of their backs and pushed into following the scarred man as he walked away.

'What are you guys doing in the forest this late at night?' He shouted from the front of the line, with Max and Will just behind. The remaining men kept up the rear.

'We're just tourists who got a little lost. I think you've got us confused with someone else!' Max pleaded with the man.

'Don't lie to me!' The man's anger seemed to peak, as his face turned slightly and Max witnessed spit shooting out of his mouth as he spoke.

'He's telling the truth! We're from England!' Will made an attempt of his own.

'I don't give a shit where you're from,' the man replied angrily. 'Did your mother not tell you it's dangerous to play out so late?' The scarred man shouted, his whole body laughing as he spoke. His cockiness added to their humiliation.

The group made their way through the forest, walking south. They never strayed from the path, indicating that even these had experience with Penny's defence mechanisms. Max and Will followed the scarred man, the guns remained pointed to their backs, bouncing off and hitting them again as they walked. This arguably was more tortuous than if it remained glued to the skin. It became a constant reminder every time their feet hit the ground, the cold metal of the barrel punching itself onto the protruding vertebrae.

With their minds preoccupied with this sensation, and the fact they walked directly behind the scarred man, the pair had absolutely no idea what was happening behind them. Silently, numbers were dropping. It was only when the party had reached the lake side, escaping from the dark forest, did the realisation occur. Only once under the glistening moonlight, that danced across the water and illuminated the shorelines where they all stood, did everyone realise something was very wrong.

'What the hell?' The expression of flabbergast escaped from the scarred man. Only the two men holding their guns at Max and Will remained. The scarred man waited for the rest of his posse to escape the trees. They never arrived.

39

It was only a subtle noise. It must have been a short distance away, though it was obvious it was not a natural noise. The person checked their leather-strapped watch. Awfully late for any dog walkers or runners. It was dark. They decided to redirect their route home and carefully proceed towards the direction of the noise, investigating further. With trepidation, they soon reached the source of the noises. There was a group of men making their way through the south track towards the direction of the lake. Nothing out of the ordinary.

Wait. They looked in slightly more detail and moved to a better position as the group continued walking. That is when they noticed the irregularity. *Of course.* Just before they were heading off to bed, how inconvenient. They almost wished they had not seen the group, and then there would not have been an obligation to offer assistance. Still, it had been a while, and maybe the rust was setting in. Time to get to work and grease the hinges.

Like a vixen, cutting through the greenery in a silent fury, they knew these woods better than anyone. Approaching from behind, a twig snapping caused the man at the back of the group to twist his head. He raised his weapon and walked towards the noise, leaving the group as they marched onwards. Then, behind him, a rock was raised and struck across his head, dropping him to the floor in a slump.

The figure moved in the dark, using the branches and bushes to alleviate being seen. The next victim was quickly dispatched as he had begun slowing from the group, wondering where the first had disappeared. Looking around, he had never noticed the figure hiding behind a nearby tree, swinging around and using their momentum to strike at his midriff. He curled over and was met with a knee to the face, shooting his body backwards and dropping to the floor. The noises made sounded too similar to walking on the track for the other men to notice.

One man was walking slightly further behind than the rest of the remaining group. He was oblivious to the recent violence enacted on his colleagues, but he heard a subtle noise from off of the track, in the woods. He stepped a little closer to investigate, turning his torch on for better visibility. There did not seem anything out of the ordinary. Just then, on a low-hanging branch, a figure dropped, swinging with all their momentum, legs extended and kicked their full weight into the man's chest. The wind taken out of his lungs, the man flew six feet backwards, nestling into a bush for a deep slumber.

Having dispatched half of the group, the figure continued their movement, plotting their next steps. However, they may have run out of time. At that moment, the group had reached the shoreline, and the figure's disguise in the forest had expired. They took a moment to consider the coming minutes and how to execute efficiently.

40

They stood and watched trees for only a moment, but it was long enough to witness everything that happened next. It was, however, not long enough to fathom or comprehend the following minutes.

'Right,' the scarred man said. 'It doesn't look like we'll be seeing anyone any time soon. Let's get them loaded onto the boat boys.' He turned and walked in the direction of the lake, where stood a small wooden dock with an inflatable mercenary boat bobbing in the water next to it. The five of them started walking, turning their back to the forest.

Suddenly, a yell could be heard from behind everyone, and Will noticed the gun was no longer puncturing his back. The men all turned around to witness as the man guarding Will had been pulled by a rope around his waist, and was now flying five feet in the air being pulled into the forest. The four remaining men stood in abject wonder for a split second, attempting to decipher the action that had just occurred.

'What the…' the scarred man began to say before the rope had returned from the forest, angling across the sky as it came down towards them. Their heads pivoted to watch the rope angle its trajectory perfectly and wrap around the scarred man's gun, the rope seemingly pulling itself tighter on the barrel of its own accord. With the next movement, a snap of the rope pulled the gun out from the scarred man's hand, flying through the sky and back into the forest.

Max seized his moment in the chaos and elbowed the man who remained behind him, forcing him to double over. Once in this position, Max used all the weight in his right leg to push him to the floor, the soldier dropping his gun in the process.

Seeing everything unfold, the scarred man's anger peaked once more, the neck muscles tightening and the rage causing redness to sweep over his face. He raised his fist to attack, bringing it down with almighty strength towards Max's face as he turned after dispatching his guard. Max saw the fist briefly and prepared for impact, of which he was ready for possibly the most painful feeling of his life. The scarred man's arms were as big as a weightlifter's legs, and he knew it was going to hurt.

Before the impact could strike, however, Will moved swiftly, grabbing the scarred man's arm back, preventing the strike from landing on Max's jaw. Will held it back with all his body weight, pushing against the strength of the scarred man's arm. Max, relieved he still had all of his teeth, thought quickly and struck the scarred man in the groin with his foot. The redness in his face arguably grew even brighter and his hands cupped between his legs, falling side wards with carelessness.

Will turned, picking up the remaining gun from Max's guard, who was just getting back to his feet. Will pointed the gun at the man and shouted for coercion and he stopped on his hands and knees.

The two shared a smile with each other once more. The scarred man writhed on the floor in unspeakable pain – he would be moving gingerly for some time – and Will held the other guard at gunpoint. They could not account for the disappearance of the others, but they were grateful to be breathing in the fresh air.

'What the hell happened to all the others?' Max said. He was out of breath, the adrenaline still flowing.

'I have absolutely no idea,' Will replied.

'Oh shit,' Max said.

'What is it?' Will was too immersed in holding his captive.

'Somebody is coming out of the trees.'

Will turned his head and began looking at the tree line with Max. The two started involuntarily walking towards each other as they watched in horrific anticipation for what was escaping the forest and arriving to inconvenience them again. It seemed like one thing after another and they were struggling to catch any sense of a break.

A figure was emerging in the shadows of the trees, sauntering slowly as the bleakness engulfed them, covering their identity. The pair watched and waited. Then, as the figure broke the line of trees and emerged into the moonlight that helped illuminate the patch of grass on the lake side, they could see clearly. It was their guardian angel. Their saviour. They carried on walking towards them, collapsing the rope they had into a neat circle and placing it on their hip. They stood over the guard Will was watching and delivered a swift kick to his head, knocking him cold and he collapsed onto his front. They walked past Max and Will, moving over to the scarred man and repeating the process. Finally, every soldier was incapacitated.

The figure smiled as they approached Max and Will, the pair in awe and disbelief. Will had a giddy smile across his face, like a child waiting for Santa Claus. Max's smile was more of a grin, of admiration and thankfulness.

The figure finally spoke. 'We have to get out of here before any of these wake-up.'

'You know of anywhere?' Max asked slyly with his grin spreading across his face as he stared.

They thought, copying Max's actions. 'Hmmm…' they considered. They rolled their eyes. 'Follow me.'

The two of them followed into the forest. Will elbowed Max in approval.

'Thank you, Penny,' Max said.

'Don't mention it', she said from in front of them. 'Just stay close, it's not far.'

41

McKenna was able to push back two further whiskeys after his phone call with Decker before deciding to worry about his subordinate's absence. Decker had telephoned to explain they would be travelling back to the boat momentarily, informing McKenna they were yet to find anything of any significance concerning their objective. He then proceeded to inform him of a pair of stragglers that they had witnessed roaming the forest particularly late in the evening. McKenna, never one to leave a stone unturned, demanded Decker to retrieve them and bring them back aboard the ship, ready for interrogation.

McKenna had some certainty after giving the order to capture them that the interrogation could have been unnecessary, but he missed the feeling he had injected into his system when he saw the fear behind somebody's eyes when they were chained to a desk, desperate to appease his every word to the letter.

He wanted to be thorough, as he always was, and wished to enact this workaholic trait to his colleagues. McKenna had persistently worked harder than everybody he worked alongside, it sickened him to see people perform tasks to such worrying degrees of laziness. Being this close to the action for the first time in many years, he was eager to make sure his subordinates learned something from working in such proximity to him during the assignment.

Having waited patiently for over twenty minutes, McKenna finished another beverage and stood on the deck once more, this time with binoculars, pulling them up to watch the pier they had offloaded their gear upon earlier that morning.

Studying the area diligently, McKenna could not see anything out of the ordinary, except the lack of movement he expected to see from the group heading back in his direction. Not helped by the night sky struggling to light up the areas he needed to see, the trees seemed to be the only thing moving according to his eyes.

McKenna noted to himself earlier during the telephone call with Decker that he sounded normal. He had feared earlier that the lack of promptness on their return could have been attributed to Decker potentially discovering the knowledge of Operation Turntable. During the call, however, he had been calm and non-assuming, McKenna happy with his judge of character and concluding Decker to still be unaware of just what was in motion around him.

Yet, the lack of the group returning still majorly concerned McKenna. He gave up with the binoculars, knowing he was losing the battle against the darkness the night cast across the lake, and retreated to his room. Decker had mentioned they had only seen two people in the forest. So why were they not back? Could these two people have escaped? Or worse, had they incapacitated the soldiers? McKenna was confident it could not have been the latter, laughing to himself his brazen suggestion of idiocy he attributed to overthinking.

Grabbing the whisky bottle for a refill, he knew that by day break he would be heading over to solid ground to find out exactly what was happening over there. He could not bear the thought of failure and the feeling ate up his stomach. He knocked back his drink to drown his feelings.

42

They did not exchange any further words on their trek back through the forest. It made sense to remain quiet, so as not to invoke any more trouble. Will and Max were just grateful to be alive, so silence was far from troubling. The birds chirping and the wind blowing sounded like music, the air they breathed was fresher than before. Max could not comprehend that Penny had just helped them escape the clutches of what seemed certain doom. By the time they had reached the house, he was desperate for a cup of tea to settle himself down. He knew Will would be the same. It would be rather difficult to sleep after such an encounter.

They approached the house from the rear, the same way as before, and it was pleasing to feel a sense of comfort and safety in the garden surrounding the building; the trees operating as their own, personal wall around the property.

Once they had got back into the living room, the pair of them took a seat, on the instruction of Penny no less, also being advised not to speak or move an inch.

'Tea, I presume?' she said. The pair both nodded, and not another word was spoken as they all listened to the kettle whistle away.

Upon setting down all the mugs on the coffee table - Penny had opted for a green tea at this late hour - she began.

'Now, I want a straight answer, please. None of your usual bullshit, Max.' Max dropped his head slightly, almost in shame. 'What on earth were you guys doing out there?'

'Well…' Max started.

'Don't tell me you were out there looking for that thing again,' Penny interjected.

'Well…' it was now Will's turn.

'I don't believe it!' Penny remarked, annoyed. She leaned back in her armchair. 'After my specific advice against it, you go and do it anyway. I told you. You were lucky I was there tonight. They'd have killed you for sure.'

'Did we say thank you for that, by the way?' Will said innocently.

'Yes, you did. But that's not the point.' Penny got back on topic. 'The reason it's dangerous is because of those people out there!' she said, pointing to the door. 'The things my family put there are the least of your concerns compared to them!'

The two of them sat. They dare not say a word, feeling very much like they were getting a telling off for late homework.

'We're really sorry, Penny.' Max sat up straight and attempted a reconciliation. 'We came all the way out here to look for it, it seemed daft not going and having another look before we went home.'

'Regardless, what you did was idiotic. Clearly, I didn't do enough to scare you away.'

'You couldn't scare me away,' as soon as he said it, Max cringed, and looking over at Will he saw him cringe as well. *Swing and a miss.* The three started chuckling, attempting to lighten the situation slightly. It was becoming a rather drab subject, so Max's pass at Penny helped to ease the tension.

They sat for a moment, content with sipping away at their beverages before Will said after a while: 'great moves back there, Penny. How did you get so good with a rope?'

'My mother taught me. She was catching stuff in these forests her whole life.'

A nod of approval from both of them. 'And what happened to the others? Whilst we were still in the forest?' Max inquired.

'My dad taught me how to handle myself when I was young. I take self-defence classes, too.' Penny was very smug in her response. It was not often she called upon these skills, but she was proud of them and appreciated the admiration from the guys.

They chatted for a while longer, about nothing important, but Penny felt it would have been rude to ask them to leave so soon, and frankly, she enjoyed the company. They were harmless and funny; it helped to take her mind off of everything she was constantly contemplating.

She was fearful she had been thinking too much lately. Thinking about what she was going to do with herself. About the future and what on earth the next step would be. She was in dreadful fear that she had missed out on opportunities, that she had been placed on the wrong path, or guilty at herself for never being able to change course. She enjoyed her solitude, but recently it had become more of a burden, a hole; something that she was unable to drag out from underneath. The boys in front of her helped alleviate her mind – the stresses – and made her think about nothing at all. It was healthy to have an empty mind with no thoughts sometimes, she was convinced. She sat in silence for a moment whilst the two of them argued about something nonsensical. When it looked like the confrontation was approaching a boiling point, she decided to wisely interject, to prevent blood stains on her sofa.

'How long were you out there for today?' She asked, moving on her chair and switching her legs around she had crossed.

'Most of the day, actually,' Max replied.

'Yeah, the kidnapping came at the perfect time really,' Will added, 'we'd just made the decision to stop looking and go back to the hotel.'

All three of them chuckled, Penny realising it had been a long time since there had been this much noise in the house. She probed, presuming to already know the answer. 'And you find anything?' She said it with a smugness as if asking a child a question she already knew the answer to.

The two exchanged a glance before Max spoke. 'Well, in fact, we did stumble across something a bit weird. You're probably the best person to ask about it, I guess.'

'Oh yeah?' Penny sat up slightly, intrigued with their findings, but not ready to admit it was anything of significance.

Will quickly scrolled through his phone and pulled up the picture of the tree engraving he took earlier that day, handing it over to Penny.

Before Max spoke, he could see Penny's facial expression change faintly, almost in acknowledgement of what it was. 'We found it on one of the trees east from here, nearer the eastern lake –'

'Manitowish Lake,' Penny interrupted to add.

'Yeah, that one. When we came across it, we thought it might be worth looking into. So we looked around the tree for ages, but we couldn't find anything.'

'I mean, the engraving is so old that you can't even tell what it is,' Will added. 'There's so much moss around it, it was a wonder we found it. It just looks like a branch has fallen off the tree.'

'Yeah…' Penny took her time. 'You're right, it hardly looks like anything.'

'Come on. Out with it.' Max said.

'What?' Penny defensively asked.

Max laughed. 'You clearly know something about this hole in the tree. It looks a bit shit now, granted, but I knew it looked a little interesting. Will took a picture just to be sure, and the way your acting proves to me it *is* something. And you *know* what it is. So you better tell us.' He smiled at the end, looking towards his friend to help back him up. Will had no idea what he was talking about, but after sharing a look with Max, he stared at Penny with a frown, indicating he was keeping up to speed with the conversation.

Penny held both of their stares, going back and forth between their eyes. After a while, she relented. 'Okay, fine,' she said and moved herself into a more comfortable position in her armchair. She picked up her mug with both hands and held it tight, feeling the warmth of the tea escaping the sides of the cup and heating her hands.

'I have never seen this before, believe me.'

'Give it a rest,' Max urged for more.

'I haven't. God's honest truth. But…' she held a finger out in silence before she was interrupted again, 'there is a legend.'

'A legend?' Will asked. 'That sounds interesting. Let's hear it.'

'Okay. It's more of a bedtime story than a legend, just before I get started.'

'Jesus Christ, get on with it!' Max was half joking, but she was dragging it out to purposely annoy them. It was working.

'So, as Max has already said, you're familiar with the John Dillinger story.' The guys nodded their heads frantically, like dogs waiting for their treats, desperate to hear what came next. 'Our family added an extra part to the story.' She cleared her throat before continuing.

'Dillinger escaped Little Bohemia Lodge into the forest, buried his money, and escaped. He decided to stay around the forest whilst the police were searching the area, as he wisely thought he could hide more easily in the woods as opposed to the main road. The legend goes that he marked four trees around where he buried the money, so he could remember when he came back to dig it up later on. When he finally left the forest, the police had given up their search, and he thought he was safe. He encountered a local farmer and his shotgun. As his only option, he offered a deal to the farmer, that in exchange for his life, he told him that he had buried $200,000 in the woods, marking four trees around where he had dug. If his life was spared, he offered the farmer a percentage of the money in exchange. The farmer agreed, and Dillinger was on his way.'

Max and Will sat on the edge of their seats, in complete transcendental amazement at the story, looking like the only way to make it better was a bowl of popcorn. They stared, not wanting to blink in fear of missing part of the story.

'The farmer just let him go?' Will asked.

'Yes. His thinking was that he could look for these trees the man spoke of, and find the money regardless of whether Dillinger returned. If he couldn't find the money, he could wait for Dillinger to help.'

'But he never found the money,' Max added.

'He didn't. He spent his life searching for it, and passed the story onto his children, telling them bedtime stories of masquerading pirates and whimsical stories of medieval Europe and bank robbers leaving lost fortunes on their doorstep. For three generations, the family has tried and failed to find these four markings in the forest, with each generation passing on more and more doubt to the story. Eventually, they gave up searching for it, believing the story to be a creation of the farmer and his imagination as he enjoyed creating stories for his children and grandchildren. That theory was helped by the fact the farmer became a part-time children's writer in the local area, meaning this version of the story had more validity.'

All three of them leaned back in their chairs, attempting to comprehend what had just been told. It was heavy contemplation for not only Max and Will, who had never heard the story before but Penny, who had not heard the story herself in years. She was coming to the realisation that the story may in fact be true, and the fortune may be out there somewhere. They sat and finished their tea in silence.

'So, this farmer,' Max said after a while. 'Is he a distant relative of yours?'

Penny played with the pendant on her necklace, running it over her fingers and holding it tightly as she spoke. 'My husband's. The family was my husband's, the farmer was his great-grandfather.'

Max's eyes flicked towards the ground in disappointment. The chemistry he felt with Penny was particularly strong, so much so that he often found himself forgetting of her relationship.

Will had been thinking. He needed validation on a certain point. 'You said the family started to believe less and less about the story as it was passed down. Are any of them that believe it still alive?'

Penny swallowed, pushing down the welling up in her throat. It was not something she particularly wanted to discuss with the pair of them, but the conversation was seemingly going to progress to a position she felt uncomfortable with as soon as she saw the tree carving.

'No, unfortunately not,' she began, a single tear beginning to roll down her cheek. 'Their family is no longer with us. My husband, he died a couple of years ago. The last was his mother, she passed last year.'

Will and Max had not realised and immediately felt awful. 'I'm sorry,' they both said in unison, with no particular desire to carry forth any more conversation if Penny was not feeling ready to. Despite the friendship they had all felt blossoming, they were both quick to remember they did not know her very strongly, and it could become uneasy for her to speak to them about such a process.

Max stood up, thinking the most respectful thing to do in this instance was to give her as much space as possible. 'We should probably go, right Will?'

'Yeah, absolutely, sorry Penny.'

She wiped the tears from her eyes, though there were not many. 'No,' she remarked. The two stopped moving momentarily. 'It's okay. I think I'd actually prefer the company if that's alright with you.'

'Of course,' Max said, and they both sat back down. If he was being totally honest with himself, he was not ready to leave just yet. She looked beautiful when she cried.

43

'You're the only person alive who knows the story?' Will continued. He had tried to wait as long as he could before asking questions, but he was fascinated and desperate to know the answer.

'Will,' Max pleaded, 'leave her alone,' wanting to change the topic to save Penny's feelings.

'No, honestly, it's fine. It was a long time ago.' There were not many tears and Max admired her strength. Penny was a little embarrassed, having only met them yesterday, but was more annoyed with herself for letting the situation bother her. 'But you're right, I am the only one.'

Max, seeing she was more than okay, decided to further the line of questioning. 'Not even the suits who wanted to buy the house and intent on killing anyone on a public footpath?'

Penny smiled. 'No, hell no. There's no way I'd mention anything to them.'

'Not that you believed it,' remarked Will.

'That too,' Penny agreed, glancing over at him kindly.

'And you think this is definitely one of these four markers?' Max enquired.

'I was hearing stories about it for over ten years. That's how they were described to me, so I can't see why it couldn't be.'

'Woah', Will reacted in amazement.

'It's funny. It seemed like a fairy tale. Something you'd share at the dinner table or after too many drinks at Christmas. I personally never thought it was true. My husband believed. I think it was because he was told the story as a boy. He even said he looked for them for a time before we got close.' Penny smiled and stared into the distance, a lovely warm rush of nostalgia taking over.

'I still don't understand something,' Max admitted.

'Which part?'

'Why, at this specific point, are the bloodthirsty suits after it? Why not in the one hundred years before?'

'Well, as I mentioned yesterday, people, including companies and suits, have been trying for decades. This particular set must have received a recent investment boost. A Babe Ruth jersey must cost an awful lot these days, enough to afford some hi-tech gadgets to look underground for a hidden crate.'

Max seemed to follow along until the last part had thrown him. He frowned, wondering what she was talking about. Babe Ruth, the baseball player? Then it hit him. He remembered back to the robbery he saw on the television back at home. The one in New York.

'You think these guys had something to do with what happened in New York?' He asked.

'Quite possibly,' she pondered. 'From what I've been reading and hearing. These fellas knew what they were doing and were well-equipped. Not to mention the boats on the lake arrived here around two days after the New York thing.'

Max nodded in agreement, seemingly being able to tie everything together. Will, on the other hand, looked awfully confused, his head turning to listen to them both like he was watching a tennis match. 'New York?' he asked innocently.

'Yeah, some people stole a Babe Ruth jersey from a private residency in Manhattan…'

'…killed two guards,' Penny continued. 'No one has any idea who it was…'

'...no leads, no evidence, and they got away with something worth $20 million,' Max finished off. The pair exchanged a smile with each other.

'Shit, they sound real serious.'

'They sound expensive,' Penny muttered.

'One more thing,' Will said. 'Who the hell is Babe Ruth?'

Penny's chin hit the floor; she couldn't believe it. She looked at Max and pointed at Will. 'Is he serious?'

'We don't watch American sports at home,' Max defended his friend. He then addressed Will. 'Think about if someone stole a Bobby Moore England shirt. Or Geoff Hurst.'

Will was quick with his comeback. 'Wow, okay. Holy shit, they *are* serious.'

Max sported a chuffed smile as he looked back at Penny, pleased with himself for being able to make them understand each other. Once again, he had felt disheartened in the process of searching today, but his mood had changed drastically since seeing Penny and being in the comfort of her home.

'I need a cig,' Will admitted, looking rather glum as he also remembered having smoked the remainder of his packet before his brush with death.

'You've run out,' Max said.

'I know, I know. Penny, are there any shops open this late?'

She did not even consider the thought. 'At eleven at night? Not around here,' she responded as if the question was not necessary, given they were in the middle of nowhere. 'Not to worry, there should be some old ones in a drawer somewhere.' And with that, the pair watched with surprise as she hopped up with a glancing smile and disappeared down the hallway to the front door. They heard the opening of a chest of drawers and a ferocious rustling that was loud enough to scare the birds away in the trees. She returned, her hair in a fluster. 'Here you go,' and handed the box to Will.

'Thanks,' Will graciously accepted the gift. 'Erm, lighter?'

'Right,' and off she turned and moved around the kitchen drawers this time. She spoke as she searched. 'I've quit for years; I threw the lighter and my box away and haven't thought about them since. It was only when you mentioned them that I thought maybe there would be some in the house somewhere.' At that moment she stood back up again and walked back over to them, handing Will the newly found lighter.

'Thanks, Pen,' Will said, the cigarette already poised at the end of his lips.

Max chimed in. 'All you had to do to quit was chuck the lighter and cigarettes away?'

'Yeah,' Penny shrugged, 'nothing else needed.'

Max smiled at her. He should not have been surprised. Penny was strong, that much was obvious. A nicotine addiction seemed like the least of her worries.

'You want one?' Will asked Max.

He thought for a moment. 'Yeah, why not,' and accepted one from the box.

'You know what?' Penny addressed them both. 'I think I may as well have one, too.'

'You sure?' Will asked.

'Yeah. It's not every day you find out a made-up story that an entire family has been brainwashed with and you assumed was a silly conspiracy theory, is, in fact, true and you own land that is home to one of the country's greatest mysteries. And that land is infested with land pirates.'

Max and Will shrugged. 'Seems like as good a reason as any,' Will said and handed her the box.

'And you saved the lives of two idiot tourists who don't know when to go home after their first brush with death,' she smiled at them.

'Okay okay, you can stop there. That's enough out of you,' Max cheekily said. 'Lead the way please.'

'I'm just gonna get one more thing before we go outside,' Penny hurried off, returning to the kitchen, retrieving a canister from under the sink, and meeting back up with the pair of them at the back door. She shook the canister, the liquid making noises from within. 'I get bugs outside. If we're out this late in the summer, you'll thank me for bringing it.'

They followed Penny as they stepped outside to her porch, each taking up a chair facing off into the forest. Max looked up above the trees, watching the sky. There was little light pollution so the stars glowed with a fiery resistance, the clouds brushing their way through the night sky. It was not dark; the moon was full and shone a mystic light across the trimmed grass that sat in front of them. The summer heat had persisted until the evening, leaving the temperature high well after the sun had disappeared. It seemed like a perfect spot.

44

They sat and puffed away at their cigarettes, the silent contemplation enough discussion for everyone at that moment. Max and Will both knew each other well enough to accept that there should be moments of quiet every now and then and accepted these situations gratefully. Max particularly enjoyed Penny's realisation and she too had opted for silence, as there were no words necessary that needed to fill the particular moment.

The only disturbances in the batches of silence were Penny leaning in her chair every minute or so, canister wielding in one hand, spraying the rodents on the porch. 'Good to keep the pests away,' she said with a grin.

'Shame you can't use that on the human pests you've got,' Max retorted. Each of them chuffed at the joke, focusing more on the smoking.

It was about five minutes later when Will was in the midst of conjuring up an itinerary for them both tomorrow – a plan which consisted of a plentiful breakfast before anything else – when he decided to confide in his colleague for confirmation. 'What's our plans for tomorrow?'

Max sat and thought through the question for a while. He was not in a rush to answer and afforded himself as much time as possible to construct an image of his plans. The most important part seemed obvious to him, so he led with that. The rest of the day will fill in accordingly, he thought.

'Well, we gotta go look for those carvings, all of them. Then we know where it's gonna be. Keep it simple.'

Will nodded his head in agreement. Penny, however, shook her head in disbelief, laughing as she did so. 'You're not seriously going back to look for them again, are you? Not when you've just almost died? Twice?'

'We're so close,' Will said.

'Yeah, and I believe no one has had both the knowledge of the carvings and the spot where they are,' Max added smugly as he raised his phone, showing the image of his blue location dot on the map he took a screenshot of earlier that day.

'Both good points,' Penny conceded. She thought for a moment, looking at both of them in turn, like a designer inspecting their models before sending them out on the catwalk. 'Let me see that,' she gestured towards Max's phone.

He handed it over gladly and stared at her face, illuminated in the darkness by the phone screen, as she studied the picture, pinching to zoom out.

'Okay,' she finally said.

'Okay, what?' Max asked, confused.

'I'll come with you.'

'You'll what?' It was now Will's turn to be confused.

'I know exactly where that is. I know the paths to take to get there from here. And you need protection.' She smiled as she finished.

'So, let me get this straight,' Max began. 'You've gone from being so against this for years, before we even got here, to now wanting to go out tomorrow and look for it?' He was dumbfounded, even as he wrapped it all up and put a bow on it for everyone.

The smile never left Penny's face. 'Yep, exactly that.'

Her face was smug, Max could see. Her gesture seemed genuine, and they both looked at each other, Max with a much more serious face than hers. It did not take long to change, however. He felt the emotions take over, her feelings were so infectious, and he could not help but reciprocate the smile, which soon turned into a burst of laughter.

He turned to Will and shrugged. 'It would be nice to have someone who can handle themselves.'

'And knows the forest like the back of their hand,' he acceptingly said.

Her charm had won them both over. She sat back into her chair and looked admirably at the stars. What the pair of them had failed to notice, was that they had inflicted a similar impact on her, and she smiled gratefully at the thought of stumbling across the both of them yesterday, and how much it had changed everything in such a short period of time.

They were bumbling idiots, she had no doubt about that, but she liked their genuine friendliness and she felt somewhat responsible for them if they were hell-bent on disappearing into the woods again.

'What do you reckon then, early start tomorrow?' Max asked the group.

'Sounds good,' Penny replied. 'Get ahead of the others while we can.'

Will let out a reluctant grunt. He had a feeling a hearty breakfast was not on the top of the others' priority list.

'We should get going, get as much sleep as we can.' Max stated.

'Don't be stupid,' Penny said brazenly. 'You can stay here, there's plenty of room.'

Will and Max looked at each other, having a conversation without speaking. They seemed to come to an agreement relatively quickly, Max prioritising time spent with Penny, and Will maximising his sleep opportunity.

'As long as we wouldn't be imposing,' Max wanted to be certain of the gracious hosting. Penny was not as welcoming yesterday. Twenty-four hours can make such a difference.

‘Of course not. At least here I can keep an eye on you,’ her eyes glistened in the moonlight. ‘And this way I can make sure you won’t be late and we can set off as early as possible.’

‘Thank you,’ Max said.

‘Yeah, thanks Pen,’ Will added his own appreciation.

‘There’s three bedrooms upstairs –’ Penny started but was soon interrupted.

‘No need,’ Max said, holding out his palms. ‘We can take the sofas. We don’t want to intrude too much. We know when we’ve outstayed our welcome.’ Will nodded to concur.

‘Yeah, it was yesterday,’ Penny laughed.

‘Shut up,’ Max snapped back in jest.

They made their way inside, Penny dropped the bug-repellent canister on the kitchen counter by the back door, disappearing upstairs briefly before returning with a couple of blankets for the pair of them. ‘Help yourself to anything you need.’

Max took the blanket gratefully, placing his hand on top of hers as he did so with careful poise. They suddenly both realised how close they stood to each other, and her face looked up from his hand to lock eyes with him. ‘Thank you for this,’ he said with a deep, gracious tone she had not particularly taken notice of before that moment. She took a second to study his face. ‘No bother at all. I have Englishmen that come for tea all the time.’ They both laughed and separated, but not after stealing one more glance as they stepped in opposite directions.

‘Well, goodnight,’ she shouted from the hallway.

‘Goodnight,’ they both joined in response. Will had already flung himself onto the same sofa he had slept on previously, pulling the blanket up to his chin. ‘Night mate,’ he said in a quieter tone to Max, who was only next to him.

Max was standing, still holding his blanket, still watching Penny. He watched as she walked backwards, she silently mouthed 'goodnight' to him, and they smiled at each other from across the hallway. She continued going backwards as their gaze held for a moment longer, Max not wanting to look away. As she reached the photographs on the side of the stairs, she spun around and walked the rest of the hallway, before jumping up the stairs, a bounce of joy in her steps. As her footsteps dissipated, only then did Max move and begin to get himself comfortable on the sofa, his smile as wide as the Cheshire cat across his face.

'Night mate,' he replied to Will, but he was already snoring.

45

Penny woke earliest and made her way downstairs to put on some coffee whilst the pair of them slept; Max stiff as a board and Will writhing around on the sofa like a cat playing in the grass. She sipped the freshly brewed coffee and wandered around the house in an oversized t-shirt, using dainty footsteps, attempting to avoid creaking the floorboards.

Max's eyes opened after his nose had smelled the coffee, rising to fetch himself a cup. Penny came back into the kitchen and they exchanged a 'good morning' with a smile. They stood in silence as they drank, looking out of the kitchen window into the forest that lay beyond them.

'You think we can actually find it?' Max asked, as he refilled the kettle up and flicked it on.

'I don't know,' Penny replied honestly. She held the cup close to her chest, her arms tucked, using both hands to warm them up. It was not a warm morning, but the sun was just appearing over the tree line, flashes of yellow attempting to sear through the window.

'Teabags?' Max asked once the kettle had finished.

Penny retrieved one from the cupboard. 'You need tea and coffee?' She asked inquisitively.

'Nah, this isn't for me,' Max said and fetched the milk from the fridge. 'I've known Will long enough to know he's not getting up for another couple of hours unless he's got a cuppa next to him.' They shared a laugh as Max busied himself around the kitchen, creating a tea-making station in preparation for the kettle to finish warming up.

Once it had boiled, he made a cup with efficiency and poise, moving across to the living room with the newly made brew, and placing the mug down on the coffee table next to Will. He shook him and pointed to the cup, and Will gratefully rose to a sit and nodded his head in appreciation as he took a sip.

Max had returned to stand next to Penny once more in the kitchen. 'Quick breakfast and go?' he said.

'Yeah, good idea. There's cereal in the cupboard. I'll get changed,' she said, disappearing upstairs with her coffee.

Max was grateful for a period of aloneness. Will was awake but he was not going to be interested in speaking to anyone this early in the morning. He made himself a bowl of cereal and leaned against the kitchen island, removing his notebook from his back pocket whilst he waited for the milk to soak into the cereal.

He opened the book and took the pencil from within, tapping it quietly on the side as he thought. He grabbed his mug and gulped down his coffee, only then beginning to scribble away on the empty pages. Regularly switching between his three tasks of drinking, eating and writing, he became fairly content with his progress after several minutes, grateful his mind was working.

The leather cover of the book had begun to show signs of discolouring, certain edges turning slightly paler than the original dark brown it had started. Pages were being filled a lot quicker since the commencement of their trip, Max was happy to pass the staples situated in the middle and took only a millisecond to appreciate his achievement before continuing. He was not sure how much longer their trip was going to last, but he knew one thing for certain, he was ready to get down to business and type up his story.

46

The three of them managed to get ready and leave the house fairly efficiently, save for a few words of encouragement from Max to Will, who was still yawning when they left through the back door. Penny had pointed toward a collection of gardening equipment sitting on the porch. Max, realising her thoughts, fetched three spades and handed one to Will, opting to carry Penny's for her. One had a strap, which he placed diagonally over his shoulder.

Max had handed his phone to Penny, who took one look at the picture of the location he and Will had found themselves in the previous day, and set off in that direction. She had chosen to take the shotgun with her, reassuring the guys it was a necessary precaution, before reminding them of the entanglements they kept experiencing. They shared a look of approval and followed her footsteps closely.

The sun had now risen completely over the highest trees, beaming across the lawn that separated the forest and the house. The neat grass was wet and full of morning dew, adding swooshing sound effects as they walked, the sun helping to warm them up before they submerged into the woods and escaped the light.

They walked for a while, Max immediately began to consider how much longer the walk could have possibly been without Penny knowing the exact route and footpaths they required to get there as quickly as possible. She understood they needed to operate quite hastily as to get there – in addition to having enough time to investigate – before anybody else could.

'This is where the mark was on the map.' Penny stopped abruptly. The shotgun was on a strap, and she had thrown it across her back. Throughout their walk, Max followed a few steps behind her religiously, her messy ponytail bouncing from left to right as she stepped and he watched with care at the gun bouncing off of her back.

'Will,' Max turned round to him. 'Any ideas?' Will began walking around the vicinity, carefully examining everything and trying to recollect what they had seen previously. After a few moments, he recalled they arrived from the opposite direction and spotted something memorable off the path. He advanced slowly, subconsciously, however, as he was aware that particular area of the woods was perfectly safe. Stepping through the bushes, his feet crunched on twigs and leaves, moving closer to the trunk that Max could also cast his mind back to remembering. He and Penny watched from the path as Will sauntered his way through the trees, settling on the one Max's eyes diverted to.

Will made the sensible choice not to shout, as he now found himself at least twenty feet off the footpath. It was rather wise not to rouse any suspicion of their whereabouts, regardless of how early it may have been, for fear of not wanting to draw the attention of the scarred man and his entourage.

Penny and Max made their way over to join Will, and the three of them stood in front of the tree trunk. The boys stood in silence as Penny looked and observed with curiosity at the marking against the wood. It was not anything of specific quality, yet the importance could not be understated. It was rather obvious the carving was made at speed with no concern for the roundness of the edges or the perfect circumference of the circle. It was designed for its purpose: to allow identification for those who knew what it was they were searching for, and blend effortlessly into the forest and the surrounding trees for anyone not aware of its importance.

Over the years, the moss gathering around the open wood, along with the bark attempting to reform around the opening, only added to the mystique and general blandness, yet her eyes could not cease staring in wonderment. After all this time, all these years, she could not quite comprehend the reality of the story, and how wrong she was to doubt the validity of it.

Her throat welled up once more, yet a smile appeared across her face. She thought back to the nights spent with her husband's family, the arguments and fights that would erupt surrounding the story. She found it so amusing how all generations, despite their differences, would come together and be utterly captivated by their family's history, and she was annoyed for having dismissed it for all those years.

Max, seeing Penny becoming overwhelmed, placed a comforting hand on her shoulder. 'You said there were four?'

'Yes,' she said softly, before realising the importance of the discovery and what it meant. 'Yes!' She said it louder this time, the excitement in her voice attempting to betray them and reveal their position. 'Yes.' The third time was in the middle, yet it still contained a giddiness that soon swept through all of them.

'Are we right to assume they'll be in a square?' Will asked.

'I can't remember exactly what they said the shape was. We shall walk this way, and loop around if we don't see anything after one hundred feet or so.'

They did not need that long.

47

The three of them had only walked ten feet when Max noticed something peculiar about the tree that stood in front of him. He surveyed the trunk at his eye-line, noting that if these marks were made in haste, Dillinger surely would not have bothered to vary the height of his markings.

He found the carving, hidden by a branch dangling in front of it, the leaves completely camouflaging as they fell over it. This would not have been found if one was not looking for something. Max turned to the others and slapped Will excitedly on the arm, pointing as he moved the branch to reveal his findings.

'Let's go left,' Penny said and they changed course. And, just as they had anticipated, ten feet or so further along, there was a tree playing host to a carving performed vigorously quickly, some parts scoring so far into the pith that moss was now protruding and escaping from these areas.

Max raced ahead of the others to what they expected to be the last marking. Instead, upon walking the ten feet, he found himself standing on the footpath. Two trees of which around the path had been resorted to stumps, on either side of the path, yet their roots joined each other in creating inconvenient steps to conquer along the track. Penny and Will had caught up, and all three stood in bewilderment, realising just how close the money had been to people walking beside it every day, not realising the distance they were away from something people had been searching for close to a century.

Penny clicked into action first. 'We can still find it; we don't necessarily need the fourth corner. Both of you, go to one of the engraved trees. Max, you go there, Will you go to that one.' She pointed as she spoke, directing orders, like a coach positioning their players for a football play. 'We'll each walk in from each tree, and if we walk at the same time, we should get to the middle.'

The two obliged and they soon found themselves standing next to the three trees with the remaining carvings. They all stood on the inside of the trees but still found it difficult to see one another as their vision was impaired by the abundance of trees and greenery that remained in the centre of the imaginary square.

Peering from a tree obscuring her view, Penny locked eyes with Max, before repeating the same process the opposite way for Will. They slowly began advancing forwards, taking slow and precarious steps to ensure not one of them moved too quickly and the measuring would be incorrect. More than once they all found themselves altering their walking path to avoid a tree or shrubbery, before rectifying the alteration and staying on course. After a minute of slowly plodding, they saw each other again as their steps finished in the centre of the imaginary square, all hoping their measurements were relatively accurate, yet all understanding the lack of proficiency in what they had just performed.

Alas, the doubt was not enough to wane their spirits. They all moved back a few steps and an all-encompassing feeling of excitement, dread, achievement, fear and anticipation swept over all of them. The realisation that they could be stood directly on top of a particular piece of history that was so sought after for so long, became hardly worth considering. They needed to see if they were right.

Max handed a spade to Penny and the three of them all stood, holding their spades downwards towards the earth. They glanced at each other, realising that not enough words of any description would satisfy their appetite at that moment. Actions were stronger than words. The pen may be mightier than the sword, but they had spades. And they were about to uncover history. They smiled and all rammed their spades into the dirt in unison, cutting through the ground. They pushed their feet down forced them deeper, and began.

48

The digging was frantic. It was not every day they had the chance to stumble upon something that had been lost for so long. As it was haphazard, it was not necessarily constructive, as short bursts of spade caught the dirt and it was promptly thrown backwards, akin to children digging in the sand. Fortune was on their side, as it remained clear that through their inference Dillinger would not have been able to dig particularly deep himself during his haste; meaning they would not have to be digging for a significant stretch of time.

After five minutes, the trio had managed to unearth around three feet, with no indication the soil underneath contained anything further than a continuation of the above. The speed at which they operated, mixed with the heat of the forest rising as the morning aged, left them all glistening with sweat, mud caking over skin and clothes.

***

It was only after they began searching the vicinity of the original hole they constructed, did any luck arrive at their feet. Their backs turned to each other, scraping seemingly hopelessly at the earth beside them, Will's spade suddenly caught itself on something immovable. Being closest to a tree, his optimism was not high, expecting a veiny root to block his advances and force him to consider an alternative route.

He moved his spade with care, scraping around the top of the root, not trying to damage it further.

It was only after he had managed to remove more dirt from around the object that the realisation struck upon him that he had misidentified the object. With this new information, he dropped to his knees, throwing his spade out of the hole they stood in, and began rummaging around the object with his hands. The mud was pushing itself under his fingernails, his fingers grimy with moist, wet earth. Yet he did not care. Like a dog digging to bury their stick, Will began furiously clawing, forming spoons with his hands and cupping the dirt away. The outline of a wooden object stared back at him, his eyes perceiving a shining glow escaping from the brown dirt around it.

As soon as they heard the spade drop outside the hole, Penny and Max both turned as quickly as their bodies could take them, desperate for any indication of progress greater than their own. Will scurrying on his hands and knees was enough optimism for them to share an embrace, for a brief second, before coming to their friend's aid.

'Holy shit!' Penny screamed.

Three of them scraped away and began to find the outline of the object, smoothing the earth around the top surface. It was rectangular, dark wooded and around one metre long. Upon removing the layer of dirt on top of it, they stood up and stared, wishing to preserve the moment and capture the exhilaration they felt between them.

'I found it, so that means I get to keep it,' Will said with a laugh whilst catching his breath back.

'I can't believe it.' Max said. 'I can't believe we actually found it.'

Max, who had attempted to remain the most optimistic, was still in disbelief himself that the feat seemed to have been achieved.

The top of the wood had two metal strips running across, splitting the wood into three pieces. But it was not the exterior of the object they were interested in.

'Quick,' Penny instructed. 'Will, you work on that edge closest to the tree, Max and I will work the other three sides and then come and help you. That looks like the most dense area, so that may be difficult to dig.'

'Not to mention the roots,' Will muttered.

'Let's hope they haven't grown around the chest, that will make things ten times worse.' Max bluntly remarked.

'Come on, let's stay positive. We've come this far,' Penny urged them. They scurried away at the ground to try and pry away the mystery.

49

Will clawed, Penny scraped and Max raked the dirt around the box, defining the edges and sides as they went. Penny and Max made quick work of three sides and promptly joined Will in tackling the condensed earth surrounding the tree trunk and its spider-like roots. It did not take long for progress to be reached. They worked furiously at an almighty speed, the tiredness in their shoulders doing little to deter them. The piercing pain of cramps shot up each of their arms, a heat as if they had held their hands too close to a raging fire. Max grimaced and Will gritted his teeth as they pushed on further.

Penny jumped out of the pit and retrieved a spade - having all thrown their spades in jubilation there was no telling whose it was originally and she did not care - before walking to face the opposite direction of Will and Max to dig from the other way. She was careful not to catch any English fingers in the process, her adrenaline ensuring safety and speed met in perfect unity.

Will could see part of the last side showing from around the dirt and began pulling from his side to try and force the box to remove its connection with the soil. With grunts of encouragement and shouts through the pain, Will finally shot backwards, falling with his back on the side of the pit. His momentum had thrown him, the soil on the last side connecting the box to the earth had given way, and Will now held the object as his coccyx burned with fury from the impact.

'We did it!' Max screamed, standing up, and jumping out of the pit to share another warm embrace with Penny, the two of them decided to leave Will abandoned in the hole.

'Thank you,' Penny said from over Max's shoulder as they hugged.

He pulled away and held his hands on her arms. 'For what?' he said with a smile.

She tilted her head and smiled back. 'For getting me up off my ass and forcing me to get on with it.' There was a glisten in her eyes, but Max remained confused, despite the elation he clearly shared with her in the moment.

'Get on with what?' He asked.

She threw up her hands. 'Does it matter?'

The smile remained between them. 'No,' he said. 'No, it doesn't.'

'Erm, a little help?' A cry was heard and their heads turned to see Will, in the bottom of the hole they had just created, with a large wooden box on his lap. 'I'm knackered, I couldn't move the box even if I tried.' He laughed and threw his head and hands on the top, imitating he was to sleep.

The three of them shared a laugh, Penny and Max jumped down and helped the box off of Will, moving it up and to the side of the tree. Doing this made them realise how tired they had also become, and they flopped down either side of Will in exasperation. The three of them sat, dirt-covered and beaten, sharing a silence, aside from their heavy exhaling and catching of their breath.

50

There were conflicting emotions shared amongst them as they sat in contemplation. The feelings of satisfaction and exuberance waved across, flowing through their bodies like live electrical currents. Tiredness, exasperation and dread began slowly creeping in; the thoughts racing from one brain to the next, passing between as if they had exchanged words and explained to one another what they were thinking.

Max was in doubt. He doubted the success. The journey had been incredibly long, yet surprisingly short. Their lives had been threatened on numerous occasions, it almost felt unnatural to him that they had yet to be placed in a death-defying situation that morning, despite it only being nine o'clock.

He attempted to push away his feelings, allowing the overwhelming reassurance surrounded by his friends to wash it away like paint in the rain. The benevolence of Will and the resolve of Penny united to create a force field of an impenetrable bubble around the three. Max sighed in relief, the doubt escaping with his breath and he closed his eyes in satisfaction.

They spent a little longer tied together, all enjoying the rest after an intense few days that neither could have possibly imagined occurring, Penny in particular. Yet, they had to know what was underneath the lid of the tremendous wooden crate they had salvaged from the dirt. She had never been bothered by the story in previous years, but the idea of being so close played on her mind, she could not take it any further. 'Let's open it,' standing up and exiting the hole in the ground.

The two followed, and they all fell to their knees around the crate. 'It's not small, is it? How far are we away from the lodge, Pen?' Will asked.

'Erm,' Penny thought for a second, 'about twenty minutes.'

'Jesus,' Will exclaimed. 'Wonder how he managed to carry it this far.'

'At least it has a handle,' Penny sympathised, pointing to the top of the container having a small handle from which to carry it.

During this, Max's eyes never left the storage container. The more he studied the object, the more he agreed with Will. The container was larger than a briefcase, yet just smaller than a suitcase. Being made of wood, it became rather heavy when they lifted it between Penny and himself moments ago. For Dillinger to have dragged it for so long was impressive, yet, Max conceded the obvious adrenaline of running for his life may have aided his strength.

The container's lid had been held down by two separate buckles; Max untangled them as he remained in silent thought. The metal was rusted and jammed full with dirt in all the places it could cram itself into, so Max had to force it open, the lid jumping excitedly when the tension released. He readied his hands and held them slightly hovering around the edge of the lid. His head looked up and he shared a look with Penny and Will simultaneously; both had finished speaking and left the air to fill with anticipation.

They nodded at each other, and Max let out a long breath. With a fluid motion, he pushed the lid upwards and flung it open, exposing the inside to eyes for the first time in almost a hundred years. All three of their heads poked over the container.

Inside the container, stacked ever so neatly, stood together in five piles rising towards the lid, were American fifty-dollar bills. All of them gazed in wonderment, failing to truly believe that what they had set out to achieve and find was in fact there, and they could see it with their own eyes. There had always been a slight inkling that it could not possibly be there, not after all those years, not to mention the likelihood they all shared that it could have been a story and nothing more. Adulation was felt, as if finding something from a fairy tale a child had been read by a relative years before; never truly believing in its reality, the comfortable nature of it remaining only words and allowing imagination to perform the rest.

Some of the notes nearer to the edge looked more weathered than the rest. They had clearly been chosen to act as a barrier between the elements and every other bill. Peering down the sides of the container, the outside edge of the notes was shrivelled and tatty in places, indicating delicate hands were to be a requirement to proceed further. Max, leaning in and removing a couple of the notes on the top of the piles with caution, soon noticed the bills underneath seemed to be in a rather impressive condition, despite their age and living conditions.

Max leaned back on his legs while remaining in a knelt position, handing the notes he had collected to Will and Penny for their own closer inspection. He was flabbergasted and beyond words of any description. He had set out on the journey with the purest intention of finding material to inspire him to create a new story. A story he would be interested in and enjoy writing about. The idea of finding the money he had always considered a secondary part of why they were there, it just seemed so easy to fall into the glorious beauty of attempting to find something that had been gone for so long.

He reached around to the back pocket of his jeans and felt for his notebook. He wanted to remind himself that despite the achievement they had made, the original goal he created for himself endured: he would write something he was proud of, without caring what other people thought of it, and he was going to make himself fall in love with his writing again. He closed his eyes, attempting to let everything sink in and comprehend all the emotions he was feeling.

Will replaced the notes back into the box after he and Penny had both had a chance to look at them in more detail. He smiled as he caught a glimpse of Max's body language and could not have felt happier for him. Having known his friend for a good number of years, he knew exactly what was going through his mind, and he did not want to interrupt him whilst he had the moment to himself.

'What now?' Will finally asked the both of them after a while.

'I have no idea,' Max admitted.

'Well,' Penny said, standing up. 'We need to get this moved. We've spent enough time in this specific spot. I'm getting a little concerned we may have some uninvited guests join us soon if we're not careful.'

'Good idea,' Max replied and stood up with Will.

'I noticed there were two handles, one on each side,' Will noted. He picked one up and half the container stood. 'Max, grab the other one.'

'You don't fancy carrying it, Penny?' Max asked sarcastically. He had begun to lift the other side as he spoke.

Penny raised the gun she now held in her hand. 'I'll cover you fools instead. You guys probably couldn't shoot a *dead* pigeon from three feet away.'

Max and Will looked at each other and shared a nod of agreement. They all had the jobs they were equipped to perform.

'Let's get this home. I'll lead the way.' Penny said.

The three of them set off once more, trudging themselves through the forest. This time, however, they were moving at a much slower pace, having acquired some additional luggage for their return journey. A local legend that had romanced an entire nation had finally found its ending, and, other than two tourists and a local, they all were none the wiser.

51

McKenna had slept, the whisky in his system providing the necessary lullaby. He awoke early, feeling no effect of the alcohol, a regular occurrence which allowed him to justify the intake. He required no alarm, not even a bed, falling to his slumber in the armchair he threw back the whiskies from. Years of fieldwork had made him not only a light sleeper but able to function with little to no sleep at all; alert and at full attention from sunrise.

The remaining group climbed into the inflatable boat that docked itself next to the accommodation ship, its small stature bouncing on the waves looking ridiculous next to the larger, unphased by the movement of the water.

McKenna climbed in last, and, attempting his best impression of Washington crossing the Delaware, ostentatiously stood on the bow as the boat advanced in the morning sun. The water sprayed all around, splashing onto the boat's occupants, ensuring they would be awake for the voyage.

They moored into the pier near the forest, slowing as they approached. Muttering began to hover around the group of sightings along the bank as they neared the shoreline. Figures and dark objects they did not recognise or had any recollection of seeing before. Upon closer inspection, as the boat's rope was tied to the wooden structure, they were all able to see the horrifying image they were looking at come into focus.

They were bodies.

Two lifeless bodies lay strewn around the river bank, contorted in a plethora of ways, helpless with their faces in the dirt. The group hurried over, McKenna pacing before the boat had the chance to park, his briskness more in annoyance at the idiocy he was witnessing as opposed to any concern for welfare. He reached the first body, throwing the body over onto its back. It was Decker. Rapidly, he felt a pulse on their neck. It was slow, but it was there. He noted another body was further along, nearer the tree line where the forest began.

'Check the other bodies.' He barked orders as the group began hurriedly panicking towards the remaining people on the ground.

'I've got a pulse!' One shouted nearer to the forest.

'Yeah, me too!' Another cried.

McKenna stood with authority, scanning the forest as his back was to the water. 'We need to find the others,' he pointed as he spoke. 'Three of you find them and get them all together, the other three come with me. When you have them recuperating on the boat, come back at once.' He started charging into the forest. 'Let's find this thing and get the fuck outta here.'

The group split instantly, some moving bodies around whilst others followed McKenna's footsteps as they ascended into the thicket of trees. One grabbed the assault rifle on his back and swung it forward, his finger hovering over the trigger as the sunlight drained all around them, swallowed up by the trees and becoming an abyss of darkness.

McKenna delegated the lead to a member of the entourage, frantically remaining inches behind them as they travelled swiftly through the forest. In a matter of minutes, they came to an opening littered with equipment they had been using to little success. He shook his head furiously, examining a specific detector, holding it in his hand and staring curiously before dispatching it back on the ground with a throw. The group loaded up the essentials before nodding towards McKenna, indicating their intent to keep moving. His head spun to the designated leader, who turned and disappeared into the forest once more.

Upon reaching the position they had last searched, the investigation resumed, meticulously searching under the watchful glare of the image they see in their nightmares. McKenna paced around the area, his hands behind his back patiently poised and keen to see just how thorough the job had been performed to this point.

As he wandered, he veered off slightly, exploring the forest at a slow pace like a grandparent would leisurely explore a museum. He absorbed his surroundings, turning his head regularly and with purpose, no movement insignificant or wasteful.

'Sir!' a cry came out from behind him. He turned to face the group. 'We haven't done that part yet!' The voice continued.

McKenna stood still for a moment, contemplating his options. 'Well let's see if I can find it before you buffoons!' He replied in a gravelly shout, before twisting around and heading into the forest.

He had no intention of looking with any particular purpose, aimlessly strolling to take in what was around him. Attempting to comprehend the foolish way they had all attempted to search for the asset, his mind racked, moving incredibly quickly in comparison to his steps.

Not only had they failed to achieve the goal within the strict time period, he now had to deal with the casualties that lay across the forest. *Just how had they been so stupid?* McKenna was becoming increasingly frustrated by the lack of intelligence that surrounded him. There was also a part of him that, the more he thought, began to express concern. *What on earth would have been able to incapacitate six armed and fully trained officers?*

He stopped walking, focusing his full attention on his thoughts, his brain working at full capacity. He knew he was able to rule out animal attack fairly confidently; he recognised that almost immediately after seeing the scene, with no bite or claw marks, it hardly seemed likely. The bodies had been spread out as if the attacker were outnumbered and was forced to take each officer out one at a time. Yet, all the officers were still alive. The attackers would have required considerable fight training and expert knowledge of human anatomy to ensure none were killed, the adrenaline usually causing strikes against an opponent to hit harder than anticipated, McKenna could testify to that. The level of poise, care and attention to detail fascinated him as he cast his mind back through the extensive case file.

He had an impeccable recollection of every file he was required to remember during an endeavour and he prided himself on that fact. McKenna tried to visualise the profile Cooper had procured of the local resident, her photograph acquired through an internet database. He remembered she was young but old enough to acquire the ability to learn and study with extensiveness the level of martial arts knowledge McKenna knew would be capable of achieving such a feat as taking out six officers. He pictured the eyes, the details of the face that he could remember - the organisation does an impeccable job of attaining persons of interest identification photographs with incredible ease. Trying to imagine the capabilities of somebody he had not encountered was difficult, but he remained confident in his judgement of character. He could not see it. He could not visualise the person he created in his mind being responsible for such atrocities he saw the aftermath of.

He walked further, self-assured in his assessment. He remained sure there would be no way of her ability to find the asset either. With the technology at the organisation's disposal, regardless of the imbeciles delegated to search for it, he was unperturbed, assuming the asset had been a creation of fiction rather than found by another party.

McKenna turned around a tree, holding the trunk in his right hand as he spun his body around it. Once he had completed his turn, he stopped dead on the balls of his feet. Flabbergasted, he remained incapable of moving any further, glad he had held onto the tree as he was certain his arm was the only thing that had kept him standing. His eyes bulged in furious frustration, his teeth appeared as he grimaced and grunted in annoying defiance. He stayed in denial, refusing to believe what he was witnessing, assuming his eyes were lying.

There, four feet from where he stood, was a hole of significant size in the ground. The inside of the hole contained fresh, wet soil, the mound of removed earth sat beside it, still moving on its hill and moving around in accordance to the wind.

He could not believe it. Someone had beaten them to the chase.

52

McKenna stormed furiously and returned to the group, all tediously searching for something that was not there. Their heads turned in unison to witness McKenna's face become redder by the second, his anger boiling to such an extent it appeared like steam was coming out of his ears.

'Does someone care to explain why there happens to be a ginormous, empty damn hole right over here?!' He seldom swore, so when it was used, it was for a good reason.

A shared feeling spread across everyone's faces, and a collective gulp was followed as they attempted to comprehend the accusation growled at them.

Robinson stood up from a crouched pose, correcting his wide-rimmed glasses which allowed for more hesitation before he spoke. 'Erm, a hole, sir?' He inquired with a sense of disbelief.

McKenna rubbed his hand over his face, preferring to not confront just how useless the people in front of him had been. 'You go over there, Robinson,' he pointed behind him, 'and you take a good look yourself. And if you can't see the crater taken out of the floor, you need to change your glasses!' The words filled with rage as he spoke, getting increasingly louder. Robinson skipped past his boss and scampered through the trees, followed by the rest of them.

There was a part of them that refused to believe in the possibility that what McKenna was shouting about was true, and, even once they had witnessed what was spoken, they still could not fathom what their eyes were telling them. Having scoured the surrounding area in such a methodical nature, they would have inevitably stumbled across this section of the forest.

They would have found it eventually. Yet, the fact that they had not, was bad enough. And even worse, it appeared as though someone may have gotten to it before them.

McKenna strolled back to walk around the hole and inspect it with more detail. He stood on the edge, looking down into the earth, shaking his head and cursing under his breath. The rest could only stare and come to terms with whatever happens next.

He closed his eyes and took a deep breath, tilted his head backwards to the canopy of leaves and exhaled, puffing out his cheeks. Repeating the process several times, he finally settled into his regular breathing of concentrated deliberateness before commencing his next steps. McKenna just required a few moments to gather composure and retain his constructiveness; he knew at this time shouting would get him nowhere. There would be plenty of time for that later.

'You and you', he barked with his finger-wagging, the pacing had already commenced. 'Get down there and see if you can find out how long that earth has been exposed. You have a look around the area. I want a meticulous search to see if you can see any fresh dirt surrounding the hole. You're looking for scrape marks, footsteps, anything. Now! Let's go! With any luck they may not be far away.'

The group hurried around and performed their delegated tasks diligently. They knew that McKenna was the best chance they had of removing the eggs off of their faces before they got back to headquarters. At this point they would willingly try anything; digging in the dirt hardly seemed an unjust punishment.

53

During their examinations, they had been joined by the three soldiers who had escorted the injured back to the large boat. They had been delegated the tasks of supporting the three others working overtime to appease McKenna's rage.

The team banded together, working thoroughly and quickly, placing utmost faith in each other as McKenna helped coordinate communication between those in the depths of the hole, and the others testing and searching for fresh dirt around the trees.

In no time at all the dirt was tested and their advanced technology allowed them to discover that the earth had been uprooted only a few hours prior, indicating the asset had been found that morning. McKenna nodded approvingly at the information he received and turned to find a conclusion as to where the asset had been taken.

He bent over a crouched Robinson, who was on his knees and taking samples of tracks to pair with a clear solution, which helped indicate its characteristics. 'Tell me some good news, Robinson.'

His head remained down concentrating on his task as he replied. 'Well, I have found some trace samples of various different soils, most of which are a combination of the numerous soils in this very forest.'

McKenna shook his head. 'English, Robinson. What does it mean?'

'It means that some of these tracks have lots of different parts of mud on them, meaning they have been tracking all around the area.'

'So they were looking around in the forest?'

'Precisely. There is one strange coincidence, however,' he rose to stand next to McKenna as he spoke.

'A coincidence?' McKenna probed.

'Yes. I have had results come back from a soil completely different to anything around here. English soil, in fact. I had to cross-reference it with some other samples I had from a previous endeavour. I don't know if you can remember Cumbria back in '09. Some years ago, mind, but I'm sure you can remember. We did a job over there and the soil is a one hundred per cent match. So it looks like some of these shoes have been across the pond. Very interesting the difference in the soil, if you didn't know. The key difference is in the pH levels –'

'Robinson,' McKenna had stopped listening after the first sentence, but Robinson had persevered regardless.

'Sorry, sir,' Robinson muttered and knelt once more.

McKenna contemplated the information and spoke aloud whilst he paced. 'So, we've got a couple of out-of-towners that have found it. Either that or someone has been vacationing in Cumbria, which seems less likely.' He stroked his chin, thinking some more. 'So, which direction is the trail is going?' He asked and continued pacing, patiently waiting for a response. After a few seconds, he heard nothing, so pressed further. 'Robinson!' He shouted.

A startled Robinson looked up, white as if he had seen a ghost. 'Sir?'

McKenna rolled his eyes for having to repeat himself. 'The direction of the soil, where does it go?' He asked in a soft tone, like addressing a child.

'Oh, yes, sir. The data is bringing back a generous spreading all around this area, yet it disperses everywhere except for that way,' he pointed with the pencil in his hand, 'where it carries on every several metres. We haven't checked any further as of yet, sir.'

McKenna remained pacing and did not acknowledge what his subordinate had told him, allowing the silence to aid his thoughts. After wandering in circles several times, he finally stopped dead in his tracks and lifted his head up. 'Get me a map. And a table,' was all he said, but Robinson listened and scurried away, returning almost immediately with a foldable table and an A3 size map of the forest.

'Your pencil please, Robinson.' McKenna asked uncharacteristically politely. Robinson removed the pencil from behind his ear and conceded possession.

McKenna hovered the pencil over the map, tracing the area and finding their location. 'We are here,' he said, talking more to himself than to Robinson, as he circled an area. 'And the trail leads…' he began drawing a line, '…that way.' He stopped his stationery, preferring to hover the pencil over the paper rather than draw the estimated trajectory of the track any further.

'So that means they would have to go this way…' his hand all of a sudden stopped. Robinson, who had been patiently following the pencil as though he was hypnotised, turned his face to look at McKenna, who circled a clearing that appeared on the map.

'Sir…' Robinson inquired slowly. 'You don't think…'

'Oh I think so,' came the interrupted reply from McKenna. 'Think about it. If they were returning to the road, the quickest way is that way.' He began pointing with the pencil towards the map. 'Even if they needed to go in that direction, they would take an alternative route. The only reason their route would ever be going that way would be if they were going back to that house.'

'But sir, what if they had simply become lost? They may have begun walking this way by mistake, and corrected their course?' Robinson attempted to talk sense into him.

McKenna raised the pencil and began tapping it against his lips, contemplating their next move. Robinson could be right. He did not like admitting it, as he was often a blithering idiot, but there was sound logic behind his theory.

He shuffled on his feet to change his standing position. If he was anything, it was thorough. The house might not be relevant at all, perhaps it was somebody else who stumbled across it and it was a major coincidence they began heading in that direction.

Standing still started to irritate him. He commenced pacing once more, strategising the next steps. Logic dictated his thoughts and constructed ideas, like a snooker player he began thinking two, three, four steps ahead, considering every possibility. He knew the most effective way to proceed.

He turned to face Robinson. 'You may be right, but I won't leave anything to chance. Get the team and find out where this trail will continue towards. Once you've done that, we'll follow it.'

'Okay, yes sir,' came the regimented response.

Robinson hurried, folding the table and turning towards the team to inform them of the update. McKenna pondered on his decision, wondering if he had made the right one. Contingency plans circulated his mind and the pacing resumed. He needed a cup of coffee, but, more importantly, he needed to find his money.

54

The satisfaction of finally getting the container back into Penny's living room was immense. Will and Max had to carry it whilst navigating tree trunks, uneven paths, low branches and, as Max had previously discovered when carrying Will, the worst part had been the porch steps up to the house.

The late morning had exasperated any remnants of white clouds in the sky, opening to allow for bright sunlight to beam down across the open grass when they had reached it. Opening the back door, the pair of them dropped the box onto the floor in the corner and flung themselves with a lack of safety at the sofas, which looked heavenly comfortable at that point.

'I've never heard two people moan and complain so much in my life, and I've been around toddlers,' Penny remarked over the groans of discontent coming from the seats as she closed the back door with caution. She pulled the curtain over its window and only then did she allow her brain to relax, walking down the hallway to the cupboard under the stairs to return the gun to its home.

Upon returning to the room, she grabbed three bottles of water from the fridge and placed two on the coffee table, gulping down appreciative swallows before leaning back in her armchair. A few minutes later, Max and Will sat up and repeated the process, the crunching of the plastic resonating as they sucked the water and air out from the bottle desperately.

'I thought you might have brought out the shampers,' Will said to Penny after finishing his bottle, chucking the deformed plastic on the table.

She looked confused. 'Shampers?'

'Champagne,' Max corrected his friend as he allowed the air to come back into his bottle and set it aside, leaving some liquid remaining.

'Oh,' Penny was slightly irritated she did not pick up the slang. 'It's 10 AM, Will.'

'That means we can celebrate all day!' Will threw his arms up in jubilation.

Max contemplated. 'We kinda need to figure out exactly what we're going to do with it before any celebrations start.'

'I agree', Penny said.

'Boring,' said Will. 'Let me know when you've decided to crack open the bottles.' And with that, he slumped back onto the sofa and rested his eyes.

Max turned to Penny. 'What do you think is the best course of action?'

'I'm not sure,' she leaned her chin on her hand and contemplated.

They all sat in silence, Penny and Max both individually reflecting on just what to do with what they found, Will prioritising his recovery with a mid-morning nap. Neither had anticipated getting this far, so the thought had never appeared as to what to do once it had been acquired.

'It has to go to a museum,' Max reasoned.

'Well, we can't do anything else with it,' Penny shrugged.

'That's true.'

'Can't exactly go to the bank. I think they might ask questions,' Penny smiled.

Max laughed. 'You're right. What would you do with $200,000 anyway?'

'I'm not quite sure,' Penny admitted. 'How about you?'

'Oh you know, the usual stuff. A big boat, booze, and use the rest to convince Oasis to get back together,' Max jibed sarcastically, receiving a laugh from Penny.

'Let's hope they give you tickets as well.'

'Surely that's implied. I'd want backstage. And the after party,' Max said, grabbing his water.

Penny began walking to the kitchen, turning her head to reply as she moved. 'Well, seeing as I helped, I want tickets too.'

Max got up and followed her, leaning against the counter. 'Don't worry, you'll be coming with me,' he smiled.

She stood up straight, resulting in them being at eye level. 'Even if they only gave you two tickets? You wouldn't take Will?'

Max looked over at his friend on the sofa, very much looking like a dead body. 'Hmmm,' he considered, 'maybe you're right. He did help too, after all.' His eyes took him back to Penny.

She moved in closer to him as he stayed against the counter, the few steps she made were deliberate and slow. She swayed, and Max could not help but stare as he took it all in. The ponytail was as adorably messy as the day before, her flannel shirt remained unkempt and unwashed. Yet, he did not care, she smelt of a sweet summer breeze, like driving country roads at sunset with the windows down.

'Although, he's more of a Blur fan anyway,' Max reasoned, his voice was deeper and purred.

Her shoes finished the movement touching his, causing an instinct reaction of them both to look at the floor, smiling as she clumsily concluded her walk, clearly an accident. Max saw the faded jeans with mud caked all over them, her hands by her sides similarly decorated. He pulled his eyes upwards, taking in the mud streaks across her face that somehow did little to distract anybody from her beauty.

Her face was inches away from his, but she still looked down, slightly nervous to see his smile stare back at her. Max was not concerned, as it gave him more time to study and absorb every delicate beauty of her radiance. She finally glanced her eyes towards him, and there they held, sharing a look of wonderment, fascination, but also confusion.

Yet it felt right for both of them. Max moved in closer and closed his eyes, his hand loose and ready to pull her close. Penny reciprocated, allowing her eyelids to close and be taken away in the moment. Max could feel her breath on his lips, sending goosebumps around his body.

Then something came through the window.

55

They advanced with purpose and intent, using a mixture of Robinson's device and McKenna's keen eye to guide them through the course. McKenna often replaced the technology, barking orders to use his intuition as a greater source of guidance, which the group was often happy to acknowledge.

Under McKenna's tutelage, he found the track relatively easy to follow. The trail was worn and the path was clear, accompanied by an assisting drop of crumbling earth, which was a different colour to the worn dirt of the trail. Like Hansel and Gretel following the breadcrumbs, the group soon reached the edge of the clearing in no time. People at the back had been following a GPS guidance system to ensure they were heading in the right direction, but never needed to be consulted, yet were surprised themselves when they discovered they had arrived at their destination.

McKenna made Robinson hold back a helping of branches so he could peer through a small gap, not wanting to give their position away in case somebody may be watching from the building. A pair of binoculars was requested, soon being passed forwards to the front and McKenna grabbed a hold of them, positioning them to his eyes.

He scanned the clearing, the trimmed grass that completely surrounded the house ensuring any unwanted visitors could be identified as soon as possible. There did not seem to be an incognito way of advancing any further towards it, a very smart construction he had to admire. His arms guided the tools and his beady eyes in the direction of the house, as he carefully scanned everything he saw, taking in every minute detail and committing all to memory. He noted the porch and the entrance, thinking of both elaborate and simple theories that may help reach it.

The most important part he double-checked was the windows. After being satisfied that nobody was watching from any of them, he restarted looking and counted them all, working out a layout of the house in his mind, the blueprints forming an outline in his brain.

He pulled the binoculars away from his face, content with his research. As he was taking a final glance without the advanced aid, something caught his eye. He stopped moving and squinted to see further. A frown took over his face as he contorted it in confusion. Not satisfied, he raised them once more.

He was reassessing the porch. He guided the binoculars all across the outside wooden structure, before reaching the part that interested him. He fiddled the zoom with his fingers, working to ensure no focus was lost as he did so. McKenna held his gaze for a moment, everybody behind him waiting diligently to discover the reason why he froze.

He stopped at the porch steps, which headed towards a door. There, on the steps he could see it. Remnants of dark mud and earth were scattered all over the stairs, an obvious contrast to the lighter colour of the steps. The earth rested upon them looked recent as if somebody had yet to clean it away. He squinted further to see the final conclusion. There were lines of dark soil marked all up the stairs, of which he inferred somebody had recently moved a dirty, heavy object up them.

Without allowing anybody else a viewing, he moved back from the clearing, allowing Robinson's arm rest as he instructed the group to form a circle. A map was requested and brought towards him, followed by the foldable table that it rested upon.

'We have come in from the south side,' McKenna began, 'here.' He circled around a small area near the clearing on the map. The outline of the building had an estimated description of the rooms and their sizes, McKenna had been correct about each and every one. 'There are marks on the outside steps, giving me no shadow of a doubt that they must have moved the asset up there recently. They may still very well be inside.'

'They? I thought she lived alone?' A voice came from the back of the group.

'We have seen too many different footprints near the scene back there to assume she worked independently. For now, we should take it that there are multiple people in the house.'

A nod of agreement flowed through the group and they all awaited further instructions.

'We will move in from here, crossing the clearing as quickly and quietly as possible. We will remain low and try to stay out of the way of the windows. I shall construct a path to avoid as much of a direct view of people seeing from inside.

'I want everyone to follow my orders, and Robinson, you stay near the back. I've seen your firearm training results, my grandmother is a better shot than you and she's ninety.'

Robinson dropped his head in shame. 'Understood, sir,' his reply muttered. The five others pushed past Robinson, cocking their assault rifles and nodding approvingly towards McKenna. Robinson, understandably dejected, offered his pistol to a fellow soldier, opting against causing more difficulty for McKenna, also with a slight frightfulness he may accidentally shoot someone. He was not lying about his scores, they were dreadful.

'Now, I would have wanted Decker to be leading you all into a situation like this, he's a good soldier and knows how you all operate on the ground. For now, you will listen to me and follow everything I say, is that clear?'

'Yes, sir!' A cry in unison came back.

'Erm, sir?' A question from the back came in a much quieter tone.

McKenna had removed his pistol from its holster and began his routine check, ensuring all moving parts were in order should its use be required. 'What, Robinson?' He shouted back.

'What makes you so sure they have it?'

'Aside from everything we've already seen, let's just call it a gut feeling.' McKenna shouted back, his head never raising as he concentrated on the task in his hands.

'Righto, sir,' Robinson replied and slinked to the back once again.

'Now, listen to the plan, and don't forget anything I say.' He cocked his pistol back in defiance. 'Let's get this fucking thing back.'

56

The smash of the kitchen window made them move apart, the moment lost, drifting away like tears in the rain. Max's first thought was not of intrigue of what may have struck the window, but rather a longing disappointment, placed alongside the bitter realisation that he may never be able to have a second chance.

His face glanced across and observed Penny, who held emotions of both fear and anger, wondering just what had the nerve to disturb her peace, hoping they would have a spare one hundred dollars to replace the damage they caused.

Will heard the noise over from the living room, half asleep yet still attentive to hear the breaking of glass, causing his eyes to widen with intrigue. He turned onto his back and sat up, like Frankenstein's monster rising, sitting upright with a rod in his back. His head turned, peering around to find what was responsible for disturbing what he thought was a well-earned rest.

The next moments flashed by, racing with an exceptional quickness that was difficult to fathom, all three processing it differently despite being in the same situation. Only once they had calmed and began to think together, did any constructiveness between the trio commence.

Penny and Max, still holding each other, moved their eyes to see a tennis ball-sized hole that had inconveniently begun letting in a draft from the window. Their eyes then followed the noise, an irritable hissing that would have woken even the deepest sleeper if it were ever used as an alarm clock. Concerned, they bent their necks down to see the source of the annoying noise.

A small canister had begun emitting a smoke of misty cloudiness around their ankles, swallowing their feet and moving its way across the room with fury. Within seconds, it had pushed itself around the room, filling and engulfing everything in sight with impassioned glee; the noise providing the evil cackle of a superhero villain as the smoke continued its pursuit of swallowing every pot, pan and person in its path.

Max looked over towards Will, sat on the sofa in disbelief, and saw his face disappear into the mist, the grey fog blinding his vision. He looked down at his hands and was helpless to see they too faded into obscurity. Panicking, he naturally shot a final glance over towards Penny, desperate to snatch one last glimpse of her unassuming beauty, not knowing when he would ever be able to see the only thing he wanted to look at ever again.

As he watched the clouds encompass her face, the look she stared back at him with made a lump appear in his throat. It said everything without needing to speak. It asked a million questions neither had the answer to. It answered questions he did not know he had. He just hoped they would be able to answer all of them, whenever that may be.

57

Penny was frozen. Attempting to process everything in the last twenty seconds was extremely difficult. Being in such close proximity to Max sensationalised feelings she had not had in years. Her spine chilled, the hair on the back of her neck pricked up, and goosebumps travelled to her fingers and toes. She was fearful of what would happen in the aftermath, but she buried her overthinking in the back of her mind and waited with nervous anticipation for the overwhelming next seconds.

Then, when she was almost on top of the world, somebody thought it was the perfect moment to break her window. Typical. Shocked, she bought herself space from Max as a natural reaction, the years spent on her own allowed her to develop a nomadic characteristic she sometimes struggled to shake. Once she noticed the smoke filling the room, she knew they were in trouble. She was glad Max had chosen to look at her just before the clouds overtook their vision, she just could not help being annoyed with herself for shooting him a sad smile of sorrow. Furthermore, she was beyond bothered with herself for being frozen to the spot, not being able to move an inch. Her feet were bolted to the ground.

She did not know what to do. She had never frozen, always being able to think on her feet and make the correct decision, letting her instinct take over and guide her. She was left with no choice but to stand, looking helpless, and hope to God Max could think of something to help shake her into action.

58

The smoke filled the room with vengeful anger. Max, after stealing his glance at Penny, tried to think as quickly as he could. Seeing she had become completely frozen, he stepped up, grabbed a hold of Penny's forearm and yanked her down towards the ground, both crouching in their swift act.

'Get down, Will!' He shouted across the room to his friend. He was too far away to help, he was just hoping Will could hear him through the chaos.

Max had come across the various types of explosives as he cast his mind back as far and fast as he possibly could. He remembered researching for a particular assignment when he was younger, just starting out working in a publishing firm. Although he despised the job - proofreading had never truly interested him - he pursued it with fiery intent, hoping to be moved onwards as swiftly as he could.

Whilst reading something he could not remember, he found himself, as always, finding the fact-checking much more interesting than the actual assignment. In a particularly wasteful afternoon, he had succumbed to a hole of reading copious websites and paraphernalia on different explosives, grenades and incendiaries. Not being of any use at the time, his memory served him well and he could now use his novice expertise.

He had come across the procedure if one was to ever be exposed to various explosives, including the best course of action to heighten chances of survival. Thinking on the spot, he identified the window-smashing object to be a smoke grenade; a way to disturb a room and provide an incognito entry. Max was fairly certain it was not a stun grenade, as these explode with more of an instant bang, followed by a flashing light to help blind those in its vicinity.

With a smoke grenade, the smoke emitted can often be lethal. He knew for both safety and visibility the best option was to remain on the ground, crawling if possible. Hoping Will had heard enough of his scream to follow the instructions, he and Penny were now on their chests, lying on the floor next to the kitchen island.

Having had all of these discussions with himself in a matter of seconds, and now satisfied they were in the safest possible position, he allowed himself a deep breath to try and calm down, the adrenaline pumping through his body coursing furiously.

Max reached into the clouds and felt for Penny's arm, despite being inches from each other they were completely blind. 'Try and follow me! Grab out for my leg and move with me!' Max shouted over to Penny.

'Okay, I'll try!' The response came from within the dark mist, yet he knew and recognised the unmistakable sound of her voice.

'Will! Crawl to the hallway, we'll try to make it upstairs!' Max cried out, but no response came from his friend. Pushing the concern away, he focused on his task. He can go back and help Will.

Like a soldier training in boot camp, trailing through the mud, he crawled on his chest, reaching out his arms and pulling his body over the hardwood, his speed aided slightly by his legs scraping their way behind him. He was slowed down by Penny's hand constantly clenched onto his calf, but he knew it was important to try and think about it being there, and how concerned he would become if he no longer felt the tightness grabbing his muscle.

Their progress was slow, neither of them could see or hear anything, and both were praying that Will was alive, having not heard him since the beginning of the debacle. Max used his arms to feel around when he reached the hallway, touching walls with the edge of his fingers and trying his best to advance forward as straight as possible.

The smoke was beginning to clear the further he crawled down the hallway, starting to see the outline of the front door at the corridor's end. Seeing this provided the necessary spark of energy, and he shifted forward with added purpose. As the clouds dissipated, he glanced to his right and saw Will's arms stretch out from just behind, his hands reaching the same position as Max's hips. He still felt Penny's grasp on his leg, they were all together again.

'Will!' Max exclaimed joyfully.

'Lovely weather in here!' Will quipped back, the exasperation noticeable in his voice.

'Glad to see you made it mate!'

'Didn't seem like rocket science. Smoke rises, get away from the source,' Will replied nonchalantly.

Max rolled his eyes but could not help smiling. Typical of Will to see this as nothing more than a minor inconvenience.

As they reached the end of the smoke, Max allowed himself to slow down slightly, attempting to get his breath back. He tried to fight off a cough, not wanting to affect his progress, also remembering the dangers of inhaling too much of certain gases that can be deployed by grenades of that type.

Yet it was no use. The smoke had wormed its way into his lungs. He began coughing and spluttering as he lay on the floor, the clouds tickling his insides with an annoying defiance. Then, as he writhed on the floor, there was another bang. He swung his head around to look back down the hallway, to see the kitchen. He still could not see any further than a few feet away, but his vision was reduced once more. As the second grenade's smoke engulfed his sight, he realised he could not even see past his knees, to see Penny. To see Will.

Will's face had disappeared into the clouds, quicker than the glee he had felt when he saw him seconds earlier. Max's heart dropped. He was set to continue ploughing on his journey to the end of the corridor, fighting the urge to cough any more than he already had. He swallowed assuredly and moved.

Then, suddenly, he could no longer feel Penny's fingers wrapped around his leg.

'Penny! Will!' Max shouted desperately into the clouds, not wanting to move so they could catch up. He waited. No one came. His eyes welled up, stung by the smoke, emotional from being all alone. The smoke surrounded him, it grew thicker and more dense. He raised his hands in front of his face but saw nothing. The grey bleakness played tricks with his eyes, with his mind as he lay only metres from the front door. As his eyes proved useless in the thickness of the clouds, his other senses took over once more. His fingers reached desperately for the handle. On the verge of finally opening the door, being able to see, to breathe again, his ears took over, aiding his lack of sight. He heard a gun cock far away behind him, far enough to be in the kitchen. He hesitated for a moment, refusing to believe what his heightened senses were telling him. That's when he heard the scream. A woman's scream. Penny's scream.

59

The group advanced hurriedly across the clearing, meticulously following McKenna's footsteps as if he had left his boot mark in fresh snow, the others never missed a step. Weaving with pace, the sun beat down on their faces, pushing their shadows across the cropped grass, moving together like a dark snake slithering on the ground.

Upon reaching the porch steps, two of them raced towards the kitchen window and stood on either side, their rifles pointed up to help conceal the weapon. Two of the remaining four mimicked the action, moving towards the door, everyone using deliberate steps to prohibit the decking from exploding with any compromising sounds. McKenna stood with the last two - of which included Robinson - all six sets of eyes staring back and hanging on his every word.

McKenna nodded to a colleague by the window, who produced a canister with a spring-loaded top, the handle drooping below a shining metal ring. He threw it to McKenna. Placing his index finger in between the ring, McKenna pulled it loose, keeping hold of the canister for a second. Knowing exactly how long before it detonated, he came to the decision to hold onto it before depositing it where he intended.

As a seasoned veteran, he was taught from a young age that if you have the courage to hold on to a grenade after pulling its pin seconds before releasing it, the grenade will detonate almost instantly upon being thrown, thus providing an added sense of surprise when it arrives at its destination. Those few seconds could be vital for evading capture, and McKenna, as a professional, could not allow that.

He glanced a mean look at everyone, nodded with intent and ensured everybody got the message without him having to speak. He took a deep breath, then aimed and threw the canister into the window, the object looping with gravitas and grace as it sailed through the air. Despite it being a simple execution, McKenna stood on the porch with the window a few feet away, the grenade appeared to move in slow motion, and the group's mouths were open in nervous anticipation for what came next.

A deafening bang came from inside the house, the windows filled up with grey smoke, and cries of desperation could be heard muffling through the mist. McKenna cracked a smile as his teeth appeared out from the corner of his mouth, making sure nobody was watching whilst the emotion slipped from his face.

The group waited, as were their instructions. Robinson stood next to McKenna, holding his arm across his body and staring awkwardly at the watch on his wrist. When it had cracked a minute, he tapped McKenna's broad shoulders, having to stand on his tiptoes to complete the action. Without a reaction, McKenna stepped forward, his hand outstretched. Somebody moved towards him and placed another canister in his hand. This time, he threw it directly after pulling the pin, not wasting a second, continuing to march in the direction of the door.

He threw the second harder, further into the room. Knowing the layout of the house, he knew anybody in there would naturally attempt to move to the front door via the corridor if they had not chosen the rear exit. Satisfied nobody had tried the latter, his soldiers strategically positioned if that be the case, the grenade was thrown into the direction of the hallway this time. The smoke began clearing in the kitchen as he strode forward to enter the house.

The two soldiers on either side of the door moved, and, in unison, kicked their boots into it, allowing it to swing forward into the house at a furious pace, the hinges pinging off and escaping into the smoke. Without having to stop walking, McKenna seamlessly entered the house as the door flung open, his neck twitching in every direction as he surveyed the surroundings.

He could see the living room, the kitchen and a portion of a corridor leading towards the front of the house. Strolling forward, he held an arm across his forehead to avert the smoke from his eyes, a natural reaction in spite of his decades of field experience which allowed him to build a sense of immunity to these types of non-lethal, screening grenades.

With his posse behind him, he wandered through the seating area, stopping once he came across what he was searching for. There, tucked into the corner, stood a wooden crate, covered in mud, mould, dirt and grime. It appeared so unassuming, as if inside contained nothing of any importance other than family photographs and heirlooms. McKenna, deciding this time to remain emotionless, remembered the full extent of his job and got back to work, eager to finish what they had started.

'Secure it,' he barked behind him, his finger wagging in the direction of the crate. Once more he set off, further into the heart of the house, now making no attempt to conceal his presence, the thick rubber heel of his boots stamping on the hardwood. He removed his firearm as he advanced, cocking the gun back once more, meticulous and eager to not make a mistake. After all, he was better than the rest of them. He was in charge for a reason.

All of a sudden he stopped. Halfway through the corridor, the family photographs on the wall beside him still black and white, having not advanced far enough down to reach colour, he stood over the top of two bodies, squirming like worms across the hallway. He glanced up briefly, witnessing the second grenade still emitting cloudy darkness further along, content the duo would not be moving particularly fast in the smoke.

This time, he smiled. A gleeful smile. A smile he had not used in a long time. A smile which indicated he was going to enjoy the next part of his day. Securing the asset was great, it allowed him to justify what he was about to do next.

A soldier came from behind him, arriving after being waved forward like a dog, a dog eager to please their owner. McKenna pointed at the body to the right, still slowly moving away. The soldier nodded and bent down, pulling at the body's shoes and dragging it back into the living room. McKenna, during this period, focused on his own job. The other body. He bent down, crouching over the top of the body with the gun resting easily in his right hand. Reaching with his left, he violently grabbed a fistful of the blonde ponytail that tousled as the body writhed on the floor. A cry came from the face he could not yet see, and he pulled harder on the hair, the head moving up as the back curved. Still holding on, McKenna rose slightly, tugging the hair as he pulled the body along the hardwood.

The woman was shaking, screaming, furiously moving to try and pry his hand off of her head, to alleviate some of the pain exuding from her skull. McKenna's grip would not budge. He held on tighter, his knuckles whitening as his clenched fist brought agony to the woman. Pulling her, he stopped for a brief moment, turning back to assess the corridor. He wanted to see further along, to see if there was anybody else.

He squinted to aid his eyes in the search. He bobbed his head, looking for any movement, a shadow even, to show somebody's whereabouts. Then, just as he wanted to investigate further, the woman he was holding increased the intensity of her displeasure at his actions. Holding his hands to help decrease the pain of the clench, she kicked and wormed her body, desperately moving in any direction to escape his clutch.

With his mind returning with full focus to the woman, he pointed his pistol at her temple, taking no care in his movement, poking the metal on the soft area of the skull. With that, he required no words, as the woman realised and accepted defeat. Her movements relaxed, and he was able to drag her easily into the living room.

Her hair was a mess, having been manhandled the ponytail had fallen loose. She had hair covering her face, allowing her to escape a solitary tear that rolled down her face as she was dragged across the floor of her own house.

60

The bodies were dragged through into the sitting room, squirming like fish out of water as they went. McKenna threw Penny in the direction of a soldier, who was holding cable ties, ready to decrease chances of hostility or escape.

Penny was drained of energy. She fought valiantly against McKenna, but the gun had deflated her optimism, and the adrenaline instantly minimised. Her eyes stung, the irritation of the smoke affecting her vision, struggling to keep her eyes open.

The cable ties zipped her hands behind her back. She peered helplessly over to Will, he was receiving a similar, rough treatment. Looking over at him, Penny could feel the sense of fear her face was exuding, assuming it would send Will into a panic once he saw her expression.

Will, however, looked back at her and smiled. He gave a little shrug of his shoulders as he was pushed down to sit on the floor. Penny could not help but smile back, the feeling infectious as it crept over her. She was pushed down on her shoulders to sit down, both of them resting their back on either arm of a sofa.

The smile they shared soon left their faces, and they started looking around the room once they came to their senses. Their heads turned and twisted, attempting to take in as much of their surroundings as possible. Their eyes met again, this time sharing a feeling of concern and dread. They did not need to speak, both sharing the same thought. *Where was Max?*

Penny's mind raced through scenarios whilst absorbing the features, characteristics and movements of the soldiers now so rudely intruding her home.

She concluded with confidence these were the same imbeciles that had been bothering her throughout the previous weeks.

These guys were not messing around, she knew that prior to their actions today, no matter how much more intense they had become.

Penny was happy she could not see Max. She would have loved nothing more in that moment of uncertainty to have him beside her, helping to calm everyone, trying to de-escalate the situation. But it was better he was not there. It meant he had gotten away, giving them the smallest of chances of being able to get out of the mess they were in.

She closed her eyes, lowered her head and smiled, dreaming her knight in shining armour might come and save the day.

61

He knew he had little time upon hearing the screams. Despite not seeing her, Max knew Penny was not far away. It was his own fortuitousness that helped the smoke cloud over his presence, whatever was the other side of the fog not realising he was there.

He blinked repetitively, attempting to process everything and plan his next move. Sweat ran across his forehead, settling in his eyebrows as he remained undeterred.

Just keep moving, he thought to himself. Staring back into the clouds one final time, thinking of his friends, in trouble and desperately needing his help, he had to fight every urge to go and try and save them.

He knew if he left, turned his back on them, and moved further away, he ultimately stood a better chance of staying alive. Only then, could he help them.

62

Max had scampered hurriedly up the stairs, grabbing steps and using all four limbs to forcibly drag himself as quickly as possible to safety.

He opted against the front door. The smoke clearing concerned him and he did not want to still be downstairs when somebody could see the front exit from the living room once again. That, added to his second-thought process of there potentially being a guard stationed on the other side of the door, made his decision to go up a second level.

Being his first time on the floor, he did his best to try and familiarise himself with the layout. He stood at the top of the stairs, the landing proceeded on his right, bending in an L-shape around with doors dotted along the journey, finally ending with what he assumed would be the master bedroom, which hung over the stairs and overlooked the front of the house.

A solitary door to his left, he decided to start there. Grabbing the golden doorknob, he pushed the dark, chocolate-brown door ajar. He wandered into a dusty but well-kept and impeccably tidy, spare room. His steps were quiet and purposeful, reminding himself at every movement to stay as silent as possible.

Max peered out of the window that overlooked the grass, the reliably resolute thicket of trees in the background. His head turned quickly, looking worriedly at the door. He had heard something from downstairs. The noise from below had remained relatively low, ensuring his conscience he was an adequate distance away.

But no, the noises were becoming clearer, closer to him. The mutterings of chatter and stomping of boots echo their sounds through the hallway, the old house projecting the noises as if it were speaking aloud. Max's heart raced. He needed to hide. He glanced around the room, frantically searching for reprieve. He thought to himself. *Under the bed? Too obvious. Wardrobe?* He looked around. *No bloody wardrobe. Bollocks.*

Out of ideas and almost out of time, he walked towards the door he had kept open. Holding the handle, he waited behind the wood, safely listening to hear how far the soldiers were from sealing his fate.

A thump bellowed from below, at the end of the hallway. *Enough time,* he thought and pulled the door back, jumping from safety and onto the landing, directly in front of the stairs.

He glanced quickly at the steps, seeing the front door from his elevated position. His gaze subconsciously flicked to a movement. He saw the top of a head as it began advancing down the corridor, becoming frequently blocked by the spindles, reappearing in between the gaps as the figure flicked along the hallway. Within seconds, the figure would reach the front door at the end of the corridor, naturally turning its head right to begin the ascension up the stairs.

Just as the head began turning, Max sprang as silently as he could further along the upstairs corridor, lowering to his knees and using the low wall the hallway possessed to conceal his presence from the soldiers. Remaining on his knees, he crawled, following the shape of the landing around to the right, reaching the final door.

It was shut. He tried reaching up from his crouched position to find the knob, but a chilling sound stopped him.

The sound of the boots returned, except louder this time. The heels angrily punched themselves into the wooden stairs, which cried out in agony. Unmistakably two sets of feet, the noises worked in stereo to pierce a fearful dread into Max's eardrums.

He looked up, reaching upwards for the handle once more. Finding it this time, he desperately turned on the metal.

It would not turn.

The stomps became louder and louder as they rose higher, escalating to their final summit.

Max rose to a more convenient position on his knees and more worriedly rattled the mechanism, praying the old handle would jump into life and save him.

'Wait.' A voice came from the stairs. Max stopped moving, his heart in his mouth. 'Did you hear that?'

'Yeah…' a slow reply came back. 'I think it came from over to the right.'

'Let's go,' the first voice finished, the military boots forcing the stairs to scream as they bounced up each step.

Max could not believe it. He was about to die because a one-hundred-year-old doorknob refused to budge. The loudness of the soldiers masked the rattling noise he was causing the handle to make, shaking it to open.

He glanced behind him. The soldiers were getting closer to the top, but still could not see him. Looking back, the other doors were all too far away. Too close to the soldiers, he would never make it in time.

His left hand frantically shook the handle. He moved his right hand to help, both clasped around the metal, pushing and pulling in every direction, pleading for the door to give way.

Ready to give up, he placed the last of his energy into a final push, not caring about the damage he could cause.

Fuck it. Holding the handle in his left hand, he momentarily moved away from the door. Standing sideways, feet shoulder-width apart, he threw his momentum with his right shoulder into the wooden obstacle.

There was a loud crack, and the wood splintered, followed by a crash. Having forced the door open, Max had ended up on the floor, face down, just inside the room.

He clenched his shoulder as he lay there, feeling a wave of unspeakable pain beginning to emanate above his arm, ready to spread across his body.

Yet he knew he was against the clock. The soldiers behind him would have started moving quicker, following the noise.

Using his left hand to pull himself up, he kept his right arm tucked close to his body, wary of the pain and not wishing for further damage, still uncertain of the extent to which he was injured. Hurrying over to the door, he grabbed it to swing shut, not bothering to look behind.

The soldiers had just rounded the corner, in hot pursuit and knew exactly which door to aim for.

Max raced across the room to the wardrobe and clambered inside, pulling himself with his left arm. He closed the door quietly behind him and began an attempt to control his laboured breathing.

He heard the door into the room burst open with excitement, the hinges creaking against a now fragmented door frame. Max could do nothing. He closed his eyes and prayed they would not find him, allowing himself the realisation that there was not anything else he could do. His fate may have just been sealed.

63

Devoid of smoke, the living room and kitchen were filled with something else. Soldiers dressed all in black, assault rifles gripped tightly as they strolled around with gloomy, monotonous defiance, refusing to acknowledge any questions barked at them from Penny.

'What do you want?! Leave us alone! Do you mind not stepping on the rugs with the boots on?!' The last one particularly bothered her, she had cleaned them all only the week before.

She knew exactly why they were there. She knew exactly what they wanted, and that they would not be leaving them alone. That was the one thing she was fairly certain of at that point. What concerned her was she had no idea the severity of what came next. She swallowed hard, pushing down her feelings, concerns and fear. Out of the two of them, she was indubitably stronger than Will, and she would have to remain resolute to ensure his spirit endured.

McKenna had been across the room, examining the wooden box. Kneeling with poise, he imagined himself looking like a historic explorer, like a conquistador finding priceless artefacts in Mesoamerica, watching carefully as the lid was raised. Peering inside, a feeling of warmth crept over him as his eyes widened to the size of car tyres, in awe of what they had found, finally letting his guard down and taking a moment to embrace his victory.

He was delighted in the preservation of much of the money. Fascinated, he took hold of a collection of notes, holding each one individually towards the light to inspect them further.

'We did it, boss,' a satisfied Robinson stood further back, patiently waiting for his turn to look into the box and see all its wonders.

McKenna remained focused on the task in his hands, refusing to acknowledge the statement. Once content with his examination, he carefully returned the notes to the home they had kept for ninety years before today.

He quickly snapped back onto the job. 'Secure the asset, secure the area. Robinson, you stay here with someone and ensure we can have this extracted ASAP. Two of you, sweep the rest of the house and make sure no one else is home. Two more of you, go out the back door and sweep the outside, I want one of you by the back door, one by the front. Thirty yards away, though. I want you to still be able to see the road, the side of the house and if anything comes from the trees.' McKenna's arms were working overtime, gesticulating each task and pointing at soldiers with paramount specificity, making sure everybody knew their assignments.

'Yes, sir!' The collective response returned once more. As they dispersed, Penny rolled her eyes, seemingly annoyed at the authoritative, managerial approach demanded by this buffoon in her house.

Not missing anything, McKenna saw this out of the corner of his eye. He smiled and moved over towards Penny, standing over her defiantly whilst she was crouched by the sofa. His hands moved to his hips and he stared down at his prisoner, taking a moment to figure out his game plan.

'I take it you are the homeowner, yes?' He liked already knowing the answers to his own questions.

'What's it to you? You gonna try and sell me some solar panels?' Penny replied sarcastically, inducing a snigger from Will to her right.

McKenna knelt down to get on a similar eye level before continuing. 'I've heard you're not the most accommodating of people,' he smiled out of the corner of his mouth.

She looked observantly, wild curiosity scanning every characteristic she could acknowledge. He was middle-aged, physically past his prime, yet he tried to hide this behind an increasing intelligence, an intellect that compensated for the slower steps he now took. The face was hard, without any soft features. It inferred many sleepless nights and sun exposure, this man had spent his best years out in the field. Yet Penny sensed he remained eager to prove his use, eager to prove father time he had not yet reached and began descending the hill.

The eyes pierced through her with a sense of maniacal, foreboding grittiness. Eyes that had seen things nobody should have been exposed to, things that hardened the outer shell but also the soul trapped inside.

'You've heard? From who? I'm not exactly running an Airbnb.' This time, Will could not contain himself, erupting into a hearty laugh.

'I must say, you're worse than your file alluded to.'

'Bite me,' Penny snapped.

He stood back up again and began pacing the vicinity, ensuring he remained within Penny's vision at all times. 'I assume you'd like to know what we're doing here.'

'I know why you're here. Just take what you've come for and get out of my house.' Penny threw her head in the direction of the wooden crate, her hands still useless behind her back.

McKenna laughed, 'We shall be out of your hair in no time, I can assure you of that.' He stopped for a moment and watched with interest as the soldiers bent over the wooden crate, whispering to each other and constructing their next itinerary. 'I want you to know that you didn't have to be a part of this. You could have stayed away and have been none the wiser.'

'Well I've recently formed a habit of bumping into strangers,' Penny quipped back, looking towards Will as they shared a smile.

'Even still,' McKenna raised a finger, 'I should tell you that you will be responsible for your friend's death, as well as your own. Unfortunately, this has been brought upon by yourself.'

'Are you just pissed cus I left a couple of your guys sleeping outside last night?' Despite being tied up, Penny was full of fire.

McKenna took a second to piece together the accusation. 'So, you're the reason five of my subordinates and my best soldier woke up near the lake this morning?' McKenna did not seem annoyed, more impressed and he did his best to hide the shock in his voice.

Penny opted to respond with a shrug, highlighting how relaxed she was staying.

'I would have liked to see you in action… Penny,' his voice held on the last word and he noticed Penny's cheeks clenched upon him mentioning her by name.

'What are you gonna do then?' Penny had genuine intrigue in her question, trying her hardest to stay stoic, but also fearful for the severity of the response.

'Details, details. There is no need to bother yourself with the specifics,' the hatred in McKenna's voice was not lost on Penny, and she lost some confidence. 'Just know that we will be taking that muddy box and getting out of your hair. It really doesn't match the rest of the furniture.'

He knelt in front of Penny again, this time closer to her face, admiring every detail he had afforded himself by being in such close proximity.

McKenna moved his hand towards her, grabbing a strand of her hair, delicately this time. 'The photograph we have doesn't do you any justice either,' he smiled and let the hair run through his fingers, Penny's nose scrunched in discomfort.

'Hey man, leave her alone!' Will cried from McKenna's left. Annoyed, he dropped the hair, standing up to move across to Will, before kneeling in front of him, inches from his face. Will was given the chance to see McKenna's face up close for the first time; he gulped fearfully.

'What's it to you, you little fucker?' McKenna said calmly, as if he was ordering coffee at his favourite restaurant. Suddenly, his face turned to anger, throwing out his hand and forcibly grasping around Will's neck. Taken by surprise, Will's mouth opened slightly as he desperately tried to breathe, noises of struggle gaining intensity as the seconds passed. Veins throbbed on McKenna's hairy forearm, the grip tightening, pushing Will's head against the sofa arm. He could feel the anatomy of his victim's neck the harder he squeezed, watching with glaring eyes as the life in front of him clung desperately. Will's face reddened, the pressure rising as McKenna grimaced, spit beginning to escape through his teeth as his concentration deepened.

'Let him go!' Penny shouted hysterically, trying so hard to move on the hardwood, slipping the more she moved. 'You crazy bastard put him down!' Her head was shaking furiously, kicking her legs out to get closer. A soldier moved towards her and attacked her with the butt of their rifle, sending her head to crack onto the floor, her hands still helpless behind her back.

She fell onto her side, her eyes facing the direction of McKenna and Will, her head resting on the floor, tears falling down the side of her face as she watched with sorrowful eyes as Will clutched to his last breath.

As she lay there, unable to move or avert her eyes from the murderous act happening in front of her, she noticed something. Just to the side of the attacker, she saw something in the reflection of the television screen. A door opened, and she detected a movement in the kitchen.

64

Standing in the wardrobe, Max was uncomfortable. He attempted to move, a coat hanger pressing into his shoulder blade, yet conscious not to move loudly enough for anyone outside to hear. He moved his head towards the doors, leaning towards the crack in between and seeing if he could see through the opening. It was in vain, as the best he could muster was the shadowy outlines of the soldiers moving separately across the room, slow enough to ensure they canvas every piece of carpet, knowing with absolute certainty of somebody else's presence in the room.

Nestled in-between a woolly, and becoming rather hot, winter coat and a pair of jeans, Max leaned the back of his head on the rail, exasperated and settling for this action as relaxation whilst he was not able to sit. In the darkness, it mattered neither if his eyes were open or closed, the only reprieve from utter blackness being the light creeping through the crack in the doors.

His mind wandered, the thoughts hazy, his mind foggy, struggling to comprehend his future and what lay in the next moments. He could be in there for seconds, maybe minutes before he was discovered. Yet, he knew with absolute certainty he would be found. It was only a matter of time before his freedom would be momentarily removed and replaced with whatever intentions these people had. It was a strange concept for him to imagine his freedom being enclosed in somebody's wardrobe. Penny smelt great, so he did not mind it happened to be her wardrobe he was restricted to, her aromas fumigating the wooden enclosure with fruitiness as he became captivated by the irresistible scent on her clothes.

He shook his head, trying his hardest to focus on something specific, to turn his attention to anything relevant, the possibility of thinking of something constructive he could benefit from at that moment. His mind was a blur. It made him hate himself, knowing that every second he spent with the inability to think of something was wasted as the soldiers circled outside.

Max lowered his head in shame. He had come to the end. And just like everything he had tried before, it would finish without having anything comprehensive to conjure in his mind. The writing was a failure. He was a failure. Tears began to well up in his eyes, he tried to hold them back but could not, feeling them drop down onto his shoes, meandering off into the wooden floor with a disappointing flow.

The self-reflection of hatred made him consider his life, all that he had not accomplished, all he promised himself he would achieve, once again falling short into a situation of self-pity and over-reliance on others. More tears flowed as his thoughts turned to his friends, blaming himself for placing them in the predicament they now found themselves in. Will, who had done nothing but be unbelievably and unconditionally supportive of every stupid venture Max thought of.

And Penny, who he had inadvertently dragged into the chaos of disorganisation for no benefit other than his own. She had warned them both of the dangers these people posed, yet he impulsively and brazenly continued anyway. Now they would both die, all because of Max's idiocy, for no reason whatsoever.

It was not possible for him to lower his head anymore, yet he tried anyway. His tears never ceased, continuing to roll down his face and into his stubble stubbornly. He felt helpless, out of his last stupid ideas, which was maybe for the best, he considered. Bending his head down, he leaned onto the back wall and slid down to the floor, not caring if his shoulder hurt anymore, not bothered about anything, the closeness of the end producing nihilism he had never experienced.

'Have you found anything?' A soldier outside asked loudly to the room.

'No, nothing yet.'

'There must be something round here,' the first voice demanded. 'We saw the door swinging and heard it open. He can't be far away.'

'We can't leave anyone behind, McKenna would be pissed. I'll check over here, you check the wardrobe.'

'If the guy's hiding, he won't be able to put up much of a fight,' A soldier said with a chuckle.

'You're right, he's probably scared, bless him. We'll let him call his mommy when we get him.'

'Deal,' the pair laughed together.

Immediately after hearing the conversation, something in Max snapped.

65

He sat, on the other side of two doors, tucked inside a wardrobe; his temporary safety secure, yet the danger heightening every second. He sat with his knees bent, arms holding them in place as he slowly rocked backwards and forwards. His eyes stung. He knew they would already be red from his crying. The crying was not helping anyone. The crying that would not achieve anything, only makes him more of a failure and the situation more disastrous, more melancholy.

He rubbed his eyes with his shirt and sniffed quietly. *This was pathetic, waiting to die in a cupboard.* His face hardened, a frown beginning to burrow across his eyebrows.

There had been an abundance of thoughts he had tried to process whilst sitting in the enclosed space. Some he rather preferred not thinking about, others he desperately attempted to continue, but to no avail.

These had all since been replaced. Removed. He began concentrating on only one thing, being able to empty his brain of negative thoughts while defenceless, the one thing in his mind focusing him, providing it with his full attention.

On the verge of death, something inside of him awakened. Stuck in the darkness, after his obvious meltdown, the waiting had bothered him. Sitting there, waiting as patiently as an old man for the bus, his sadness replaced itself with rage.

The thought remained as he stood up defiantly and without care of provoking noise. It mattered little at that point, they would be coming through the doors at any moment. Holding his right shoulder, he tested its strength by moving the joint in circles. There was a slight sharpness of pain during every completed rotation, but he knew he would be able to manage for the foreseeable future. Most importantly, he knew that once his adrenaline started pumping, the pain would disappear and his hindrance would cease.

A grizzled look of determination came across his face. The one thought struck a fire of absolute certainty, knowing he had no choice but to continue to believe and place all his faith into his ideology.

I'm alive. I'm still alive. The thought waved over his body, consuming him, and providing a sense of confidence in a moment of increasing hostility.

However, this was only part of his motivation. *I am alive, and I can still save them. I either die trying or die anyway. They would do the same.* His fury had reached its peak and he was jittering on his toes like a footballer waiting to take their penalty; a nervous energy of anticipation, fully confident in the result concluding the way he wanted.

He would be ready for whatever was behind the doors. They had come so far and he would be damned if they all gave up now. He was certain the pair of them would be fighting downstairs if they were still there.

And if they were not, he would find them. He just hoped the soldiers behind the doors came at him one at a time, to give him the best chance possible.

He had never been in a fight before. He had never even punched anyone. With three lives on the line, it seemed like the perfect time to start.

66

One of the doors flung open from the outside with an almighty pace, but Max was ready. Reacting within seconds, knowing he would only be able to use the element of surprise once, he lifted his right leg and pushed with as much force he could manage into the unsuspecting soldier's chest. The momentum caused the soldier to fall backwards, stumbling with his assault rifle flailing as his arms desperately tried to assist in balancing himself once more. Falling back for more than a few steps, he reached the foot of the bed, his legs hitting the wooden rail.

Going from falling whilst standing to his momentum suddenly stopping, the soldier's legs bent at the knees and he was sent falling onto the bed, his arms outstretched and having no control of his movements. He bounced backwards onto the bed, falling into the plethora of pillows, decorative cushions and throws, all of which aided his landing, reclining him onto a crash mat of indescribable comfort.

His back bounced onto the bed, and his arms did the same, resulting in his grip of the rifle loosening, sending it flying out from his grasp and settling on the floor in a heap.

The second soldier in the room, completely flabbergasted, could do nothing but watch as his colleague had seemingly been pushed backwards from the wardrobe, not being able to see Max's leg behind the open door.

Not resting on his laurels, Max continued moving at an exceptional speed. He stepped out of the cupboard, dropping down the step as the soldier he had just attacked was looking rather ridiculous falling whilst standing up. Stepping past the door, the other soldier stood, finding it difficult to avert his eyes from watching his friend make a fool of himself trying to balance, not aware of Max's movements to the left of him. By the time he acknowledged Max's presence, it was too late.

Max moved towards the second soldier. He placed his left hand on the rifle floating near his midriff, pointed off to the side in a non-threatening position. Keeping his hand fixed firmly to the barrel to prevent an attack, Max swung back his right hand and curled his fist as it wound up, before proceeding to bring forward his entire body weight and use the force generated to direct his fist into the soldier's left cheek, giving him his meanest, right hook.

Taken by surprise, the second soldier staggered backwards. Whilst the soldier moved further away, his weapon remained, his hands releasing the rifle, only for it to remain in position. Max's left hand had stuck to the barrel, causing him to acquire possession of the gun. Realising his good fortune - he had only meant to prevent the rifle from being pointed in his face - he grabbed the butt and swung it around, grabbing hold of the trigger once it was positioned correctly.

He was in a position of strength, the only person in the room holding a weapon. The first soldier was still in the effort of comprehending the proceeding events, which caused him to be lying on the bed and without his rifle. The second soldier, however, took less time to realise. Max's punch had thrown his balance, but once recovered, the soldier was now only a few feet away.

He looked at Max in disgust, observing from the way Max held the weapon that it was his first time holding a gun, providing the soldier with a boost of confidence. Max observed the expression, a look of concern spreading over his face. He knew that the longer this conflict endured the likelihood of success would decrease. He needed something, and quickly. He held a stare with the soldier for a brief second, looking closely and carefully in case he made a move. Both of their eyes dropped towards the rifle situated in Max's hands, the only thing of slight concern in both minds.

Max knew he was not going to use the gun, and his fear was the soldier had realised the same. Looking at the weapon, a spark ignited. Just as the soldier began slowly moving in his direction, a grin wrapped across his face in glee, Max spun the gun around, holding the barrel, yet this time with both hands. Confused by the movement, the soldier was undeterred and advanced further. Max, doing his best baseball swing, pulled the rifle back behind his head and swung it forward, wrapping the butt of the gun across the soldier's head, the metal making a cracking thud as it made an impact with the bone.

The force of the swing caused the soldier's eyes to roll back into his head, unconscious before he even hit the ground. Max watched as he fell backwards, like an old tree being felled, standing over him and holding the gun over his shoulder in triumph.

He only allowed himself a second to revel in his victory, soon remembering the first soldier he had temporarily subdued moments earlier. The speed in which he dispatched the second soldier meant the first had little time to recover from a soft fall onto the bed, wrestling and wriggling to move in any direction and land on solid ground. He flapped all four arms and legs, aggressively attempting to navigate through all of the comfortable obstacles and retrieve his weapon from the ground.

Max moved across the room, watching in silence as the soldier desperately tried to make progress getting off of the bed, failing miserably. *Thank God for girls and their cushions,* Max allowed himself a brief smile before interjecting the soldier's movements, pointing the gun so the barrel was inches from his skull. This did the trick, and the soldier stopped, realising Max had moved his chess pieces into checkmate.

'Cuffs, now.' Max said towards the man, hoping it would come across with a sense of authority and urgency.

One of the man's arms reached towards his belt, making Max very nervous in case he had a sidearm around his hip. A hand returned with cable ties being held out to him, and he let out a silent sigh of relief in his mind.

'Come on, up,' Max waved the rifle to indicate instructions. He pointed to the radiator underneath one of the windows, 'Down there, please.' The man obliged and sat on the floor next to the radiator pipes. Max, holding both the gun and the ties, started to crouch down to begin the process of tying the man to the metal fixture.

All of a sudden, halfway crouched, he stopped. He realised if he performed the restraint himself, he would require two hands, therefore having to forfeit the weapon somewhere. Not wanting to find out whether the man would grab an undefended rifle, Max thought better of it and stood once more.

He threw the cable ties towards the man. 'Put them on yourself. Tie them to the radiator, if you don't mind,' Max said as he pointed the gun in the man's direction again. The man shrugged and put the words into action, Max only bending down to assess the ties once the man had finished zipping them tightly to his left wrist. 'Give me your rounds too, please.' Confused, the man handed Max the spare two rounds on his hip, not understanding why.

Max stood up. 'Thank you,' Max nodded in appreciation. He walked across the room and fetched the man's weapon that had bounced off of the bed, before making his way to the unconscious man and retrieving the spare bullets situated on his belt.

There were two windows, one overlooking the front, and the soldier now sat next to the radiator underneath. Max moved to the second, located to look outside the side of the house.

He opened it and let the mid-morning breeze slide in. He threw all the spare rounds out, falling onto the grass below, before repeating the process with the round in the magazines of each rifle, being cautious to remember the bullet that sat in the chamber.

He stuck his head and shoulders out of the window, looking towards the front of the house, he could just work out a soldier, positioned about twenty metres from the front door. It appeared he had been tasked with watching the front exit and the road that led out onto the main highway. Max raised a smile, knowing he had made the correct decision to go upstairs, he would have been spotted by the lookout as soon as he had opened the door.

'Ta ra fellas,' Max spoke to both men, regardless of how conscious they were. He walked out of the room, dropping the now useless rifles, and shut the door carefully behind him, grimacing at the door frame apologetically as he looked at the damage for the first time.

I'm sure she won't mind. Two down, let's see how many are downstairs.

He began descending down the steps, aware that it could be a lot worse down there.

67

Max carefully descended the stairs, aware of the creaks that may cry out at any moment. Moving to the bottom step, he peered down the hallway, leaning to show only his head to the corridor. His survival instincts worked overtime, he was cautious of a soldier on watch at the end of the hallway, so he snatched a look around the corner subtly.

Checking his surroundings, the front door sat to his right. *Freedom.* Pushing the idea of escaping away with frivolous anger, annoyed with himself for even contemplating it, he noticed the door directly opposite, across the corridor.

Having never noticed it before, he wondered where the door might have led. Taking one last observation down the corridor, ensuring with absolute necessity no onlookers, he jumped down the final step, leaping across the four-foot hallway, striding with one step, like jumping over a creek, before silently turning the door handle and successfully moving inside.

Fortunately, the doorknob was significantly more accommodating than the one upstairs.

He had entered a dining room, noticing by the furnishings the room appeared to be the most outdated, old-fashioned, and least occupied. There stood a thick, grand, and expansive wooden table in the centre, capable of entertaining no less than ten people comfortably. Numerous cabinets housing varieties of crockery scattered the two longest walls, the exterior wall also housing a supremely dusty fireplace. The smaller walls to the sides contained a large window overlooking the front of the house to the right, and directly parallel stood double doors escaping into the kitchen on the left.

Max admired this last detail with confusion, struggling to accept its existence and assuming he would have observed this addition during his time spent in the house. Pondering, he soon reasoned it must have largely been because he struggled to take his eyes off of Penny, which he attributed as a worthy excuse.

He heard a scream. His eyes darted in the direction of the sound, panicking and overthinking as to just what the reason for the noise could have been.

Moving sharply, he navigated past the grand table to the glass-paned doors on the other side, positioning himself against the wall to avoid anybody potentially seeing him from inside the kitchen.

Each of the doors had four, even panes vertically stacked, separated by a thin slice of caramel wood. The second from the top, which was directly at Max's eye level, created a perfect option for him to rapidly turn his head for a brief second, assessing if anyone was situated in the kitchen. Although it was only a second's glance, it was successful; revealing that the kitchen remained unguarded. *Result.*

Max opened one of the doors slowly but stayed in position behind the wall, pushing the object and allowing its momentum to carry it, opening further. He withheld from moving just a second longer, his ear pressed against the wall, listening for the slightest indication of movement from the other side.

The cries returned, louder this time, more frequent and seemed to emit greater agony. Max concluded with the presumption he was safe to move, the cries hopefully providing an adequate cover for his advancement. This, coupled with running out of time, the shouting emanating from the next room only heightened the intensity, the danger worsening.

He saw the kitchen island directly in front and walked in a crouch with precision, finishing with the island in between him and the living room, concealing his presence. Crawling to the end of the fixture, he made it nearer to the back door.

Readying himself to look around the corner, he finally needed to see for himself the extent of the tragedy in the adjacent room.

He could identify the owner of the screams by ear alone, but he refused to believe until another of his senses acknowledged. He did not want them to belong to her, he heard the pain in her voice as she released emotions of incapability. The anguish pierced his chest after every outcry, the noises causing him to wince as they filled the room.

Please be alright, please be alright, he kept telling himself over and over.

Just before he moved, he leaned upwards and reached into the island's drawers, removing a small kitchen knife. There was no way he would use a gun, but he decided going in weaponless would be insanity.

Like a soldier going over the top, out of the trenches and into the unknown, he jutted his head from the obstacle and tried to comprehend what he saw.

68

Max's head scanned the living room situation with a hastiness he had never utilised before, his neck aching from the speed at which he contemplated the predicament. On the right, tucked slightly into the corner, stood a small, spectacled gentleman with a quiet demeanour assessing the wooden crate the trio had salvaged earlier that morning. Presuming him to be little more than a technician, Max allowed himself to infer that he would provide little difficulty or resistance if he were to notice him.

To the left carried an indubitably severe confrontation which contained an eye-popping time sensitivity to it, requiring Max to move almost immediately. A soldier stood over Penny, another rifle perfectly positioned with its barrel pointed directly at her skull, all while she lay on her side near the sofa, hands tied oppressingly behind her back. The reason for her cries and sobbing soon came to fruition, although Max failed to believe he would have ever assumed the situation to have been what he was laying witness to. No more than three feet from Penny, defenceless with her head on the hardwood floor, she could only watch as a middle-aged soldier was attempting to squeeze the life out of Will, a firm grip tightening every second around his throat. Will appeared as though his head was about to burst, sporting a red-coloured face Max had never seen before.

If Max did not move now, it would be only seconds before his friend would be dead.

The adrenaline moving furiously around Max's system turned to anger, his entire body hardening with a feeling of despicable hatred. Hatred towards the situation, towards everyone not welcome in the house. Everyone who wanted to cause them harm, who wanted to harm Penny. Everyone who wanted to harm Will, especially the soldier desperately trying to choke the life out of his best friend in the entire world.

He marched into the living room, holding the knife with a clenched fist, tight enough for his knuckles to have whitened, poised and ready to be deployed. The guard standing over Penny was the first obstacle in his path, the soldier's back facing Max, allowing him the option of a surprise confrontation. Without wasting another moment, he made a split-second decision about his attack strategy.

Reasoning that a stab wound may not completely incapacitate the soldier, Max was concerned she would still retain possession of the gun, rendering his attack pointless and shot within seconds of his rescue mission commencing. Arguing with his subconscious, he concluded his itinerary to begin with attempting to displace the rifle, ensuring to perform the action at a sufficient enough volume to rouse the middle-aged man, who in surprise would hopefully let go of Will's neck.

Having made his decision, Max had arrived at the first soldier, before proceeding to kick the back of her right knee with terrific precision. Taken aback, she fell to her knees, not particularly aware of the reasons behind her falling over. Max dropped the knife to the ground and followed the first move by grabbing hold of the rifle, which had now been eligible for grasping as her arms raised separately from each other to aid the balance of her fall. Grabbing the rifle in her right hand, the force of Max's pulling on the weapon caused her to turn slightly, aided by her knees being able to slide along the wooden floorboards. Now facing her attacker, she looked up with a troublesome expression, only then contemplating the severity of the situation as it stared directly back at her face. With two hands controllingly placed on the rifle, Max was able to move the object freely, in spite of the soldier's hand remaining on the grip, and he swung with as much force as he could muster, angling the trajectory in the direction of the soldier's face. The continuous movement of attack resulted in the side of the weapon crashing into the side of the soldier's head, sending her reeling backwards, finally forfeiting complete control of the rifle as she fell to the floor beside Penny in a slump.

Beyond outraged that he had been interrupted and therefore unable to finish the job, McKenna released Will from his epic clutches upon hearing metal crushing against bone directly next to him.

Will gasped thankfully at the fresh air around him, desperately consuming as much oxygen within his vicinity as he found humanly possible, his face returning to an ordinary colour despite him feeling an extraordinary sense of pain around his neck and his crushed Adam's apple.

McKenna stood in his typical stance with a straight back, showing a height difference between him and Max, who remained unfazed, however, as he stood with his recently acquired rifle pointing in McKenna's direction. Holding the gun towards the aggressor, Max slowly bent down, retrieving the knife and cutting at the cable ties holding Penny's hands behind her back. She shuffled on the floor and stood, rubbing her reddened wrists in discomfort.

Max noticed McKenna's sidearm at his hip and they stood watching each other, McKenna's hand delicately hovering over the holster.

'Come on then, hero, show me what you've got,' McKenna said, a smile across his face, seemingly undeterred despite being within four feet of Max's firing line.

Max's face remained emotionless and resolute, refusing to allow the man in front of him to goad him into a game of chicken. Penny stood by Max and patiently observed the scene, ready to interject at the commencement of any swift movements should she be required.

McKenna moved his glance around the room to see slightly behind him. In the corner, resided Robinson, standing like a statue after the ruckus that had been caused since Max's presence in the room disturbed his job in assessing and securing the crate.

'Robinson! I order you to shoot this man!' McKenna cried out orders.

Max began worrying momentarily, believing he could have underestimated the small man in the corner. He wanted to shoot Penny a look, but he dared not to move his eyes as they stuck to watching McKenna closely.

Robinson gulped. 'I left my service weapon with Collins outside, sir. After your rather insulting remarks about my firearm ability.'

McKenna rolled his eyes disappointingly. 'Robinson, once again you prove to me just how much of a useless bastard you really are!'

'Yes, sir. Sorry, sir,' a quiet reply came from the corner.

'You better hope this asshole kills you because if he doesn't, I'll personally shoot you myself!'

'I look forward to it, sir.'

McKenna contemplated. 'Go and get Collins from outside the back, now!'

'Very good, sir.' Robinson moved to the back door and fled as quickly as his short legs would take him.

McKenna's full attention now resumed towards the weapon pointed at his stomach, knowing that soon enough these imbeciles would once again be outnumbered.

Penny shot into action. 'Max, hand me the gun. Go and untie Will.'

Max nodded in agreement, handing over the rifle and taking the knife over to his friend. He was cautious and took the longer route, around the side of the room to reach Will sitting behind

McKenna, who was also being understandably cautious - finding himself on the wrong end of a three-to-one deficit for the time being - stepping backwards further into the corner.

He reached Will and helped him with his binds.

'Five seconds longer and that guy would have been dead,' Will remarked sarcastically as he stood up, still trying his hardest to get the air back into his lungs. Max smirked, thankful his friend once again could make light out of such a drastic situation.

'Penny,' Max said from across the room. 'We'll deal with these guys coming in, you okay there?'

'Yeah,' Penny cocked the rifle back and raised it with purpose. 'I'll be fine.'

Max and Will raced across the room to the back door and waited on either side of it for Robinson to return with his backup. Penny stared directly at McKenna, who returned the favour with a smiling frown as he awaited a flinch from Penny, ready with his hand to pull his pistol out.

The pair reached the door and waited patiently. Max still had the knife in his hand, but decided he no longer wanted to wield it. *Who do I think I am?* he thought to himself. *This is not Tarantino for God's sake.* He turned behind him and looked at the counter, throwing the knife and it slid, scraping over the kitchen side before settling with a wobble, its movement stopped by the bug spray canister Penny had wielded the night before when they had sat on the porch.

'You sure you're alright?' Max asked Will with genuine concern.

Will waved his friend's question away nonchalantly, almost as if his life had not almost ended minutes earlier. 'Yeah, grand mate, don't worry about me. Let's just get these fuckers and get outta here.'

'Deal.'

69

Penny watched through the corner of her eye as Max and Will raced across the room to the back door, ready to try and rid the intruders from returning inside. The majority of her attention stuck with dedication towards McKenna, however, who returned the favour with a resolute stare of his own. The pair engaged in a quiet, brooding staring contest, both refusing to relent, both refusing to move.

'Why don't we settle this the old-fashioned way, eh?' McKenna broke the eerie silence, gesturing with a nod for Penny to remove the rifle as if it were an obstruction to them.

'My gun is perfectly happy where it is for now,' Penny tried to ignore the provocation.

He moved onto his toes, lightening his weight, ready for any movement to jump into action. 'You know, I'll be walking out your front door with that crate, whether you like it or not.'

'I don't give a shit about the money.'

McKenna was momentarily confused. 'Then why are you making it so difficult?'

''Cus you're taking something that we found first. You try and kill my friends. And you're trespassing, and I have a right to protect what's mine.'

McKenna tried running a different play. 'You're right, Penny. You have every right. But what if we compensated you for your cooperation? We can arrange a handsome finder's fee for you.' He smiled and tried his best to come across as warm. His strategy of deception would still end with them all dead, but she did not need to know that for the moment.

Flabbergasted by the offer, Penny was amazed at how little McKenna valued her intelligence. She saw directly through the ploy, 'I'm okay, thanks though,' is all she replied with.

Penny's thoughts raced. There was no world where she was about to give up the ending of the story to the man in front of her now. She had spent her entire life growing up with the stories and legends being told at bedsides, campsites, and sleepovers; the mythical narrative that could be true, waiting to be found. She had never believed the story, yet her husband and his family always remained entranced by it. They held onto the legend, the belief it could be out there was more glorious, more romantic than it not being there at all. She finally understood. She owed it to them for the story to end more romantically than leaving it in the hands of whoever these people were, that conclusion particularly unsatisfying.

'I can arrange it all for you, Penny. I'm responsible for all of this, all the incessant bother we've troubled you with. Let me give you some closure and go on with your life. We reached out to the local town council weeks ago,' McKenna's monologue finished.

Penny looked confused. 'The council?' She inquired with disbelief, she had heard him but needed confirmation.

'We know everything, Penny. There is nothing you can hide from us. We went to the council and made sure there were more definitive land ownership rights set out. It seemed like they needed to be reminded of just who owned the land.' He smiled gleefully.

'You *bribed* the council?'

'Technically, you now have no claim to any land other than what your house now stands on, we made sure of that. That box is not yours, it was on our land.'

Penny took a moment to understand what he was trying to say. That was it. They had stolen her land, all for the sake of a one-hundred-year-old box. No. They had stolen her *family's* land. She was beside herself. She wanted nothing more than to break down and sob uncontrollably. How could they steal her family's legacy? Her face contorted in various expressions as she held back her emotions, remaining as strong as possible in front of McKenna.

Out of everything that occurred in the previous weeks, all the inconvenience, the trespassing and uninvited visits, this was the worst. All she had left from her family was the house and the land. An old rickety house that was falling down and nothing else. In a matter of seconds, it had been reduced to nothing. The area had been in her husband's family for over two hundred years. And she had inexplicably turned it over.

A rage boiled all over her body. Her sadness had depleted, her emotions drained of all feeling. She had a choice. She could either blame herself for everything, for being responsible for all the fuck-ups and disastrous consequences and give up. Or, she could fight. Honour her husband's legacy, and his family's legacy, and fight to the very end for everything she had been entrusted with.

She sniffed hard, the last remnants of being upset erased in a flash. 'Come on then, you throw yours away first,' she nodded at McKenna's gun.

'Okay,' McKenna replied with a smile, throwing his gun to the ground before kicking it behind him.

Penny dropped the rifle with a sense of tiredness. Not of wanting to be asleep, but of tiredness of being completely fed up with their bullshit. 'You're gonna have to kill me if you wanna walk outta my house, you bastard.' She spoke firmly and with a toughness she had not used to address McKenna so far. Suddenly wary, he slowly advanced closer, his fists raised.

70

Collins entered the door first, followed by Robinson. The next moments happened so quickly, Collins getting the wind knocked out of him and Robinson being pulled around by his shirt collar.

Max took Collins, they had agreed on that beforehand. A foot had entered the door first, being kicked down by the mighty, black boot worn by Collins' right foot. As soon as he saw it from behind the wall, Max grabbed the leg it belonged to and yanked it into the room, sending its owner reeling towards the ground and sliding over the hardwood, spinning in all directions like a poorly thrown bowling ball hurtling down the alley.

Before Collins had the chance to acknowledge the situation, Max ran towards him and pulled the rifle loose from his grasp, tossing it with disregard into the room. He finished his assault with a kick to the ribs, forcing Collins to curl over in pain, before he spun the helpless soldier onto his front and kneeled authoritatively on his back, pinning Collins into submission and holding his hands together.

Will, however, made slightly harder work of arguably an easier opponent. Grabbing Robinson's collar was his first step, moving to swipe a punch at the face he held in position from the neck.

Robinson retaliated subconsciously, instinctively. Not one for violence, he still found it within himself to throw a jab into Will's stomach, who keeled over in a mixture of shock and pain. Robinson took a few steps backwards, struggling to acknowledge the action his adrenaline had caused him to perform. Once recovered, Will stood straight once more and readied himself for a fight, raising his fists.

Unsure of what to do next, Robinson threw a weak, half-hearted hook in Will's direction, his adrenaline seemingly dropping back to a normal rate. Will was able to counteract efficiently, catching the non-flying fist, twisting the wrist and moving Robinson into a one-hundred-and-eighty-degree turn to finish with his back to Will, who remained holding the arm and pushing it further up Robinson's back into a position of significant discomfort.

Max, knelt over his victim, and Will, pushing his victim's arm dangerously close to a fracture, nodded at each other approvingly, grateful they were able to successfully tame the uprising. Will forced his prisoner onto the ground, both Collins and Robinson had their faces pushed into the floorboards, two Englishmen kneeling atop their backs. Max had witnessed Will being punched by Robinson, but ultimately voted against ridiculing him, opting for a more opportune moment of calmness to bully him further.

It would be worth the wait. He looked across the room, both his and Will's conflicts had moved them towards the far corner, next to the wooden crate and all its fortune contained inside.

What the hell was happening with Penny? He watched in awe at the struggle now moving into the kitchen.

71

Penny felt powerful when she disposed of the weapon, the seething anger guiding her infuriation towards McKenna, imagining unspeakable descriptions of violence directed on his face. She was younger and could move quicker, the adrenaline aiding to provide a confidence boost as they moved closer to one another.

Patiently waiting, they stood and observed each other's fighting stance, both insistent on the other making the first move.

McKenna reasoned he may be older, yet wiser and more experienced. Twenty years of fieldwork in combat altercations would undoubtedly supersede whatever credentials Penny may be hiding from him.

He moved forward with his left foot, readying his hands before stepping into an unconvincing and half-hearted left jab, eager to see a response. Penny defended with a side step, evading the slow fist, countering with a swiftly executed right kick into McKenna's undefended and recently exposed right rib cage. McKenna faltered backwards with a spin, correcting his footing and attempting to play off the pain emanating from his side.

Shaking his fists in an act of restart, he moved with increased directness and speed, throwing a combination of well-constructed left and right punches in Penny's direction. She parried successfully, keeping her arms tight to her face, using her forearms to deflect advances and staying on her toes for ease of movement. She swerved after the last punch and threw a jab of her own, hitting him square on the nose, his face thrown backwards from the impact.

McKenna waited for a retaliation, knowing he needed to wait to break her down. Having gained additional confidence, Penny moved to strike, attempting a right hook. Seeing the move, McKenna stepped back and knocked the flying fist away, before attacking with his own right fist, aimed at Penny's stomach.

The impact threw her, shuffling her feet and trying her hardest not to fall. Seeing her close to falling, McKenna stepped forward and hit her again, this time a left hook to the cheek, the noise deafening as the bone-to-bone meeting cracked in horror; Penny's arms were no use as a defence, being used to aid her balance.

The second punch sent her stumbling further, moving across the hallway entrance and into the kitchen, desperately reaching out for any object that could help steady her. She found the kitchen island to her right and grabbed it tightly, leaning over it to catch her breath whilst McKenna was a few steps in front.

Insatiable, he moved forward purposefully, ready to enact his next attack. Penny had gathered herself and was able to parry a further strike aiming for her right side, pushing it away with both hands and settling for her retaliation to be a weakly struck kick at the side of his knees. The strategy worked, as McKenna's legs momentarily buckled, bringing him down a few inches, making a strike to his face an easier job for Penny to complete.

She followed with more severe punches, acknowledging McKenna's weakened position as he almost fell to his knees. Striking downwards, Penny landed a well-timed uppercut as McKenna had just begun holding his arms up defensively once more; the hit to the chin lowering them as quickly as they had risen. Penny added with a selection of various jabs, alternating hands for maximum confusion.

Using her other limbs, she opted for a kick, trying a swipe on the ribcage again, having it bear fruit upon its previous use. Bending her leg back, the swing came, but her leg suddenly stopped moving, not following through to complete the movement. McKenna, his face bloodied and starting to swell from Penny's recent handiwork, had caught a glimpse of her leg pulling back in the nick of time. He managed to catch her foot before it made contact with his side, holding it there for a second, taking the chance to shoot Penny a smile to discomfort her.

She stood on one leg, her right foot hovering in McKenna's clutches. Before having the chance to alter her attack strategy, McKenna twisted her foot, forcing her to spin, losing her balance and finishing with a collapse on the floor. A chuckling McKenna found his footing once again, standing tall and making his way over to Penny, who was now dragging herself further away, desperately trying to stand as quickly as possible to avoid being in her position of weakness any longer.

McKenna spat out a mouthful of darkened blood, the smile reappearing to show a hideous red glaze forming over his white teeth. His tolerance of pain had always been a boastful personality trait to his peers, and as he stood there, there was a part of him that missed working in the field.

He missed being in the firing line, down on the ground. Hunting his prey, seeing the fear in their eyes and watching their soul being sucked out of them. He liked playing God, being in control of whether someone lives or dies.

Still exasperated, Penny still took steps behind her, her last flurry of successful hits only slightly hindering McKenna's advancement as they moved past the kitchen window and further around the island. Clenching his fists once more, he attacked with vengeance.

Penny did her best to deflect the punches aimed at her, but the fury they now carried was greater than before. It seemed as though all the hits and kicks she had inflicted on McKenna had only made him stronger, awakening something dormant inside of him. His eyes carried more terror behind them, and for the first time, Penny was beginning to doubt her ability to best him.

She retreated further, reaching the corner of the island and she moved around accordingly, sensing the right time to move without having to look. Trying to think of something, anything, to conjure up an attempt of defence against McKenna as he unwaveringly moved forward, she racked her brain furiously searching for an answer.

Almost immediately it came to her. She constructed an idea within milliseconds, but she was severely uncertain how successful it could be. It was not necessarily rewarding, she would be depending on assistance from somebody else, but, despite the negatives, she doubted she was able to think of something else so quickly. McKenna was only steps in front, and soon he would be close enough to strike again. She had to do something.

She thought intensely about whether she would be making the right decision. It was important she was correct about the next few moments, as she would have to live with the consequences for the rest of her life.

Her thoughts kept recalling her adopted family, her husband's relatives who had taken her in and accepted her as one of their own. They had been so kind to her, she could not have asked for better support from them upon her husband's death, allowing her to stay with them and treating her as much a part of the family as if she were blood related.

That is why she wanted to ensure their family's legacy remained intact. Previously resolute and statuesque in good times and bad, the ups and downs throughout two centuries of memories, changes, generations and unexpected circumstances. Their legacy was important to her and she wanted that protected more than anything in the world.

It was unorthodox, but she was steadfast that their family, *her* family, would have wanted it to come to this if they had been here to experience the events of recent weeks. If it could not stay within the family, they would do the same thing instead of handing it over willingly to anyone of such a despicable nature that stood in front of her now, incessantly stalking her in her own house. *This is our house.*

'Will!' She shouted across the room. Her back to the pair of them, she had no idea where they were until she allowed herself a quick glance backwards before McKenna advanced too closely. They were across the other side of the room. It would be difficult, but she had faith.

She moved closer to the back door. 'Lighter!' She shouted louder this time. McKenna was momentarily frozen in confusion by what was happening in front of him. Penny's head turned, only for a moment, to see the instructions she screamed were being followed. In flight, the lighter flew across the room, being caught in Penny's right hand as she twisted back around to face McKenna.

Next, she grabbed the insect repellent canister that had sat on the countertop since the previous evening and pointed it purposefully at McKenna, her right hand holding the flame rising up from the lighter underneath.

Finally realising the danger he had since been placed in by her unconventional, strategic method, McKenna began stepping backwards, this time it was his turn to hold fear behind his eyes.

72

'Now, be careful with that, Penny,' McKenna instructed like he was addressing a child.

Penny ignored him, not even listening, careless of his words, regardless of what was said. Her eyes teared up with a resolute sadness as she continued to hold the canister and the accompanying flame in McKenna's direction. She had made a difficult decision over the recent moments, but the choice was concrete and she was not going to talk herself out of it.

She had already convinced herself this was the best choice. The *only* choice. But she allowed herself a moment of emotional vulnerability as a part of her life flashed before her eyes. Core memories, happy moments and sad endings, a chapter concluding not because of someone else's decision, but because of *her* choice.

Her left index finger pressed down on the aerosol can, releasing the liquid-gas combination in a spray into the room. Reacting with the flame Penny held closely to the nozzle, the flame courtesy of the lighter, the reaction sent a gloriously colourful projection of fire across the room, at least a metre in length, in McKenna's direction. Having acquired the skill of fire-breathing, Penny stepped forward with confidence, continually spraying her vicinity with the hot flame, like a dragon waking up from a slumber to save its treasure from intruders.

Max and Will, at this point holding down their helpless prisoners, turned to find the source of the almighty scorching they recently heard. They both turned and could only watch and stare with astonished looks at the bedlam that had erupted in the next room.

McKenna stepped back and shielded his face, trying desperately to protect himself from the intense heat that so suddenly attacked him from a considerable distance away. He took hurried yet careful steps, retreating past the kitchen window and back in the direction he came, towards the corner of the room, of which sat close to the doors entering into the dining room.

Penny, unrelenting, continued torching the air around her, making certain to withstand McKenna's unwanted advances. Even as he stepped back, she charged forward, refusing to release her finger on the aerosol, the fire heating up the room at a ferocious pace.

McKenna let out a cry of pain, seemingly injured by the fire. Penny was not able to see particularly far, her sight being blocked by the enormity of the flame.

As McKenna scarpered, Penny's strategy changed. Refusing to yield the torching fire, she sprayed the flame with more inaccuracy, yet the movement seemed deliberate. As she reached the kitchen window, the accuracy wavered further, and she began aiming the flame towards the walls.

Seemingly allowing McKenna the chance to recover after being removed from the firing line of the makeshift flamethrower, Penny's actions were deliberate; only she knew the true intentions behind her actions.

The fire unyielding, pointed at the kitchen walls, it was instantaneous as she reached the curtains that hung decoratively open next to the window. What seemed in a fit of unknowingly blind rage, Penny had inadvertently torched her furniture, the curtains wasting no time sparking alight thanks to the enormous ignition of heat she had handed them.

With the curtains ablaze, the fire spread quickly across the flammable material, the heat rapidly moving across and engulfing both sides of the curtains. As the charred furniture hung carefully to a blazing, wooden curtain pole, the fire had spread once more, jumping onto the wooden walls and rising higher, clutching a hold of the support beams that ran across the ground floor's ceiling.

Whilst the fire continued advancing with purposeful intent, Penny's flamethrower faltered. The aerosol can empty, and the source of the flame ceased as the liquid ran out. Then, no sooner after discovering the can to be empty, Penny wasted no time, throwing the canister and lighter to the floor, capitalising on everybody in the room somewhat distracted by her show of brazen disregard.

McKenna stood directly in front of the dining room doors. Penny let out a rageful scream of anger, and, like a sprinter hearing the starting gun; she exploded into a run and covered the two-metre distance separating herself and McKenna in seconds. She remained low, and with her arms outstretched, aimed towards his legs and grabbed them together once she reached them, pinning them and holding them tightly. After completing the successful rugby challenge, Penny used the momentum she had gathered and all the strength she had left to run with the broad and heavy McKenna, his legs raised off the ground, and threw him directly into the dining room doors, his back taking the impact of eight glass panes and falling to the floor with a smash once in the room.

Max and Will, on the other side of the house in the corner of the living room, adjacent to the wooden crate, had witnessed the previous moments with amazement. Having seen the conclusion, McKenna being thrown into the glass-paned doors, the sounds of crashing and breaking glass momentarily erupted over the fire now dangerously spreading across the walls and ceiling. Max stared at the blaze in horror. *What has she done? And more concerningly, was she okay?*

Despite not requiring prior assistance, Max could not help but conclude Penny would desperately need them to step up and end this once and for all. He looked towards Will and contemplated their options.

73

'Will,' Max turned to face his friend. 'We need to go and help her.'

'Yeah, you're right,' Will said.

Max scanned his surroundings, hoping for some inspiration. He soon found it in the form of an assault rifle, one of them had been disregarded near to where they now held Collins and Robinson, pinned with their faces squished to the floor.

'Watch them,' Max did not wait for a response and shot up, scrambling across the floor to cover the distance between him and the weapon. He grabbed the gun and retraced his steps, turning around to walk backwards to where Will and the soldiers were.

Will had performed valiantly in trying to guard both of them, but Collins saw an opportunity and began fidgeting on the ground, realising the lack of Max's presence potentially working in his favour.

Max, upon turning, saw Collins and his movement, jumping into action to thwart the uprising before it began. Half crouched, Max soon returned, the long strides he took in his position making him appear frog-like. Holding the rifle, he soon pointed it in Collins' direction, who had just planted his hands and feet on the floor, ready to perform a push-up motion to escape. Once Max had cocked the rifle, Collins defeatedly returned to the floor, his chest once again pressing onto the wooden floorboards.

'Here, take this,' Max instructed Will, holding the rifle to him with an outstretched hand. 'I'll go and check on Penny.'

Will held out his hand, stretching to receive the gun. 'Yeah, go, go,' the hastiness in which Will spoke was not wasted, the fire continuing to spread across the ceiling, not to mention the almighty crash they heard from McKenna's collision with the double doors. Will decided he would point the gun directly at the back of Collins' head, pushing his face into the floor, whilst staying with his right knee pinned on Robinson's back, ensuring neither moved an inch.

Max ran across into the kitchen and past the island. Looking down the corridor, he saw the extent of the damage Penny's tackle had inflicted on the house. The doors were completely shattered, shards of wood and glass littering the dining room carpet. McKenna and Penny both lay in the middle of the rubble neither moving, which concerned Max greatly.

He pulled open cupboard doors, searching frantically for something to try and tame the rapidly expanding fire. His luck was out, not able to find an extinguisher, he settled for a collection of novelty tea towels, waving them with both hands in various directions; his left flapping the curtains and walls, the right reaching for the roof and support beams, the latter aided with him jumping up and down in order to reach the ceiling.

Performing the task incessantly, refusing to stop even as lactic acid filled up in his calves from the constant jumping, Max was taming the flames the best he could. Yet his work seemed futile. As he was preventing further growth in certain areas, the parts he left unsupervised continued ragefully engulfing everything in its path. Finally, after several minutes, he decided to stop, realising his efforts were of no use.

He turned his head towards Penny, seeing if there was any movement from across the room, even though he had not heard anything above the roaring flames. What he witnessed horrified him, and he wished he had stopped flapping his arms like a pigeon and checked on her long before he noticed the severity of the situation now unfolding in the next room.

74

Penny was in a lot of pain. Having fought off McKenna, being impacted by several heavy blows, she ended the exchange by running through a pair of glass doors. Despite using McKenna as a shield from the glass, when she fell to the ground she landed awkwardly on multiple shards, piercing her skin and heightening the agony through her body. McKenna's punches reared their ugly consequence, the pain now being felt where he had targeted his blows.

She only hoped McKenna was in worse pain than she was. It took the majority of her remaining strength to roll off the glass and try standing, her torturous cries trying desperately to be heard over the crackling fire taking over her house. She stood and tried walking, stumbling on the uneven floor, her head lighter than a balloon with dizziness and shock. She clung to the table for support.

Penny could hear the fire burning in the room behind her, not needing to witness the extent of the damage she caused, the noises alone troubling enough, like the sounds of a nightmare cutting its way through every wooden beam and plank that tied the house together.

McKenna was beginning to writhe on the floor in discomfort, twisting over and placing his hands onto the glass, desperately moving to a stand. He was conscious that regardless of the pain coursing through his back, he needed to get back up, in case another attack was imminent.

Penny watched as McKenna rose once more, she was too concerned with her own recovery to launch an assault on him at that moment. As the air started to fill her lungs again, she noticed idiosyncrasies as to how McKenna's posture had changed. After the extent of their fight was impacting his body, he looked like a shell of the man he appeared earlier. Now 1 much looking closer to his age, he moved much slower and more carefully, not due to his experience and poise, but rather his body failing him, disapproving of his mind for putting it through such rigorous physical activity.

The pain spread across his facial expressions, wincing and grimacing as he held the most agonising parts of pain, unsettled and less confident with his movements, stepping out of the way of the glass shards.

Despite feeling similarly pain-struck, Penny knew this was the perfect time to finish what he had started. Her pain was replaced again by her rage, the disgust she had for McKenna far outperforming any sense of stinging discomfort waving across her entire body. Knowing he had been responsible for the misgivings, the crux of her animosity with the organisation, he could be singled out as the person overseeing the complete breakdown of her life. Of her *family's* lives. She was grateful he was standing there, so she could beat the living crap out of him for their sake. He was the reason it was all ending.

Penny screamed furiously as her mind filled her with dark thoughts of violence and depravity she desperately wished to enact against McKenna. His breathing was laboured and he held his back with a hand, seemingly ageing ten years in a matter of moments.

She pushed off of the table and stood facing McKenna who had decided to remain next to the dining room furniture, ready to use it as an assist to keep him standing if his legs failed him. He looked back at her with a worried look, she stood in the doorframe and this was McKenna's first opportunity to see the extent of the fire in the next room. As Penny stood, her eyes filled with hateful vengeance, the fire continued to blaze all around her figure in the next room, encompassing the walls, ceilings, and fixtures.

McKenna could only watch as Penny leaned forward and delivered a tenacious kick, connecting with his stomach and sending him shooting backwards, his momentum only concluding once his lower back made an almighty crash against the side of the table. He let out a scream of pain as his back cracked on the wood, the edge of the furniture nestling in between his vertebrae and he slumped to the floor helplessly.

Seemingly finished defending himself, McKenna lay immovable on the floor, crying out as the nerves tingled around his spine, no longer able to feel his legs. Penny was far from content, however, releasing a scream of her own, hers of passionate fury, and charged for McKenna on the ground. She placed her knees on either side of his stomach and continually beat, struck and hit his face and head with all manner of different punches, the defenceless man not able to do anything as blow after blow came raining down from above.

Penny screamed again, letting out all of her emotions and she cried, sobbing incessantly, the tears rolling down her face like a flooded river, her arms still punching her victim. Blood started to escape McKenna's face in regions Penny had opened with her fists, spraying around the room and splashing up against her shirt.

Her emotions had taken control, she was no longer able to rationally consider what she was doing, unable to stop, just wanting to vent her anger on McKenna's face until the trance was over.

Suddenly, long after McKenna's face and body had gone limp in unconsciousness, Penny was pulled from behind by something; being dragged off her victim. Even as she was pulled away, her arm movements never ceased, continuing to throw punches in the air with the hopes of landing them on McKenna. Like a boxing match, her adrenaline had consumed her, not knowing when to stop, yet luckily for her, her referee was there to save her.

75

Max struggled to move, frozen solid like an ice sculpture, the temperature rising from the fire performing its hardest to melt him into moving. He watched from the kitchen as, just inside the dining room, Penny knelt over McKenna's body and continuously thrust punches at him. Max could not see any sense of life from McKenna, no fighting or attempt at defending the onslaught being inflicted upon him. That is when Max knew he had to act, to prevent Penny from leaving the man with no face.

The aggression of the hits was extraordinary. No energy was lost as Penny seemingly drained all her strength into the repetitive throws, using McKenna's face as a punching bag, a bag that would have fallen off its fixture a long time ago due to the severity of the attacks laid upon it.

The fire melting his statue pose, Max raced across the room and proceeded to drag Penny off the limp body, grabbing her under her armpits. He moved around to face her, the rage contained in her eyes sending a shiver down his spine as he looked to see life behind them.

'Penny! Look at me! It's over! Okay? It's over.' Max tried desperately to get through to her, to pierce the protective layer she had put up, to break down the walls around her.

She sat, her face dripping with tears, hair all across her face, dark blood drying across her neck. Her breathing was extremely heavy like she had just run a marathon.

Max moved his hands to her face, pushing the hair away and using his thumb to dry her cheeks. Her eyes blinked repetitively, almost as if the daze was over and she had returned to the room, frantically contemplating the last moments. The film over her eyes dissipated and Max was once again able to see the strikingly blue eyes stare back at him, immediately relaxing him and sending a rush over his body.

'Oh, Max,' Penny said languishingly, lunging at him and they embraced in a warm hug.

'It's okay, it's okay,' Max kept repeating, holding her head as it was cushioned on his chest, and reassuring her.

They separated and stood, briefly staring at each other before each of them remembered their current predicament and stared hopelessly around the house.

The fire had spread extensively, swallowing everything it could claim. The walls had changed to blackened charcoal, the fire leaving remnants of light as it tried to cling onto the wood. It had taken over, using the support beams to weave its way across to the living room, the furniture closest to the edge made victim of the rapidly advancing heat that became unbearably warm.

Will sat, remaining guard with the two soldiers, helpless to the heat rising, thankful he was not closer to the walls or he would have been toast.

Max looked over at Penny, not needing any words and finding it very difficult to hide the sadness in his eyes. He eventually found his voice. 'What can we do?'

Penny took a moment to herself, strolling in circles as the fire was becoming increasingly dangerous, readying to collapse the ceiling as the beams trying to support the floor above began to lose the battle.

She watched as her life crashed down in front of her, the extent of the damage too much, futile to try and salvage anything. Tears began forming in her eyes again and she sniffed, wiping her nose with her sleeve. She swallowed down the tears, knowing that she had made the decision herself. On *her* terms rather than anybody else's.

Walking over to Max, she stretched out her hand, waiting for him to reciprocate and hold it. He held on, first delicately, and then squeezed it tight and she obliged, holding it firmly as they let out some of their emotions with the gesture.

Time seemed to stand still as she watched it all crumble. Once she was satisfied she had seen enough, she looked longingly at Max, the sadness escaping her once her eyes met his once more. Despite the fire raging all around her, she felt incredibly safe in Max's gaze, knowing what they had done to protect each other already, and what they would continue to do to protect each other in the future.

'There's nothing *to* do,' Penny spoke for the first time since being pulled off of McKenna's body. 'We need to leave. Now.'

'Surely we must do something?' Max knew it was a long shot, but he was not ready to give up fighting.

'No. This is it, we need to go before this ceiling collapses.'

'Okay,' Max replied, smiling at her and pulling her closer to him, releasing her hand and placing an arm over her shoulder.

Max supported Penny as she limped towards the back door. Penny looked over her shoulder, stealing a final glance at her world crashing around her. She saw McKenna's unconscious body begin to move without conviction, allowing his fate to be sealed at the hands of the family home as opposed to her own.

They made their way over to Will, stoically above his two captures. His demeanour was calm, yet he spoke frantically. 'What do I do with these?' He asked them both, gesturing towards the two lying on the floor.

Max and Penny looked at each other in bewilderment, neither of them having anything particularly constructive to suggest. Finally, Max spoke calmly and softly, 'Let them go,' the conviction in his voice acknowledged by his friend.

'Let them go?' Will was eager to confirm.

'Yeah, they're not gonna do anything, right lads?' His voice moved to direct it towards the soldiers patiently waiting for their fate.

'No, no,' Collins spoke up. 'We're gonna forget this ever happened.'

'We are?' Robinson seemed confused with the developments.

'Of course we are. What's gonna happen if we go back and tell them what a fuck up this whole thing turned out to be?' Collins asked his colleague, both their faces squashed onto the floor but looking at each other.

'Well,' Robinson considered the prospect for a moment. 'I suppose they might kill us, shouldn't you think?'

'Exactly,' Collins reasoned, 'we'll go out the front, you go out the back, we'll never mention the whole thing to anyone.'

Max looked to his companions, eager to deliberate. They both returned looks of satisfaction, not requiring speech but rather sharing nods of approval between the trio. 'That works for us. Will, let them go, let's get outta here.'

'The sooner the better,' Will threw the rifle away and stood quickly, eager to put his words into action.

'There's two of your lads upstairs, they'll both be awake by now I bet,' Max added a final remark, which was acknowledged by a nod of gratitude by Collins; now standing, relieved he was no longer licking the floorboards.

The three of them, Penny, Max and Will, headed for the exit, a short distance of only a couple of metres, before escaping the heat through the open door and onto the porch for a necessary reprieve. As they turned their backs on the two soldiers, Max could hear the mutterings of a moral quandary, the pair arguing with each other on whether to tend to McKenna's aid and recover him from the flames. Max looked behind as the door was closing, content in witnessing them help the remaining soldier in the room, being firefighter-lifted onto Collins' shoulder, before quickly moving down the hallway, proceeding to the stairs and leaving McKenna to lay in his coffin.

76

They moved promptly down the porch steps, not stopping until they had paced at least thirty metres from the burning building. Only then, when they realised they were at a safe distance, did they turn around and see the full extent of the damage that the fire had caused to the house.

Through the windows they saw the fire, progressing purposefully across the rear rooms, the area where they had stood moments earlier falling victim to the blazing flames as it engulfed everything in sight. Standing in silence to watch, they saw the fire entangle itself around the exterior walls, clinging to the wooden structure and wrapping around any part it had yet to conquer. Moving swiftly, it soon took the second floor, rising higher and higher as it took over, the three of them no longer being able to make out the walls. Crashing noises exploded from within the fire, the floor and walls giving way, the house accepting the end of its life.

Max turned to Penny, still in somewhat disbelief. 'You did that intentionally, right?'

She did not turn, her eyes fixed on her house crumbling in front of her. 'Yep. Yes, I did,' she spoke with defiance, almost gratification, brimmed with confidence and she stuck her chest out assuredly.

'Do I dare ask why?' Max probed with a hint of a smile in the corner of his mouth. He could see Penny's emotions rushing over her, releasing something, a weight off of her shoulders. He had never been more attracted to her than at that moment.

'I made a decision, to get us outta there,' she deliberated, 'and it worked,' she smiled as she finished.

'Seems a little drastic, don't you think?' Max inquired.

She sighed. 'It was time to move on. It was only then I realised I was ready,' she turned to face him, her smile capturing Max's heart. To him, it seemed strange, but, after looking at her face, and how proud she seemed of herself, he knew he agreed with her; it was the right decision.

'I don't see him complaining,' Penny said, jibing a thumb in Will's direction.

He straightened up. 'Absolutely not, I thank you for it. Cheers Pen,' the genuine nature behind the statement caused them all to smile, returning their eyes to stare at the burning wreckage.

'That's it, I'm quitting,' Will pulled the cigarette packet Penny had gifted him from his pocket. He gestured it towards her, asking her permission before the disposal. She nodded approvingly. His eyes moved to Max, ensuring his friend felt the same.

'Hey,' Max started, 'if you don't have any, I can't smoke any.' The response sufficed Will, who proceeded to walk back closer to the house and throw the box into the flames.

He spoke upon returning. 'I've tempted death enough for now, let's not bring me any closer,' he smiled triumphantly to the other pair.

Having seen enough, Penny started making her way around the house, cautious to leave sufficient allocation to the wreckage. Will followed behind, leaving Max momentarily standing on his own. He thought about the journey, spending his second alone to contemplate the madness of the previous days, how he would never have dreamt such a scenario ever occurring upon making the decision to go and search for the money. And yet, despite almost dying, multiple times, he concluded to himself he would not change a single moment.

He felt the back pocket of his jeans, removing his notebook. The ends that had stuck out of the pocket had bent over, the leather cover curling at the corners and the pages inside separately slightly, indicating the book had been written in. Briefly flicking through, he saw his writings, his scribbles and all the nonsense he had conjured for his story. He knew at that moment exactly how he was going to finish the book.

He smiled to himself. *Nothing like some real-world experience.*

Will's voice came calling after him. 'You not bothered about losing the money?' The conversation starter was close enough for Penny to overhear, and, intrigued to hear Max's answer to the question, turned around to listen.

Max instinctively looked up at his friend, contemplating the complexities of what he had been asked. He pondered with exciting deliberation, acknowledging just how close they had been to actually retrieving the money. His gaze fell to his notebook, holding it in both hands, and he gripped it tightly, pulling it close to his chest. It was never about the money. He would not argue the financial benefits of keeping it, but what he held in his hands was far more important to him.

This was it. This was to get him back on track. And he was eternally grateful.

He looked up again, his eyes finding what they were searching for, behind his dear friend. A girl, looking perfect in the shirt she had not washed in two days, the filthy blue jeans that were caked in mud, her face covered in blood and dirt, her hair looking a week unbrushed. She held her arm across her eyes, shielding the sun as she stared back at him, the warm glow showing her radiance and making his heart beat uncontrollably quickly, filled with a desire burning as high as the fire next to him, ready to unconditionally support a girl with all his heart having only met her two days before.

Max's smile was enormously large, he struggled to contain his happiness as it almost burst out of him, his teeth forming into an irritably happy grin that took over his face and never ceased.

Penny watched him walk towards her and she bit her bottom lip in nervous anticipation, not wanting to overplay her emotions of jubilation and giddiness. She could not wait to start her next chapter, and she could not wait to start it with the person she had found. No, the person who had found *her.*

He got too close for her to keep her disguise and she returned a smile as wide as his. He held out his hand, open and ready for hers. She glanced at it, then looked back into his eyes and accepted it. This time, the holding was tender and loving.

'Absolutely not. I have everything I have right here.' His eyes never moved from watching her face, grateful he had the opportunity to study every portion of it once more. He clutched his notebook in his spare hand, knowing he was going to be very busy when he got home.

'So,' Penny started, 'what now?'

Max and Will looked at each other. 'Well,' said Will, plunging a hand into his pocket to retrieve his phone. 'It's past midday…'

He trailed off and Max filled in the blanks. 'Pub?'

'Pub,' Will smiled, reaching into his other pocket and producing a collection of dollar bills. 'First rounds on me.'

Max and Penny were watching his movements and acknowledged the gesture of him removing the money from his pocket. He held it out in front of himself proudly. Max nodded appreciatively and turned his head to face forward. Then he took a double take, his head spinning back to look at the notes in Will's hand.

'Will, you cheeky bastard!' He chuckled once he had realised.

'Only a couple, no one's even gonna know they're missing,' Will laughed.

There, in his hand, he held American dollars. These, however, were slightly different. The seals were different on the front, the edges of the paper were older and more weathered. Penny glanced over to see the commotion. It was unmistakable. Will held in his hands part of Dillinger's lost fortune, the only surviving notes from the legend, safe in his grasp.

They all shared a laugh, overcome with joy, knowing they were the only three people in the world to know the real ending to the legend.

Acknowledgements

I'd like to thank a few people who have made this possible for me, many of whom continually remind me of the achievement it is to have a book published.

To my parents, for always being there, for always supporting my decisions, even if you don't agree with them.

To Paige, my editor and advertiser. I've lost count of how many times you've been forced to read parts of this book, reassuring me every time it wasn't boring and motivating me to finish it. For helping to brainstorm on our travels, your support is invaluable.

For Tom and Krupa, for being perfect examples and amazing people to look up to. You're always there if I need help, and I'm grateful I've finally been able to give Tom his National Treasure sequel.

– Kieran –

Available worldwide from Amazon
and all good bookstores

Michael Terence
Publishing

www.mtp.agency

mtp.agency

@mtp_agency

Printed in Dunstable, United Kingdom

72082710R00161